Praise for

BECAUSE YOU'LL NEVER MEET ME

A William C. Morris YA Debut Award Finalist

★ "The pacing is impeccable, as letters move from sunniness (Oliver) and bemused distance (Moritz) to both writers exploring their darkest fears, experiences, and worries for their futures." —*BCCB*, starred review

"A witty, unusual take on friendship and parlaying weakness into power." —*Kirkus Reviews*

"Ollie and Moritz are memorable characters with engaging and often humorous voices. . . . A quirky, almost whimsical feel even as Thomas grounds it in heartfelt and often painful emotion." —*SLJ*

"The two may be eccentric outcasts, but their conflicts, heartbreak, and eventual bond form a relatable and engaging narrative." —*Publishers Weekly*

"Readers will enjoy . . . the candor with which the author explores some of the more challenging realities of adolescent life—especially for a teen who feels 'different.'" —*VOYA*

"It's the distinct, deeply memorable voices of Ollie and Moritz that make this novel an affecting page-turner." —*The Horn Book*

Books by Leah Thomas

Because You'll Never Meet Me
Nowhere Near You

BECAUSE YOU'LL NEVER MEET ME

leah thomas

BLOOMSBURY

NEW YORK LONDON OXFORD NEW DELHI SYDNEY

First published in the United States of America in June 2015
by Bloomsbury Children's Books
Paperback edition published in February 2017
www.bloomsbury.com

Bloomsbury is a registered trademark of Bloomsbury Publishing Plc

For information about permission to reproduce selections from this book, write to
Permissions, Bloomsbury Children's Books, 1385 Broadway, New York, New York 10018
Bloomsbury books may be purchased for business or promotional use. For information on bulk
purchases please contact Macmillan Corporate and Premium Sales Department at
specialmarkets@macmillan.com

The Library of Congress has cataloged the hardcover edition as follows:
Thomas, Leah.
Because you'll never meet me / by Leah Thomas.
pages   cm
Summary: Ollie, who has seizures when near electricity, lives in a backwoods cabin with his mother
and rarely sees other people, and Moritz, born with no eyes and a heart defect that requires a
pacemaker, is bullied at his high school, but when a physician who knows both suggests they
begin corresponding, they form a strong bond that may get them through dark times.
ISBN 978-1-61963-590-6 (hardcover) • ISBN 978-1-61963-591-3 (e-book)
[1. Letters—Fiction. 2. Epilepsy—Fiction. 3. Blind—Fiction. 4. People with disabilities—Fiction.
5. Loneliness—Fiction. 6. Friendship—Fiction. 7. Bullies—Fiction. 8. Single-parent families—Fiction.]
I. Title. II. Title: Because you will never meet me.
PZ7.T366996Bec 2015   [Fic]—dc23   2014024670

ISBN 978-1-68119-021-1 (paperback)

Book design by Amanda Bartlett
Typeset by Westchester Book Composition
Printed and bound in the U.S.A. by Berryville Graphics Inc., Berryville, Virginia
2 4 6 8 10 9 7 5 3 1

All papers used by Bloomsbury Publishing, Inc., are natural, recyclable products
made from wood grown in well-managed forests. The manufacturing processes
conform to the environmental regulations of the country of origin.

For my sister
and all the things that make us

BECAUSE YOU'LL NEVER MEET ME

chapter one

THE LASER BEAM

Dear Fellow Hermit,

My name is Oliver, but most people who meet me end up calling me Ollie. I guess you don't really have to, though, because odds are you'll never meet me.

I can never travel to wherever you are, because a big part of what makes me a hermit is the fact that I'm deathly allergic to electricity. This is kind of massively incapacitating, but hey—everyone has problems, right?

I think never being able to meet me is sort of a shame, because I'm not *too* boring. I can juggle forks like nobody's business, for starters. I'm also pretty great at kanji calligraphy, and I can whittle a piece of pine into anything—well, anything made of pine. Dr. Auburn-Stache (I swear that's his real name) is impressed by how quickly I can list every bone in the human body, from the distal phalanx of my ugliest toe all the way up to the frontal bone above my eyes. I've read more books than I've got hairs on my head, and I am just months away from mastering the glockenspiel. (In case you didn't know, the glockenspiel is like the metallic, cooler older brother of the xylophone.) I know what you're thinking, but you'd be surprised how living alone in the woods can warm a person to the delights of glockenspieling.

But beyond all that stuff, the most interesting thing about me is that I'm lovesick.

I don't mean all that poetical nonsense about feeling the urge to carve a girl's name into notebooks and desks and trees. I'm not talking moonlit serenades, either, because even my wheezing *cat* is a better singer than I am.

I mean that if I wanted to be around this girl—Liz, her name is Liz—under normal circumstances, I could die. If I ever wanted to take her out to—I dunno—an *arcade* (isn't that what you call those mystical places that are just wall-to-wall electric games?), the moment I walked into a bleeping basement full of neon lights and racing simulators, I'd collapse and start seizing like there's no tomorrow. Which there might not be, if I hit my head the wrong way.

I don't think that's what most people mean by lovesickness, Fellow Hermit.

If I took this girl out to a movie (and I would love to—what are movies like?), the buzzing of the projector behind us would make my eyelids twitch. The shrill screeching of phones in other people's pockets would drive emerald ice picks into my temples, and the dim lights overhead would burn white and gold in my retinas. Maybe I'd even swallow my tongue.

But I read somewhere that people who have epileptic fits can't actually swallow their tongues. They do *bite* their tongues, though;

one time after a big seizure I chomped right through mine, and it took Auburn-Stache, like, seven stitches on the top and five on the bottom to make it heal up afterward. For more than two weeks, I wandered around our cabin saying things like "Waf gongan?" and "Yef, pleef" while Mom just shook her head at me, all exasperated.

Mom's always exasperated. Her face is pretty creased up most of the time, especially around her eyes, even when she's smiling. That's mostly my fault, I think. I would never say anything to her about it, because I think it would upset her that I noticed, and then she might lock herself in the garage again for a day or two, or even longer this time.

Mom's amazing, but she and I have had some pretty bad days lately, days where neither of us really enjoys the winter sunshine. She's watching while I'm writing this by candlelight, and she's probably wondering if you'll even be able to read it. Mom says I've got the handwriting of a drunk doctor. One time I asked Dr. Auburn-Stache if he would consider drinking some moonshine (isn't that what people are supposed to drink out in the woods?) and then write me a sonnet so I could compare our penmanship, but he just snickered behind his goatee and patted me on the shoulder.

But—what was I talking about?

Was I talking about Liz? Probably I was, because that's what it's like when you're lovesick. The first side effect is uncontrollable word-vomit:

When Liz is around, it seems like nothing else is! She smirks and teases me just like she did on the day I met her in the woods, and then I think that maybe I'm going to be okay, maybe I'm *not* losing it after all. Because Liz told me that no one should ever say his illness before his name. And I told you my name first, Fellow Hermit!

But . . . Liz is hardly ever around anymore, so . . .

Sorry if I wasn't supposed to be talking about her!

Liz's parents are social workers, and she thinks I have some kind of attention deficit disorder because sometimes my thoughts careen away from my brain and I blab, blab, blab.

But tell me about you! What's your deal?

Mom won't say where she plans to send this letter. All she says is that Auburn-Stache knows another kid somewhere out there a couple of years older than me with his own set of bizarre medical issues. What with everything that has happened to me this year, she thought I could use someone to talk to. She thinks I need help, but she's overreacting. It's not like I've stopped *eating*; sometimes a guy just doesn't want tuna sandwiches. That doesn't mean I'm sick. Or at least any sicker than usual, because you can't get much sicker than being allergic to electricity.

About that—I'll try explaining it to you, but if you ask *why* I'm allergic to electricity, I'll just throw my hands up and sigh. I've always been this way. It's the ultimate mystery in my neck of the woods.

It might have something to do with a *top secret* laboratory, though! This is just a hypothesis, and it doesn't *just* come from reading *Frankenstein* in blanket forts during thunderstorms as an impressionable ten-year-old. Half the superhero characters I've read about, from Captain America to the Hulk to Wolverine, got interesting abilities after being test subjects in laboratories.

I think being an experiment sounds way better than being sick, you know?

So here's the working theory: maybe Dr. Auburn-Stache met your parents at a secret, hush-hush laboratory? Maybe the same one where my dad got radiation poisoning!

Because, see, I do have evidence to support my hypothesis. I don't know much about my dad. But I do know he was some sort of doctor or *scientist*, because Mom keeps his lab coat hanging in her wardrobe. One time, when I was seven or something, I snuck into her room to steal her keys from her bureau (sometimes she padlocks us in, but I really wanted to go outside because it was prime cricket-catching season), and she was fast asleep with the faded white coat draped over her like a blanket. I saw that and stopped looking for the keys.

She won't tell me whether I'm right about the lab, or about dad, beyond saying that he was sick before he died. (I guess it wasn't *necessarily* radiation poisoning.) But I am an expert needler, Fellow Hermit. Over the years I've tried all sorts of tactics to get the story out of her. These tactics include but are not limited to

a. leaping out from behind her armchair and screeching: "Who'smydaddyyyy!?"

b. waiting in the dark pantry until she dives in seeking flour, at which point I moan in a low whisper, "What about . . . the laboratory?"

c. moping extensively (it's an act, I swear) with the shiniest damn puppy eyes you've ever *seen*.

Mom is unshakable. Her usual response to all tactics is an eye roll, but every now and then she pats me on the head. When I'm in the pantry, she just shuts the door on me.

So I don't know who my dad was, but I know she misses him. If she misses him anything like how much I miss Liz, then no won-der she locks the doors.

Maybe you can tell me anything you know about laboratories in your letter, since I went to bug Mom about it again just now, and she told me to sit back down at my desk and try, for the love of pajamas, to stay on topic for once. How? I've never really had to stay on topic before. When it's just you alone in a forest of pine trees for your whole life, there's really no reason not to meander. No one's ever around to tell me to shut up.

I mean, apart from the mailman and a few others, hardly any-one around here has ever even seen me. Liz told me that some people believe my cabin is an urban legend! I wish I could ride to town and show them what's what.

But there's this power line halfway down our long driveway, right, and the orange tendrils of electricity that dangle down from it never let me pass underneath. Those little wisps of tangerine light actually yanked me off my bike once and threw me headfirst into a tree trunk.

What I've got is a bit weirder than an allergy, when you get right down to it. Sometimes it's more like mutual repulsion or something, like when you put two magnets with the same polarization nose-to-nose and they catapult each other across the table. Doesn't that sound almost like something from comics? Compelling, right?

Mom says I'm not explaining myself properly. She frowned at the part I wrote about the lab coat but didn't scratch it out, and then she read about the repulsion stuff and reminded me that my sick-ness is basically like a tongue: it's hard for most people to swallow.

Epilepsy basically means that the electricity in your brain is

somehow out of whack. A lot of people in the world have this problem, but most people don't have to be hermits because of it.

Having epilepsy means sometimes having seizures—um, shaking fits? I think of it like this: my head gets stuck on something and
then the whole rest of me gets stuck, too, and it's like those times
when you stutter, but it's not my words—it's all of me. Head to toe,
just stuttering. And later I can't remember what I was trying to do
or say in the first place. All that's left are throbbing temples, a swollen tongue, lost time, and so much bone-tiredness that I don't want
to move ever again.

I've read *tons* of pamphlets on epilepsy. Mom brings them
home from the clinic and we go through them together. I've read
that some people only develop epilepsy after a nasty head injury,
like from a car crash. Others start having seizures as a side effect of
a disease or drug abuse.

But some people just have rotten luck. See also: me.

Pamphlets are also how I learned about auras, when I was six or
something.

" 'Before having seizures, many people have some sense that a
seizure is imminent. This sense is referred to as an aura.' And *imminent* means 'close.' Head up, Ollie. This is important."

"Can't I go outside?"

"Homework first. 'During an aura, sufferers may experience
acute sensory dissonance.' "

"Are those *all* real words?"

"It means that many people's senses start going haywire before
a seizure, Ollie. They might taste pepper—"

"I'd rather taste ice cream."

"—or smell sulfur. Or maybe they start to see the world

differently. I think you know about that last one." Were we outside in the yard, or inside by the kitchen window? I can't remember. But I remember that Mom squeezed my hand and I squeezed my eyes shut.

For sure I see things differently, Fellow Hermit. I can't look at *anything* electric without seeing blobs of color. It's like my vision measures electric currents on a spectrum or something. If getting blinded by multicolored electric hazes is because of an aura, then I must have an eternal aura. It never goes away. It's downright immortal. *Dracul-aura.*

Mom says I'm almost off topic again and that I should focus. I swear that lately it's just: *Ollie, stop moping! Ollie, eat your tuna sandwiches!*

Focus!

Do people ever tell you to focus? What does that even *mean*? Whenever Mom or Auburn-Stache says "Focus, Oliver!" I try to wrangle my thoughts into the shape of a laser beam. I've seen laser beams on the covers of my favorite sci-fi novels; I've even painted some. I usually paint what my aura shows me when I look at electricity: saffron-slashing walkie-talkies, sunbursts floating out of headlights. Before it knocks me flat, electricity can be really cool to look at.

All the MRI machines I saw, back when Mom and Auburn-Stache still bundled me up in rubber clothes and dragged me to hospitals, were wrapped in scarves of golden light that gave me pounding headaches. X-rays emit rich scarlet ringlets. Fluorescent bulbs exude a silver mist that drifts downward like craft glitter. Power sockets? They spit out blue-white confetti curls. Batteries in use are little twists of bronze radiance that shatter to gray when they run low. Every single machine gives off its own brand of color-ful energy, and my seizures are triggered by all of them: anything and everything electric.

I know this does sound unswallowable. But it's so real to me. It's the reason I'm bored but not boring. Why I'm stuck out here by myself.

At least when Liz used to come by I could act like I was normal, just like she is. I listened to her talk about her school stuff, and it was almost like I was the sort of kid who could go there with her, who could text during class and type essays and later come home on a bus and plop myself in front of a television and eat food from a microwave. (Those sound *magical*, Fellow Hermit.)

But I've never looked directly at a television; that would proba-bly send me tonic-clonic in seconds. Televisions are bursting with inorganic light and organic color, a miasma of noise. I'm told that's all televisions are to anyone. I'm not sure I buy that. (I think I would love cartoons.)

And motor vehicles! Engines are hard for me to see because the smog of energy around them is pitch-dark. I can't tell you what color Mom's truck is; every time I've stood at my bedroom window and watched it pull away, it has been surrounded by a gritty, opaque nebula.

My favorites are all those electrical things that people seem to superglue to themselves, things Liz used to show me: phones, music players, laptops. When they're switched on, their colors bounce off the skin of their users. Phones lend the faces they are pressed against a luminous green sheen. Headphones coat ears in minty residue. But laptops are the best. Fingers on keyboards are traced by trails of light, like long blades of grass.

You may be wondering whether I'm complaining or not. I'm not really sure myself. Mom says the way I see things sounds beautiful. But I'm not sure the sight of rainbow explosions is worth toasting a bunch of my brain cells over. It's not really beautiful when I'm drooling on the floor and rattled with tremors.

What was I saying about laser beams?

I'm going to try to beam my life story to you, as directly as I can manage. So these letters will be my autobiography. You don't have to read them if you don't want to, but I would appreciate it if you could write me your story back. There's enough boredom to drown in around these parts. And please don't tell me that people can drown in an inch of water. I know that. I'm being figurative! I'm just trying to tell you that it's a *lot* of boredom.

Especially now that Liz might never stop by to see me ever again.

I'll tell you about that later because Mom says that good autobiographies are linear, like life. Like, I should tell you about being a toddler before I talk about being a kid.

That's good. I don't think I want to talk about what it feels like when I'm waiting outside in the dusty driveway and Liz doesn't come biking down it, smiling. When she doesn't come biking down it frowning, even. When she doesn't come biking down it at all, and I just stare at the same old jack pines as ever and the same old stumps and breathe the same old smell of emptiness and sap, until it gets dark out.

First I want to make sure you exist. I can't wait to hear from you, Fellow Hermit! I doubt I've ever done half of what you have. I would trade all my glockenspiel skills for a chance to go online. Or to ride a school bus or feel air conditioning. Are you also hypersensitive to electricity?

Mom says that fifteen double-sided pages are enough to scare anyone away, so I'll stop here at page fourteen.

Write me soon. It's getting boring here. Did I mention that?

~ Ollie Ollie UpandFree

P.S. Here's a teaser to make you want to read my autobiography: I've *died* before.

chapter two

THE PACEMAKER

Oliver:

Firstly, my father has confirmed that your penmanship is atrocious. At least you can spell. I would hate to outmatch you in your own language. How embarrassing that would be for you. I am sick of people deciding that being young means being ineloquent. Yet the idiots who attend school with me are too preoccupied with *gossip* to care about language. I do not expect them to meet my standards, but you needn't be a *Wunderkind* to educate yourself.

I despise other people my age. *Jugendlichen*. Let them rot.

You mentioned Japanese. But the glockenspiel is a German musical instrument. Can't you speak and write *auf Deutsch*? I doubt you are aware, but the glockenspiel has rarely been used in hip-hop music. I pity your ears for never having been graced by Public Enemy.

Secondly, you are correct. We will not be meeting. This has little to do with your deafening personality. I am electric. Exposure to me would floor you.

Doubtless that hyperactive mind of yours is already jumping to outlandish conclusions: "My, is he an android? What sort of monstrosity is he, the son of one of my doctor's old friends? What is he, that he is electric? A reanimated corpse, veins coursing with lightning? Oh boy!"

Calm yourself. This is not science fiction. This is not fun.

For the past five years, my heart has remained pumping only with the assistance of a small apparatus that feeds electric pulses into the lower-left chamber. If I ever met you, the electricity in my rib cage would trigger your seizures. If I shut off my pacemaker to spare you that, my blood flow would weaken. I could go into shock or even cardiac arrest. You could kill me.

Your postscript teaser fails to impress me. I have died also, Oliver UpandFree. (I feel foolish writing that. I will call you Oliver.) Dying was not an enjoyable experience. It's enough to say that I woke from death with an electric heart. You and I will certainly never meet.

And yet I do have a morbid interest in continuing our correspondence. I may have chuckled once while Father read your words to me yesterday evening. If I were sickened by phones, by vehicles and amplifiers, and not merely sickened by my classmates, perhaps I would resort to babbling as well. Not that this excuses you.

I thought I had seen EVERYTHING. But your mother

is right. Your worldview is remarkable. So is your earsplitting enthusiasm. So I do not blame her for hiding in the garage.

I am not certain that I want to share the details of my life with you. I do not trust you, Oliver. I am uncomfortable with spitting every thought I have ever had onto paper. People like you do not realize what power words have. Words are impossible to see. Words can be twisted in so many directions. Some of us are more careful with them.

As for your questions about "secret laboratories," I am not nearly as interested in this subject as you are. Talk about something you know about. If you don't want to be bored, don't bore me. There's nothing fascinating about laboratories, in my experience.

Tell me more about your life. If you must.

Besides. It is more entertaining if I do not speak.

Moritz Farber

P.S. Yes. A man can drown in an inch of water. But in Germany we would call it 2.54 centimeters of water. The metric system is altogether superior.

chapter three

THE COMPUTER

Well, riddle me this, riddle me that! Do you read comics? Wait. Let me rephrase that: Marvel or DC? Also, you didn't tell me whether you like cartoons.

Way to write a letter and tell me almost nothing about yourself, although I guess I'm impressed by your refusal to reveal your tragic past! Now I *really* want to know your thoughts on laboratories. But at least you know I exist!

So you're German? What's that like? I've read a lot of history books, and a lot of fairy tales. Germans are featured in both, and not always nicely, but you probably already know that. Are all Germans as stuffy as you? No offense, but reading what you wrote felt a little like I was *conversing* with a Victorian gentleman, by Jove! Do you read Oscar Wilde? He was Victorian, but, like, the *exact* opposite of you! He was way less *reserved*, by gum!

I think language *is* pretty awesome, so we already have something in common! But don't you think English is the greatest?

Sometimes I just sit here at my desk and chortle because *but* and *butt* sound the same. The other day I was just snickering about it in bed, and Mom got all wide-eyed because I started coughing and she thought maybe I was hysterical again, but—*butt!*—sometimes I need something to laugh at.

Oh! I looked up "*Jugendlichen.*" So that's German for "teenagers," huh? Well, say what you want. I would *kill* (not actually, because I'm not a psychopath) to know more idiotic teenagers. I want to be one of them!

And Auburn-Stache says you're sixteen. You've got two years on me! I'm not your age, so you can't despise me yet.

Despite your depressing response to my awesome I-Died-Once teaser, I'll attach Part One of my autobiography. This way Mom can keep believing that writing to you is helping me focus, helping me get better, and stopping me from standing in the driveway all day.

Here goes:

The Linear Autobiography of
Oliver Paulot, the Powerless Boy
Part One: Screaming

When I was born, I was born screaming. It was the same for almost everyone I've ever heard of; if you weren't born screaming, then you were probably born with too much optimism.

But my scream made even the most jaded night nurses in the natal center cover their ears. The old doctor at the bedside nearly dropped me. Auburn-Stache told me that old doctor probably wanted to holler at me to "put a sock in it," but that's usually frowned upon. Besides, I bet the socks of a full-time doctor are even less sanitary than the socks of teenage boys, if Auburn-Stache's grubby feet are anything to go by.

Mom was quiet. She claims that I was making enough commotion for both of us.

The old doctor pulled a penlight from his lab coat and aimed it down my throat. The beam shot past my empty gums and into the center of me, and finally I stopped screaming.

The room exhaled. . . .

And I had my first seizure.

Last time I asked Mom about it, it was a snowy afternoon and we were both biding time by firelight in the living room.

"The day I was born—what was it like?" I tucked my calligraphy brush behind my ear.

She put down the heavy tapestry she was cross-stitching, letting it drape across her legs. To me it looked like the most violent quilt known to man. Mom is always making things; she gets as bored as I do. This was her seventh tapestry or something, and it depicted a pretty gory stag-hunting scene. She jabbed her needle into the arm of the couch. It was still trailing the red thread she was using to sew the eviscerated innards of the unfortunate stag.

"You've read about childbirth. *Tch.*"

Sometimes Mom makes a slight clucking sound near the front of her teeth. It's her type of sniggering. I used to wonder if it was something everyone did. Now I know it's a family habit.

"I was a *huge* pain in the vagina, I bet."

"Ollie." In the half-light, the lines of her face seemed deeper.

"It's a medical term, Mom." I rolled my eyes. "What else do you want me to call it?"

"Most people wouldn't call it anything. Most people have *tact.*"

I held my arms wide apart to illustrate the vast nothingness outside our cabin. "Wherefore, Mother? *Wherefore?*"

"Yes. Fine. You were a *huge* pain. Like I was splitting in two."

"Nuclear fission!"

"I don't know about that. But putting you on this earth was the most painful thing I have ever done. Since you asked."

"Sorry."

"*Tch.* I don't think what I felt compared in any way to what you felt during that first seizure." She grimaced. "Your face was so red. It looked as though you might burst."

"Nuclear explosion." I stood up and stretched.

"*Implosion.* You stayed in one piece. But something was collapsing and burning under your skin, in your skull. You know how it feels better than I do."

I shrugged. I've had enough seizures that I can't imagine the shock of the first one.

"You were so small," she said, picking up her needle again. "No wonder it killed you."

Anytime I was conscious, I was seizing. They were all worried about my brain cells because seizures burn them up pretty rapidly. I was sedated and stuck in an incubator while Mom was on bed rest.

Last spring I asked Auburn-Stache for his side of the story. We were on the back porch early one warm evening, and he was taking my blood pressure by the pinkish light of sunset over the tree line.

"Tell me about when I was a baby, Auburn-Stache."

"What? Yet again?"

"Yeppers."

"Sometimes, Ollie, you sound unnervingly like a five-year-old."

"You mean right now, or when I stamp my feet and demand ice cream?"

He smirked and adjusted his glasses. The armband tightened on my upper arm. "Ice cream is serious business, kiddo. It renders us all five, as you well know."

"Once more with feeling, Auburn-Stache."

"*Tch.*" He raised a mocking eyebrow. The armband released. "You were weeks early, or I'd have been there. Already you couldn't stay put!"

Auburn-Stache had been friends with my dad ever since they both worked together (at the mysterious laboratory no one likes to talk about?), and Mom called him the moment she went into labor. She probably screamed at him, like anyone being split in two would. He was working as an on-call physician a few counties away. He jokes that he got out of work and on the road so fast that he left his previous patient on the table with two limbs too few. Very funny, Auburn-Stache.

"I couldn't stop thinking about the penlight. It left the faintest trail of hives on your skin! 'Aha!' " He re-created his moment of epiphany, standing up from the lawn chair with his finger in the air. "Photosensitive epilepsy!"

"Sit down, you kook."

He knew that flashing lights sometimes cause seizures. Many people's auras are triggered by cycles or patterns of lights or images. Auburn-Stache bugged the hell out of the old doctor until he agreed to put me in a dark room. But I was still in an incubator, so I still got sick. I got so sick that I flatlined. Auburn-Stache resuscitated me.

"But I never got around to actually placing the defibrillator paddles on your chest and back! The moment I held them near your diaphragm, the shock of their proximity alone somehow restarted your heart"—he clapped his hands—"and set you to seizing again."

"Man, sounds like it was a party!"

"It would have been rather exciting for me, had you not been in pain." His face went unusually still. "You should not think I'm so terrible as that, Ollie."

I couldn't think of what to say. The fireflies were beginning to hover around above the grass when he said, "But you aren't entirely wrong. There are all kinds of adventures in the world. In that moment when you woke back up, the paddle was repelled from you. It was as if you had an electric charge of your own."

He had me released into his care, and then he bundled me up in rubber hospital gear and wheeled Mom and me out to his Impala while the hospital staff looked on without much hope, all teary eyed. (Artistic license, okay?)

I bet that car could have killed me all over again. Even the tiny lights that come on when the door opens could have done me in! Even the FM radio. Even automatic window switches!

I don't know what he and Mom talked about while he drove out of town. Maybe they talked about my dad. Once we were past the last gas station, on the brink of the forests where tourists liked to go camping, he pulled me out of the car and laid me in the ferns.

But I still trembled, so he tore off his jacket and his phone and left them behind. He carried me deep into the woods, Mom following behind him. He asked her to wait in the car, but that just wouldn't be like her. I bet she looked comical, stumbling over branches in a hospital gown.

At some point under the trees somewhere, the seizing stopped. I opened my eyes.

Mom told me later that Auburn-Stache laughed then—with joy, or relief, or the sort of mad glee that doctors and scientists get swept up in when they solve a puzzle. But Mom didn't laugh.

"I knew then that there were things you would always be powerless to change about your life." She spoke softly. "And that I couldn't protect you from all of them."

Bleak, Mom. Bleak.

You can await Part Two with bated breath! I can leave out some of the finer details of my toddling years, like every time Mom burped me or the time I decided to pee on our blue Persian cat, Dorian Gray. I can be mysterious, too, all right.

As much as I like mystery stories, it's hard to solve them when you're stranded in northern Michigan. The only Watson candidate I have is a cat who still resents me. I've read a lot of Sir Arthur Conan Doyle and Agatha Christie and a ton of Case Closed, but I'm no detective. I don't have a pipe, for one thing. I think that's required.

Here are the clues you've given me, Moritz Farber:

1. You have a pacemaker. Oh, and the name of your lower-left heart chamber is actually your left ventricle, or your *ventriculus cordis sinister*. You may win at languages, but *you* didn't spend four months handcrafting a life-size model skeleton complete with clay organs, Styrofoam lungs, and hand-spun alveoli!

2. You can't read by yourself. Your father had to read my letter

to you. But this paper was typed on a computer in, yes, *real good* English. So although electricity is no problem for you, there is something wrong with your eyes. But in that case, clue #3 seems strange. . . .

3. What the heck do you mean, you've "seen EVERYTHING"? Why was that part of your letter typed in capital letters? To me, capitalizing things doesn't come across as italicizing. It looked like you were SHOUTING AT ME! ANGRILY!

4. People have said cruel things to you in the past. This one is speculation. I mean, you hate your peers. But not just because they're idiots, because I think idiots are probably nice people sometimes. If it's about abusing language, I don't have to go to school to know that words can really suck, even when they aren't insults. I'll do my best, Moritz Farber, not to slash at you with them. OR WRITE AT YOU IN AGGRESSIVE CAPITAL LETTERS.

5. You typed your letter, so I know you have a computer. Don't even get me started on what a bottomless sense of emptiness I get when I hear about the Internet, a weird electric Neverland where everyone giggles at cats and updates myyouface pages or something. I mean, when I read manuals for old Internet browsers, it feels like I'm reading a really bland cyberpunk novel, and half the time I end up falling asleep and waking up with newsprint on my face.

Part of me wants to ask you all about it, but what would be the point? I try to be optimistic! It doesn't do me much good to hear about things I can never have.

But anyhow. I want to tell you about the first time I saw a computer, because it was also the first time I ever saw Liz.

*   *   *

It was at Junkyard Joe's, many years ago. Joe's trailer is the only place within a few miles of ours. The cars in his yard are the only safe ones I've ever seen—dead, scattered across the lawn like rusting bones in some mechanical elephant graveyard. I used to sneak away to crawl between them.

The little girl on Joe's porch didn't see me crouching behind an old pickup truck, spying on her. It was Liz, but I didn't know that yet. She was sitting at the lopsided picnic table and biting her lip, poking away at what would now seem like a massive brick of a thing, oblivious to the strips of verdant energy that gathered around her fingertips whenever she pressed the keys. The white light of the screen was reflected in her eyes. It made me think she was staring at the moon.

Did the screen reflect her like she reflected it?

I knew that if I got closer to her, my stomach would knot. Veins in my temples would bulge. I would convulse and fall and hit my head on the wooden steps.

But maybe seeing whatever she saw on that screen would have been worth a seizure.

Thanks for writing me back. The boredom's already shallower! I even got my lazy butt out of bed and went downstairs for a couple of hours to dig out the English-German dictionary, so Mom'll be singing your praises soon. You know, when she gets out of bed herself.

I'll leave the rest to you, Moritz. (Can I call you Mo?) And I've written way too much again, so I guess I'll save the questions about laboratories for later, but I hope you can start to trust me. I don't know why you think I would ever want to say anything cruel to you.

I mean, I've already given you lots to make fun of me for. If I'm ever an asshole to you, I hereby give you the right to call me a "cat-pisser"!

Don't tell me this isn't a *little* fun.

~ Ollie

chapter four

THE FOUNTAIN

You are a difficult tic to ignore, Oliver. I cannot despise you. Yet.

I am no Oscar Wilde and no Mo. I *am* an expert in oral storytelling. I have listened to hundreds of books. Dozens of authors and readers. Yet I have rarely heard a voice quite like yours.

My father has a strong Schwäbisch accent. He is not the best reader. His voice is like gravel. When he speaks, I must lean in close to find what he means within what he says. Before he knew me, I doubt he spoke to anyone. Now he tries to be heard. For my sake. During his reading yesterday evening, I heard you. On the fifth-floor apartment balcony overlooking the cars driving across Kreiszig's noisome *Freibrücke*, I discovered something about you. Something you are unaware of:

Even if you are powerless, your words are not.

You are a natural storyteller, Oliver. That may be *why* I

do not trust you—your sincerity is implausible. You and I are very different. Yet you made me understand something of what it means to be you. Most people aren't capable of making me feel anything. Let alone sympathy.

Most people would have been angry after my last letter. I was condescending. I mocked you outright. But you respond by telling me exactly who you are. You offer me new insults to use against you? It seems cruel to withhold my story when you are incapable of doing so. It is as if I am avoiding a puppy for fear of it drooling on me.

And your detective skills are not entirely wretched. You are right about my eyes.

I doubt I can be as endearing about it as you are. But let me tell you who I am.

I am Moritz Farber. I was born listening.

I was born without eyes. Do not ask if I am blind. I have never been blind. But I was born with no eyeballs in my sockets. While I doubt I wailed as loudly as you did, others have since screamed bloody murder at the sight of me.

Oliver, you should be grateful you were raised in a cabin and not a laboratory. I spent my earliest years in a testing facility. I do not intend to talk about it. Needle me as much as you like. I have felt worse. I have felt actual needles.

Yet I have also thought this: at least scientists could bear the sight of me.

You have never seen an eyeless boy. Perhaps not even in all those comics and books that occupy your time. Imagine you are looking at your dear Liz. Imagine that above her button nose and her sunshine smile there are no eyes reflecting a computer screen. Imagine that there is nothingness there—just skin. No expression whatsoever. Imagine this. Can you say you love her still?

I have no eyes, no eyelids. No eyebrows. I grow my dark hair long in the front so that my fringe hides the worst of it.

But there is nothingness on my face. Who would not scream?

I do not say "*tch!*" like you and your mother do. That would be irritating.

Sometimes I click my tongue against the roof of my mouth when I wish to see anything with greater clarity: If I am curious about the pores in someone's nose. The dust in the cobblestones outside. Anything minuscule requires this extra effort on my part. A focused click and, yes. I can see EVERYTHING.

Such clicks are usually unnecessary. My surroundings create enough sound waves to see by. This is the only advantage of living around other people. Kreiszig is a city of bustle. Of bodies and movement and clatter. No one can see what I see in the morning fruit and bread markets, where people haggle and stack and chop and banter. The noisier an area is, the clearer it is to me.

During school I can see well enough to avoid those who might be looking for me. See hiding places that others miss. Empty closets and classrooms. I can duck beneath tables when familiar footsteps trudge closer, scraping against the floor. At least my nothingness gives me warning.

*   *   *

Surely you have read about echolocation. You seem to have read about everything else. Surely you have read about whales using echolocation to find one another in the dark depths of the sea. About dolphins using sound waves to communicate with one another across great distances.

I see with my ears. My brain uses sound waves to determine the shapes of objects and barriers in my vicinity. How a bat might by using sonar. I can "see" how far away things are, can see what they look like by the way my ears interpret sound bending around them. I am not the first person to accomplish this. I *am* the only person, so far as I know, to have been able to do this from birth, and with more clarity of sight than a person with flawless vision.

My ears are so sensitive that I can tell individual eyelashes from one another when someone blinks. Because I can hear the sound of eyelids closing.

Imagine what I see at hip-hop concerts, Oliver. I always have the best view at any venue. At the summer festivals in the park, when the bass pounds hardest through the speakers, woofers, and amplifiers, I can see the droplets of sweat on thirty thousand people at once. I can see right into the performers' teeth. The hair follicles on their chins and the lines in their fingers as they clutch microphones. Darkness and light have no bearing on my sight. Darkness has no sound.

But color is silent also. I do not envy you the colors you have seen. Color is an alien concept to me. Probably much as the Internet is to you.

*   *   *

Many of the scientists at the facility thought my oversensitivity should be wreaking havoc on my brain. Certainly, they speculated, if I can hear eyes shutting and bones creaking and hairs sliding against one another, I should be incapable of processing the ceaseless input. How can I sleep over the sound of my own blood flowing in my veins? They believed I should be clutching my head. Wincing and whimpering in an anechoic chamber. A soundless room.

One thing about having no eyes, Oliver, is that you can never close them.

Yet I have never known anything else. I don't have to ignore the sound of water in pipes. Or wind in stairwells. Or a slightly squeaky nostril when someone speaks to me. My brain adapted. It labors on my behalf. This is something you can understand, Anatomy Expert.

If I whimper now, it is because of what I am. I have seen, if not everything, enough to despise myself and the rest of the world, if not yet you.

Many otherwise intelligent people severely underestimate the human brain. May all those scientists forever scratch their heads. I have no patience for their antics. They can rot.

Of greater concern to me is the chronic weakness of my heart. But that is a story best left untold. Leave it be. Needling won't reveal it.

I am not a fellow hermit, Oliver. If only.

For the past year I have been enrolled at Bernholdt-Regen Hauptschule, attending public school for the first time in my life. I did not want to attend any school at all. But Father came home early from work with brochures one evening. Brochures he had been collecting in the hopes that I would at least mime excitement when he presented them to me.

The schools in those brochures. As if we could afford half of them. But Father is proud. I could not say that. Not while he was sitting before me, grease on his uniform. A hopeful smile on his lips. He has tried so hard to raise me well. No one asked him to. Still, he has tried.

I have not even taken the required assessment that would allow me to pick from decent schools. To say nothing of procuring a letter of recommendation. There *are* some schools suitable for the likes of me. I chose Bernholdt-Regen because it was nearby.

I chose it because I deserve nothing better. Because I have reasons to whimper and reasons to despise myself.

Father was pleased that I made any decision at all. He believes *Hauptschule* might raise my awareness of the world. Discourage some of my alleged "antisocial" habits. I do not know why he believes I need *more* awareness. I see 360 degrees at once even at nighttime. And he's one to murmur and mumble about antisocial habits.

My teachers have been informed that I suffer from a cardiovascular disease, photosensitivity, and a severe reading impairment. They don't precisely understand. Sometimes they speak loudly to me. Move desks and chairs out of my path as if they think I will deliberately stumble over any piece of furniture foolish enough to get in my way. They think I am blind.

I am *not* blind. I have never been blind.

It is fair to say I have a reading impairment. Echolocation does not allow me to see the contents of screens or most books. Flat surfaces are impenetrable to me.

Father suggested I feign blindness at school. To raise fewer questions. To make it easier to belong. But I loathe the notion of using a cane when I don't need one. To pretend to be blind, for the sake of fitting in with people—with *children*—who have no interest in me in the first place? What a repulsive idea. I'm nothing like them. They can rot.

For almost as long as I have lived, I have worn opaque goggles in public. I am told they are black. On the left side I wound shoelaces around the strap to make it thicker. To obscure a pitted scar directly behind my ear. I've been told the goggles make me look like a Gothic owl. But they obscure my eyelessness enough to discourage the shrieking of strangers.

I can recall the exact moment I became aware of what I am to strangers.

I was just shy of six. I had begged my nanny to take me into the bakery one morning. The smells that were wafting out into the street drew me in. I was sniffing the egg tarts and custards nearest the window. The ovens in the back were hot, filled with croissants and sandwiches. The room was sweltering. There was a little boy around my age standing beside the *Brötchen*. Watching me. Waggling his tongue at me from the opposite side of the room. He winked at me and snorted into his hand. What good fun it would be to "out-wink" him!

I was an imbecile.

I was happy to remove my goggles in the heat of the room. The boy screamed and screamed. His father clenched his cracked, floury fists and hollered at the nanny. She nodded. Dragged me away in silence. Pulled me close to her side. Placed a hand over the upper half of my face to spare the world the sight of me. All the while I was clicking, clicking, and seeing too much in all directions as the boy's father tried to console his stricken child. With his apron he wiped the wash of tears and the dribble of snot that slipped down the boy's lip.

Here is an adage you must know: *The eyes are the windows to the soul.*

I can see so much of others. But no one can see into me. On some primitive level, this makes it seem like I do not have a soul. Perhaps I don't. If I am less than human somehow, I don't expect humanity from others. And do not doubt that I am less. I *know* that I was created as much as born. There is nothing comforting about it, Oliver.

I have pondered this too much. My peers at this worthless school don't even consider the state of their souls; they are too preoccupied with pop music. With eyeliner and sport.

You talk about being lonely and unwell in a cabin in the woods, even though you put on a great show of being cheerful. Your personality is as colorful as your vision. You really should be grateful.

There is nothing so lonely as being surrounded by people. I waste my days in a massive pool of bodies that, for the most part, cannot be bothered with the "disabled" boy in goggles.

For the most part.

There is a boy named Lenz Monk who has taken to tormenting me. Today I was on the second floor, leaning over what must be the last drinking fountain in Saxony (of course Bernholdt-Regen would maintain something so unhygienic), focused on the filthy grime on the mouth of the faucet. Lenz, passing behind me, kicked the back of my knees. Of course my legs folded. Of course water shot into my face. Perhaps if I had not been so fixated on the gunk, I would have heard the swish of Lenz's pants as he aimed his kick.

Instead I came up dripping. At least this time he did not leave me bleeding.

I did not turn to look at him. I do not need to turn to see. I only walked away. Lenz does not taunt. He merely grants his bruises and watches in silence. Last week he slammed a door on my fingers. I heard the door as it fell and I could have moved my hand, but Lenz does not stop until I whimper. If I whimper sooner, he leaves me sooner. If his first attack succeeds, he is satisfied.

I am typing with my left hand only today, because the skin on its knuckles is unbroken.

The number of times Lenz has done his best to shove me against walls or bathroom stalls or concrete. Lenz often tries to pull away my goggles. To pull them taut and snap them back into my face. He walks the same street home that I do, toward Ostzig on the city's east side. Often I must hide behind a kiosk outside the train station where smokers gather. They don't look at me while I listen, trying with all my might not to cough on their smoke and waiting for the drag-scrape of Lenz's feet to pass by.

He waits for me to whimper.

Eventually he will catch hold of me again. Once he squeezed my throat until I could all but hear the bruises forming beneath my skin, could hear the blood vessels creaking under his fists. I had to wear a scarf so that Father would not wor—

Why should I stain your simple ears, Oliver? You can be spared such things.

Appreciate your isolation. Public school is true torture.

There is something I have been considering since you first began writing to me. I have never heard you speak. Yet I imagine that you chitter and chatter like birds and traffic in the morning. I imagine you are a very noisy person.

The noisier someone is, the more I can see. Perhaps you could help me see something that I have never seen before. Perhaps I could see the world with your optimism?

But I will never meet you.

I have exposed enough of myself for the time being. I await Part Two. Not with bated breath, but with gracious anticipation. I still don't comprehend why, precisely, you are so fixated on this Liz of yours. It seems she is mistreating you.

Excuse my caution. I am not used to such abrasive honesty.

Moritz

P.S. To address your curiosity, specifically:

1. Marvel or DC: I could not care less. I do not listen to comics.

2. Cartoons: They are irritating. Bangs and explosions. Some people do enjoy them.

3. Oscar Wilde: I have listened to the audiobooks of *The Picture of Dorian Gray* and *The Importance of Being Earnest*. Why is he so verbose? Who has that much to say? Apart from you?

4. Computers and the Internet: I prefer the radio. Flat surfaces frustrate me.

I never learned Braille. I am not blind. But I learned the shapes of letters long ago. I learned my keyboard home keys early on as well. When I am typing to you, my computer dictates what I am writing back to me in a robotic voice. It is not lovely to listen to. It is like tone-deaf Daft Punk.

chapter five

THE POWER LINE

I didn't think you were being rude to me in your first letter, although I'm sort of annoyed that you're slandering Liz in your second one. Look, I may whine about her a bit, but when I LINEARLY get around to telling you more about her, I think you'll get it. It's not like Liz *asked* me to shut down. I mean, none of this is her fault. She's not the one who made me like this.

As for whether I could still love her if she had no eyes: for that I have to take more extreme measures.

Please follow these instructions:

1. Stack the pages of this letter neatly.
2. Roll the pages up into a cylinder.
3. Smack yourself over the head with it.
4. Repeat.

You complete ass. Of all the stupid—sorry, stoopid—things to say. You think that Liz would lose her soul if she lost her eyes? She could look like anything, so long as she was being Liz. I mean, come on, Moritz. What you look like isn't who you are.

If Liz wouldn't be soulless without eyes, neither are you.

Haven't you ever fallen for anyone? I mean, I know fewer people than I've got phalanges, and I've found someone I can't stop thinking about. But you haven't? I find that really hard to believe. Look closer. What are you . . . *blind*?

Also! What. The hell. You've been holding out on me, Mo! You've got no eyeballs? And instead you wear goggles and you've somehow developed bat vision? Um, okay. I understand you can't read comics, but please try to get your ears on *Daredevil*. Don't you get it? You see like a bat? You're bilingual? You're more than half-way to being a superhero already!

And whatever happened to you growing up (needling you about the lab again), you aren't *subhuman*. I mean, look at the X-Men. Rogue can't even touch people without killing them! And Beast is freakin' *blue*. So you have no eyes? At least your eyes aren't flesh-burning lasers! But if they were, you'd still be worth knowing.

As far as echolocation goes, when I was nine or so I went through a pretty sizable dolphin obsession. We have a small fish-pond a few acres away from our cabin that I've hiked to before. But there are, surprisingly, no dolphins in it. (Why couldn't I be a hermit at a beach house? I'll never see the ocean. . . .)

Here's what I've learned about echolocation: dolphins can click at frequencies so high that most people can't hear them. Most humans can hear sounds as low as 20 hertz, which doesn't sound like anything but feels a bit like being underwater with pressure on your ears, and as high as 20,000 hertz, which is probably like ALL CAPS, if ALL CAPS were a seriously pissed-off tea-kettle. But there have been a few documented cases where scuba divers swimming with dolphins could feel vibrations in the water. And here's the weird part:

Some people felt some emotion in the vibrations. They could sense if the dolphins were happy, or sad, or scared that a boat was gonna come and make tuna of them. These dolphins were sending their feelings into the world. What if I could see sound waves instead of electricity? What color would dolphin feelings be?

(Liz said this was the "girliest" question I've ever asked. I know that cowboys are manly, but why? And somehow dolphin noises are . . . girly? Who writes these rules?)

Anyhow, maybe the reason people avoid you is because the emotions your brain sends out when you click are kind of . . . negative emotions? Clicking is a nervous habit. And you do it more when you're worried about this kid who follows you home. Is he what folks call a "bully"? Is there a German word for that? I checked the German dictionary, and it said *Tyrann*, which sounds like *tyrannosaurus*. But he sounds less like an awesome tyrannosaurus and more like a loser. Maybe you're clicking unhappiness at people, and they're sending it right back in echoes.

I hope this doesn't sound dumb. What I'm getting at is some people can be really terrible. But you have to work harder not to let it faze you, because if you let them make you feel that way, you're just adding to the mess of unhappiness in the air.

I don't understand why you're so self-conscious. You seem pretty cool to me, even if you are kind of stuffy. I'm wondering what could have happened to make you despise Moritz Farber. Moritz Farber is not even a little boring.

Like I said, you've got all the makings of a comic book superhero! If people give you shit for being pretty cool, stand up and peel your goggles off and scare them away. Laugh maniacally and send happy dolphin-waves—

Actually, I mean it. I think you *should* try pulling the goggles off sometime. Have you ever done that? If you're so ugly (shut up and hit yourself over the head with the rolled-up pages again), you can send them running for the hills! Maybe then you won't have to whimper anymore. Lenz won't stop if you don't stop him.

What are you so afraid of? I can't even ride a bike down my driveway, but you can do anything. Anything you want, wherever you want!

In fact, your Magic Brain Vision (henceforth called MBV) makes my allergies look pathetic on all fronts. So I'll try to get to the good parts of my story. I'll try to hurry and get to Liz, to stop you from "talking smack," as kids say.

I'm going to rush my earliest years. I want to get to when I was old enough to read, old enough to wonder why the heck I couldn't handle batteries, old enough to stop peeing on household pets. Since you trust my storytelling so much (which is one of the coolest compliments—stories are everything to me), I think I'll tell you three stories from when I was a little kid. Three memories of three accidents that really stick out in my mind. Three's okay, but I kind of wish it were five. Because you know who really *was* a good storyteller? Shakespeare. He wrote plays in five acts.

Focus, Ollie.

The Linear Autobiography of
Oliver Paulot, the Powerless Boy
PART TWO: EARLY DAYS, IN THREE ACCIDENTS

1. The Fire

Mom used the money from my father's life insurance to buy our cabin in the woods. The cabin is shaped like a triangle; apparently it's part of some sort of ancient worldwide tradition to let your rooftop trail all the way down to the grass. The almighty A-frame! There's moss and ivy creeping up the roof from the ground, and sometimes it gets mildewy in the peak of the house, where my bedroom makes up the top floor, and it starts to smell a little like pond scum and cedar. Downstairs, there's Mom's bedroom, the kitchen, the living room, and the bathroom, all paneled in dark wood that Mom calls "too seventies to abide." Maybe that's why she hangs tapestries and quilts and paintings on every surface. There's a porch in the back, and one in the front with an awning that doesn't really offer enough shade in the summertime.

The cabin is on the outskirts of Rochdale, Michigan, hours away from where Auburn-Stache lives. My whole life long, he's come to check up on me at least twice a month. He's a kook, but I suppose I love him or something.

Anyhow, one of my weirdest memories begins with one of those checkups.

I've never seen Dr. Auburn-Stache drive. He's too careful about my allergies. So he parks the brown smudge of his latest Impala at the end of the two-mile-long driveway. (That's some nonsense number of kilometers. I'm just saying that our driveway is more like a long, thin dirt road.) Then he buzzes and flits to the house with a suitcase in hand. He doesn't wear a lab coat, which is kind of disappointing. He wears paisley dress shirts and corduroy pants. For a long time I thought this was how men dressed, but Mom smirks and says Auburn-Stache is "quirky."

Usually I get a standard physical check from him, but he has to be creative about some things. For years I've had this sort of awkward, deflated Mohawk haircut. Not by choice. By the hand of Auburn-Stache! Whenever he gives me a physical, he has to look into my ears and nose and mouth without a penlight. (You remember how penlights and I don't get along.)

So he has this wacky old apparatus that's like a small adjustable gas lantern with a pane of magnifying glass in front of it, and a funnel attached to that. He holds that against the side of my head whenever he wants to check my ears for infections. (It's his makeshift otoscope.) He says having hair on the sides of my head is a fire hazard, but I think he just likes to make me look like a rooster.

He used to sit me on his knee out on the front porch, where the light is better. One time when I was pretty little, Dr. Auburn-Stache pressed his otoscope against the side of my head and I didn't feel like sitting still anymore. So I wriggled away and somehow knocked the otoscope onto the wooden porch, and the lantern shattered. There was a sudden burst of heat as the doormat went up in flames, and then the nearest potted plant, and then the wreath on the open door, and then the carpet in the breezeway. I remember feeling like the fire had a mind of its own, sort of like electricity—like it was out to get me.

Good thing Dr. Auburn-Stache is always so twitchy, because he bundled me up and flitted and buzzed away from the porch. He deposited me on a stump pretty far away from the cabin and told me to "Stay!" like I was the drooling puppy you compared me to.

I think he was going back to rescue Mom, who'd been inside making tea. She needed no rescuing. She strode right out through the fiery doorway and onto the porch with Dorian Gray pinched under her arm, both of them looking more annoyed than anything else. He was clawing her up pretty good. Out on the lawn, she thrust the cat into Auburn-Stache's arms before sprinting to the garage to call the fire department.

I sat there on the stump, just blinking, watching the flames lick the brick chimney. The roof was catching fire by the time we heard the sirens. I wish I could describe what it looked like. The fire engine, I mean. I thought Mom's car was gritty, but that was before that diesel engine. I could feel the humming electricity even in the soles of my feet, even when it wasn't within sight. I could feel that thing coming like an electric stampede of red weight and light at my temples, and that must have shown on my face because Auburn-Stache lifted me up into his arms and jogged me away from it as it pulled up. Dorian Gray was meowing like nobody's business, and Auburn-Stache's chest rose and fell like running was the last thing Englishmen in paisley were used to.

There was Mom, staring at our house going up in flames, watching smoke and ash pour from the haven she'd set up for herself and her kid, and she still looked at least halfway exasperated about it all. And I only had eyes for the flashing lights and bleeding black smog that smothered the fire truck. It's what I imagine an old locomotive might look like, if that locomotive came roaring out of hell. Like some massive battering ram, all black and red smoke and bursts of white light that churned and spat into oblivion before my watering eyes. Grond! Grond! (Read Tolkien!)

I remember seeing some other amazing things. I saw policemen with walkie-talkies that left trails of saffron dust in the air whenever they buzzed with noise. I remember the blue light atop cars piercing through the clouds around the fire truck, but they didn't look only blue to me. They were spinning fronds of multicolor, fanning streaks of chartreuse and aquamarine that stabbed through puffs of burgundy and umber.

I should have looked away. My skull hummed against my brain. My nose was running, my eyes poured, and it had less to do with the fire than it did with the electrical auras buzzing in the air, making me itch from head to toe like I had some sort of volcanic sun rash.

But I saw so many colors that night, so many that maybe even you should be a little jealous.

Mom wouldn't let anyone near me. She couldn't be sure they weren't stashing phones or Tasers in their utility belts. Auburn-Stache chuckled when he saw I'd singed the side of my pants, but his eyes were shining. When Mom stomped back over to us, I rounded my shoulders in preparation for an almighty reaming.

Mom flew right past me and had Auburn-Stache by the shoulders, shaking him.

"What did you do? Another *harmless* digital watch?"

"Of course not!" he protested. "It was an accident! Electromagnetism wouldn't simply light a fire!"

"Don't say 'of course not,' as if you've never pushed him before. Oliver is not one of your experiments!"

"You don't need to tell me that." The fire in his eyes was only halfway due to the reflection of the flames behind us.

"He isn't *your* son."

I was gaping at the pair of them because this was a bigger spectacle than the fire, even. Mom and Auburn-Stache *never* fought. They sipped beers on the porch some evenings, got teary eyed and red faced when they thought I wasn't peeking down with binoculars.

Now Mom was looking at Auburn-Stache like he'd been beating me.

"Meredith," he said slowly, eyes reflecting the firelight, "I would never harm him. You have to know that."

Mom let out a laugh like a bark. "I think I can cut Ollie's hair from now on."

"Please." The blood left his cheeks, Moritz.

I rushed forward and grabbed her elbow. "Mom! He didn't do anything!"

She slumped. "Not this time, he didn't."

Mom, covered in black ash, let go of Dr. Auburn-Stache, wrapped her arms around me, and squeezed too tightly.

I could see Dr. Auburn-Stache over her shoulder, white against the red-black.

We stayed in a tent for a month, which the police thought was weird. But camping out and cooking hot dogs was an adventure while we waited for the cabin to be repaired. When we finally moved back in, Mom set our suitcases down in the untouched living room and sighed.

"Tch. Even hellfire couldn't kill the seventies?"

I threw myself across the orange tartan couch, burying myself in cushions. "Nope!"

Mom sat down beside me. "Ollie. Look at me."

She was so quiet that I did.

"You're too young to remember the digital watch. But if Greg—Dr. Auburn-Stache—*ever* tries to show you something electric, you have to tell me right away."

"But . . . he's my doctor."

"I'm your mother."

I think I was just relieved to hear he'd keep visiting. That I'd get to see color in his face again.

We've got a living room *covered* in bookshelves, Moritz, and one shelf is entirely stacks of encyclopedias. A couple years after

Auburn-Stache and Mom argued, I read the word *electromagnetism*.

Basically, electromagnetism is as strong a force in the world as gravity. I mean, if you can count on anything, you can count on things falling when you drop them and the air being full of electricity. Subatomically, electric particles are attracting and repelling each other *all the dang time*.

But if I'm allergic to electricity, how come static doesn't kill me? I've had a few shocks in my socks on the wooden kitchen floor, and those didn't give me seizures. And I know about anatomy. There's electricity in *our* brains, Moritz. Walt Whitman doesn't need to sing any body electric. We're all a little electric already, with or without pacemakers.

So how come I'm not permanently dead yet?

This is my working theory: my epilepsy isn't due to allergies. It goes beyond that.

I don't *get along* with electricity. I repel it and it repels me. Nobody's just *born* that different. It defies science and logic, Moritz.

It's just easier to say I'm sick. Easier for Mom to coop me up like an invalid.

So you *have* to tell me about the laboratory, Moritz. Even if it bores you. I'm not needling you now. I'm *asking* you. If you were created in a lab, was I created there, too? I mean, how else are you and I connected?

What else can explain the mess I'm in? If I'm an experiment like you, I need to explain that to Liz. I need her to know that there were bigger issues than me being a walking disaster to excuse—well, not excuse—but to *explain* that I couldn't help what happened when we went camping. I couldn't help her and I couldn't—

Focus.

I'm puffing on my bubble pipe, Watson.

2. Junkyard Joe

Mom put up "No Trespassing" signs everywhere around our property. You know. The kind that said, "VIOLATORS will be SHOT." Which I don't think is legal, but made for a decent threat. The reason that signs like these were even necessary had a lot to do with open season.

Do people hunt in Germany, Moritz? When I try to imagine it, I think of men in pantaloons prancing around chasing stags, like on Mom's tapestries.

Anyhow, open season here is a big deal. There are a lot of white-tailed deer in the forests, and every November people travel here with beer bottles and rifles and tarps in tow. They say they're after ten-point bucks, but it's really more about getting drunk with your buddies and sitting in trees, Auburn-Stache says. He's not the hunting type. Too British or something.

The last thing Mom wanted was a hunter stumbling near our cabin. Most moms would be worried about drunks carrying guns. She was more worried about drunks carrying flashlights.

Well, sure enough, when I was seven or so, some man wearing camouflage walked onto our property with a rifle over his shoulder.

Mom was teaching me how to bike-ride. I still had training wheels on the back, but I was getting really into pedaling as fast as I could and then braking hard enough to leave deep gouges of tire tracks in the dirt driveway. Mom jogged along behind me, always watchful.

On an autumn day, when the leaves smelled wet and rich and they were browning in the driveway, I pedaled slowly to put her at ease.

"I hear a woodpecker, Mom."

She kicked at the leaves. "Really? I don't hear a thing."

"Listen!"

"Nah, I'd rather smell. Smell that air." She closed her eyes.

And when she opened them, I was pedaling away as fast as possible. She shouted my name. I hadn't gotten all that far ahead when the hunter in orange appeared right in front of me, stepping out from between the pines. His eyes widened. I could see that something electric was glowing limelike in his pockets, so I slammed on the brakes and spun out, and the next thing I knew I was being carried and my head hurt, and I'd scraped my face along the dirt.

"This ain't your property," said the man who held me. Not the hunter, but someone else. I was too spaced out to recognize him. "Go on, before I report you. Police in this town are always lookin' to fine idiot flatlanders, you know."

I could see the treetops and a scraggly chin overhead. I don't know if the hunter—the flatlander—vamoosed or not.

"Waf gongan?" I said. It could have been right then, or it could have been minutes later. Sparks were in my eyes, rattling my teeth in my ears.

"Got yourself a nice concussion. And here comes your mom, lookin' likely to give you another one."

I heard her call my name, and the next thing I knew, I was in her arms instead, out on the porch and woozy still. And leaning over her shoulder was all the rest of the scraggle-chin: Junkyard Joe.

Joe, a bearded mechanic who perpetually wore a baseball cap, was our only "neighbor," although his trailer and junkyard are a mile away. He didn't mind Mom's signs. Last thing he wanted was more hunters on his turf. As far as he was concerned, all that deer meat was his. He used to stop by to drop off Tupperware containers full of chewy venison stew.

"Rise and shine, sonny jim," he said, showing off his missing teeth.

I blinked.

"Can you hear me?" Mom's voice was so loud, this close to me.

I nodded, but it felt like half my face had been torn to shreds.

"Just look at you. Now people'll think we're abusing you." She pulled me closer. "If you ever run away like that again, I don't know what I'll do. So don't. Never again."

This might have been when Mom started putting padlocks on the door, Mo.

Eventually Mom tucked me into bed, but it was early afternoon and I wasn't sleepy. Mom and Joe were on the back porch. My window was open. It was a warm day and the wind was blowing leaves against the screen and Mom was right—they smelled pretty great.

"Thanks for your help, Joe."

"Just lookin' out for my neighbors. Keep an eye on your boy."

"I'm trying. If I don't, he'll vanish. Gone before I know him."

"Aw, it won' happen like that. He gettin' any better?"

Mom must have shaken her head. I shied away from the window.

"Maybe I'll have him meet my niece sometime. She's around his age. Name's Elizabeth."

"Yes," said Mom, after a second. "Maybe."

Okay, so next I was going to tell you a story about the one time I had a babysitter and it was a big disaster, but I've changed my mind. Because the Elizabeth who Joe mentioned was the Liz I'm always going on about, so jumping right ahead to the day I met her is still more or less being linear. And I have to clear her name! I have to tell you what she means to me. I have to tell you why I wait at the end of the driveway every Wednesday.

3. The Girl

Playing huntsman in the woods is a lot less fun when your mother's sneaking along behind you, lurking beneath trees with all the grace of a drunken amputee. But if I was in my bedroom, Mom checked on me almost every seven minutes. Sometimes she brought warm macaroni from the woodstove or cold milk from the garage.

I told you she has hobbies. She's got a brain like mine, a brain that wants to be busy all the time. She knits, sews, paints, crafts model train layouts, collects flowers and presses them, makes mobiles and pottery, and binds books. But her favorite hobby is watching me, I think.

She watched me from my bed while I studied or folded or drew at my desk. Occasionally she spoke. More often, she only peered at me with fingers on her lips, that expression (you know which one) on her face.

"Can you go do something else?"

"*Can* is a fun word," she answered. "But if I *can* put up with you, you can put up with me."

She told me once, when I asked about Dad, that she'd promised not to trap me. Whether my dad wanted what was best or worst for me, I don't know. He died and left us enough money to live on, but with one condition: if I ever decided to go, Mom must let me. He put it in his will. Mom can't just keep me here forever.

She *promised* him.

But the way Mom looked at me, I didn't think she could keep that promise.

Maybe that's why I was always trying to leave.

I was almost eleven when Mom finally let me take the training wheels off my bicycle.

She and I played mechanic. Mom used to be a lot more playful. She lay down on her back on the grass with the bike frame over her nose while I watched, suck-chewing a banana.

"Screwdriver!" she cried.

"Don't you need a wrench first?" I passed her my banana peel and she didn't flinch. Just dropped it and held her hand out again.

"Scalpel!"

"But you're not a doctor." I held out the socket wrench. "Doctors have goatees. 'Staches of auburn."

Her fingertips were cold when she took it, because even in those days her circulation wasn't great. The rusty bolts ground when she twisted them.

"Ollie, does Dr. Auburn-Stache talk to you about the past?"

"I wish. He's too scared of you to answer my 'lab!' attacks."

"*Tch.* He'd better be." It was a murmur, but I could hear it under the clicking of the tool in her hand.

"Isn't he your friend, Mom?"

"Not exactly, Ollie."

"Then . . . what are friends like? Do you think I'll ever have any?"

I was smiling, but Mom dropped the wrench. She frowned at me through the wheel axle. "I wish that . . . well, for now you have me, Ollie. Better than nothing?"

"S'pose." I grinned wide to scrunch up my eyes because for some reason they were damp and I didn't want her to see that. "S'pose you'll do. Tell me about Dad?"

Needling immunity! Mom inched out from under the bike frame and stood up to look at it. "There. But you have to be careful. If you kick up the kickstand now, the bike will just fall over."

"That's okay. Mom?"

She was wiping her eyes, just staring at that bike. I felt like if I climbed on it she'd push me right off it again, or she was fighting a powerful urge to reattach the training wheels or cement the whole frame to the ground.

I let myself fall to lean against her—she put a foot out to her left to catch herself.

"I'll be your kickstand."

She snorted and rested her elbow (*articulatio cubiti*) in my hair. The bone was sharp. "Nah. You're my armrest. You aren't going anywhere."

Mom means well. But do you see why I couldn't buy her promises, Moritz?

I'm a lousy kickstand.

A few days later, I stole the keys from their most recent hiding place on the second oak bookshelf (I *always* find them), burst out onto the lawn, and pulled the bike from the tangled hoses in the shed. I pedaled down the driveway that led out of the woods. Tree roots jutted into the path. They looked a lot like outstretched hands. Every time I ran one over, I thought I was running over someone's fingers.

It wasn't just about escaping Mom. I was chasing after humidifiers, semitrucks, and cash registers. Stereos and movie theaters and tablets and tennis shoes with lights in them. I wanted to see the things everyone else saw, even if it was just from a distance. I wanted the world.

That power line halfway down the driveway all but blew me off my bike. Orange electrical tendrils dangled from the overhanging cable, probably draping from the wire like your Goth bangs drape across your forehead, Mo. The moment I neared them, my stomach clenched up. Definitely we had opposing charges, that power line and me.

A spasm went through my right foot; it slipped from the pedal. It was like the tendrils had grabbed me, had wrapped hot wires around my cranium and squeezed. The roots on the path had done nothing, but that silver cable in the sky threw me sidelong into the ferns.

But just as there had been something hypnotic about the laptop, there was something about those billowing, tangerine tendrils that made me determined to cross them, even if their licks left me twitching.

"This isn't over," I told the power line. And so began our legendary rivalry.

* * *

When I returned to the break in the pines, I rode one-handed with an old fishbowl lodged under my other arm. (Dorian Gray had shown the beta fish it once held a proper burial inside his stomach.) I dismounted, let the bike fall, and shoved the bowl over my head. It caught on my ears. I fought it down. Soon my breath was fogging up my vision. Trying not to tremble beneath my makeshift helmet, I approached the tangerine agitators that swung from the power line.

I'd read pamphlets about hazmat and NBC suits, about scientifically insulated clothes (although Mom always told me they just weren't worth the risk—whatever). I'd also read that glass doesn't conduct electricity.

Besides—glass seemed to work for spacemen, right?

Liz must have been laughing at me. She lived in town, but her father loved blackberry pie and there are lots of berry patches near our driveway. Picking berries wasn't really what other kids did on the weekends, but Liz wasn't other kids, Mo. I didn't see her standing in the ferns, watching me; I assumed that no one was around because no one ever was.

Liz crept up beside me while I was craning my neck to stare at my ropy nemesis. She could have taught Mom something about being quiet, or else the glass muffled sound pretty well, because I didn't even notice her until she pressed her face close to the fishbowl and hollered:

"GOING DEEP-SEA DIVING?"

The sound echoed in my ears. I fell backward into the leaves.

"What the heck are you wearing?"

I wiped pine needles from my palms and raised my eyes to her. Through the distorted glass, she could have been anyone, anything. I pulled the bowl off my head.

She was the girl I'd seen with the laptop. Her dark hair was tied back in a ponytail. Her tanned face was freckled, completely at odds with my pasty complexion. She was wearing short overalls with pockets full of blackberries that were staining the jean fabric purple. One dirty kneecap had a wet leaf stuck to it.

"Oh no." Her expression softened. "You aren't developmentally disabled, are you? Do you maybe suffer from a mental impairment?"

"No . . ."

"Oh. Well, my parents are both social workers; my mom works crisis calls, which means she stops people from killing themselves." Liz smiled. I'm sure she thought it was reassuring, but it was such a wide smile. "If you have a mental illness, I'm totally cool with it. I could probably even help you with it."

"I'm not mental!" My ears were burning.

"And you are—?"

"I'm sick. Um, allergic to electricity."

Liz raised her eyebrows. "So you are crazy."

"No." I stood up on wobbling legs and pointed at the power line. "Watch."

I ran full tilt at the break in the trees. It was the most reckless thing I'd ever done, and when the tendrils tossed me back and I ended up shaking on the forest floor with a nosebleed, I was amazed that I'd suffered nothing worse.

"Whoa! That was weird. Almost like you hit an invisible wall or somethin'. Did it hurt?"

I nodded.

"*Cool.*"

My face flushed.

"But that's *not* why I said you were crazy." She suddenly became stern. "I said you're crazy because you said your illness before you said your name. That's like one of my dad's clients." She pointed a reprimanding finger at me. "DO NOT DEFINE YOURSELF BY YOUR ILLNESS, Mr.—?"

"O-Oliver."

"I'm Liz." She reached a hand out. I thought she was going to help me up, but she proffered juicy purple berries. "You want some, Ollie? Or do you wanna sit there and bleed some more?"

"Thank you." I plopped one berry into my mouth, but I could taste blood over top of it. "Thanks a lot."

"No biggie, Ollie."

It was a biggie, Moritz. She had no idea how big of a biggie.

Tomorrow is Wednesday, so maybe Liz will stop by. Or maybe not. I mean, it's okay either way. It's not like I don't have anything else to do. I've been trying to get into origami, but I can't even begin to fold the dragons right, because you're supposed to build them up from cranes, but every time I fold a crane it goes all saggy in the middle. It's taking up a lot of time. It's better than just lying around and tearing my hair out, though.

You have to tell me more about whatever else is worth knowing about your life and times in Kreiszig. Cure the boredom again, won't you?

~ Ollie

P.S. Hey, why do you have a scar behind your ear? Was that Lenz or the laboratory? You can't just tell me you aren't interested in SECRET

LABS and then strongly hint that people did *actual experiments* on you. That's like dangling the carrot after cutting the donkey's legs off! Please, Moritz.

There's no one else for me to ask. Just squirrels and trees. Hey?

chapter six

THE WORDS

Why, Oliver? WHY DID I LISTEN TO YOU?! You complete cat-pisser!

I am not implying the use of italics. I am SHOUTING at you! I am writing this damned letter after being awarded a one-week suspension from Bernholdt-Regen Hauptschule pending my potential expulsion! I am sitting alone in my apartment with a bloodied nose and battered face. Both of which I hold you responsible for. But why should you care? I'm not boring you.

I was so pleased about your last letter. That is why I have acted like a fool. Acted as you might have. When someone tells you for the first time in your existence that you are *heroic*, it is difficult to remain sensible. That charming nature of yours has made an *Arsch* of me. You don't understand me, Oliver, any more than you understand the world. I can only *hope* that your dreadful advice was not an act of cruelty but of ignorance.

But if my hopes are justified? How terrible. It is as if your ignorance is being passed to me simply because you wrote something that moved me. I am furious. But then I am also to blame. I chose to trust you. You have a misleading tendency to sound wise.

But what could you possibly know? All the words you have ever written to me are words you learned in books. Words you learned in a cabin far removed from the real world. Or they are something worse: they are words you learned from a teenage girl who strings you along like you are a mindless plaything. Are you eating, Ollie? Why is getting out of bed a victory? You try so hard to sound happy, but what would you do without distractions? Are you so lovesick that you would whimper for eternity if Liz never returned?

You are the one who needs to *stand up*.

So how could I find solace in your words?

You have never gone to school. You have never had objects thrown at your head. You have never watched your classmates feign illness. Coughing and spitting and sighing when they are assigned your partner during science courses.

You have never walked through an indifferent city in the afternoon and waited for Lenz Monk to knock you down, worried that the whooshing of the wind might obscure some of his movement. You have never hurried home on cold afternoons with eyes on your back. When you can almost feel hands clawing at you and snagging at your hemlines. The hands of someone who is itching to grab you, just to hear you shout.

"MBV" does have some benefits. MBV tells me whether

someone is looming along the path up ahead. Whether someone is following me. I can hear their paces quickening. Footsteps. The sound makes my heart strain, my lungs soften.
Rattles my very brain, Oliver.

But you wouldn't know anything about this. You have not
seen the shape of words in echolocation. It is not the same as
seeing electricity. It is not beautiful.

"Freak!" bounces off every surface until it reaches me. It
seeps right into my forehead.

"Fag!" pierces me in the chest. Coils around my loins, my
fluttering heart.

"Retard!" is one I can hear forming on lips. I see it in the
spittle that casts it out, because I click, click, click my tongue
twice as much when I think someone might utter it. "Retard."

To say nothing of the laboratory. You ask why I am
scarred? You wonder about my *heroic* origins? What a fun
mystery! I am scarred because when I was small, people in
that laboratory cut me and put electric machines inside my
skull. For the sake of science. Are you pleased you asked? You
want to know more? Do you really hope that you and I have
that place in common?

You say people may be cruel to me because I poison the
air with, what, negative energy? You imply that the way others treat me might be my fault? Because I show them I am
afraid?

How can I help but show that, when I can hardly breathe
and sweat pours off me and I wish only that I could close
eyes I don't have so that I don't have to see the looks on their
faces?

You don't have to tell me I deserve this. I know that already.

Fick dich, Oliver.

To think I had begun to consider you a friend.

Our parents wanted our letters to be medicinal. This is bad medicine. I want no further part of you. Consider this the end of our correspondence.

chapter seven
THE CABIN

Okay. You need to calm down. Part of me is afraid to say anything that might upset you more, but part of me wants to scream right back at you. All of me is wondering if you've gotten any help. Where's your dad while you're busy bleeding all over and screaming? You're sitting all alone in your apartment? Have you told anyone else about Lenz Monk? Anyone who isn't powerless? Or do you just close your mouth and accept it?

So what the hell happened?! What triggered this? I would *never* say you deserve to be hurt, so why are *you* saying it?

I may have an attention deficit or whatever, but I think you might have manic depression or a mood disorder, Moritz! I've read about these things, and I don't pretend to be an expert, but I think you should get a counselor or social worker or psychiatrist to help you, if you haven't already. I even asked Auburn-Stache to have a look at your last letter, but that was pretty pointless. Here is what he said, while taking my pulse:

"Sometimes friends in crappy situations can be unfriendly and crappy themselves."

I'm worried about you, and it sucks that I can't do anything about it. Maybe we've never met and never will, but I think I've made it clear that I *want* to be your friend. And if friends are just crappy to each other, I guess I'm allowed to be a bit crappy, too. So I'll tell you that I *won't* be sorry until you tell me what happened and why you got suspended and how on earth that's supposed to be my fault!

You're right. I don't know much about how other kids act around one another. I've never stood in a classroom. I've never waited at a freakin' bus stop. So maybe I am the worst person to listen to. But I think you're taking this out on me because you're too scared to face the people who actually hurt you. Like the people in the lab I don't know about, I guess.

Do us both a favor and tell me what the hell happened before you start screaming at me! Because here's the truth about how I feel about our "correspondence" so far: I have been really honest with you.

But you, Moritz?

You talk around everything like you're talking in those waves you see by. You don't say what you mean! You pull your punches. You say you don't want to hurt my "simple ears." I call bullshit. You're just too scared to trust me because you think if I ever met you I might shove you into a drinking fountain just like Lenz does.

As if I needed one more reason to feel like a leper.

Next time you talk to me, actually *talk to me*.

If you really don't want to write to me anymore, I guess that's okay. I mean, I'm getting pretty used to the whole abandonment thing. It's been four months since I last saw Liz. Four months since she stopped by after school and told me how her days were booked with basketball games and acting competitions and basically filled with lots of people who aren't powerless.

Anyhow, I hear the word *freak* all the time. I hear it in this empty house. It's so quiet here sometimes. You would be blind. You think my talk fills up the space? Who is there to talk to?!

And you know what? I'm not sorry about asking about the lab. It's easy for you to ignore because you have other distractions. It's easy for you to just forget about where you came from because you're going to go other places.

I may never get out of here, Moritz. What do I have to look forward to but the past?

Sorry I told you to enjoy the "real" world. Sorry I told you not to take being surrounded by people for granted.

Mom says she feels like maybe I shouldn't have tried writing you to begin with. She's trying to lock this door like she does all the others. She says I shouldn't even reply. But there's not really much to lose if you're already ditching out.

As for my terrible advice—I told you to stand up and face your troubles. Blaming your troubles on me isn't heroic at all. You could have had a cape and mask, Moritz. I guess I thought you were braver than this.

chapter eight
THE GOGGLES

Ollie. May I call you Ollie? As an apology? I do not have a lot of experience with apologies or friendship. I do not know where to begin.

I was prepared never to speak to you again when I wrote that last letter. Because you'll never meet me, I wrote like a coward. Wrote knowing that you could not fight my accusations, at least not to my empty face.

But after I screamed at you, you replied first with *concern*. That was humbling. I am two years older than you, Ollie. I don't feel those years. You . . . you could not let me rot.

Thank you, Ollie.

No, I do not have a psychiatrist. I have no intention of contacting one. I admit that my temperament is sometimes unstable. I attribute this to unfortunate genetics. A troubled upbringing. I have had enough of people in lab coats. A doctor regularly visits to ensure that my pacemaker is functioning. Beyond him I will have no one.

But I am grateful for your concern. Father is concerned as well. Quietly. Sometimes when I sit on the balcony listening to Kreiszig at rush hour, cars and horns and the echoes of footsteps far below, he sits beside me. He puts his hand on my shoulder.

But family is compulsory. Family that does not care is not family. Perhaps friends who do care are something more than family? How sanctimonious I sound. Let me speak plainly: I appreciate your friendship. Apologies for making an awkward dirge of it.

Did I deserve all your reprimands?

Firstly, I resent the accusation that I do not trust you. I may never be the extrovert that you are. But I *am* learning to trust you. You know more about me than almost anyone.

Secondly, you aren't being objective. As much as I admire your honest writing, you aren't always honest with yourself, Ollie. Let me elaborate:

You say you see no point in dwelling on things you can't have. But you think of these things constantly. Take the Internet. You insult it. You express a desire to see it. Then you claim a lack of interest once more. Why pretend? Can you tell *me* to treat my temper when *you* are so contradictory? Hypocrisy.

Perhaps I vented my anger at my circumstances on you. You have done the same to me by feigning happiness. Trying to be funny even when you are in pain. I am not a hero and you should not pretend to be one. Wearing a mask cannot change that you are wincing underneath it!

I would like to visit your empty house. To give you some-one to be noisy to. I cannot. So when you write: Be angry! Be upset! How else will I ever "meet" you?

Which brings me to Liz. She seems . . . *charming.* In a way. But you cannot decide that without her there is no future. I am trying to withhold judgment until I hear more. Is she entirely composed of confidence?

I don't speak in school. Yes, perhaps a brooding smog of unhappiness permeates the air around me. In my defense, no one ever reached out to me like Liz did to you, with berries or a hand or anything else. Hearing how you met—how she supported you while you fought to overcome that power line, armed only with resentment and a fishbowl—

I longed to be half so heroic as the pair of you.

Let me tell you why I blamed you. Let me tell you about the miraculous moment that inspired this apology.

Let me counter your story with a nosebleed fable of my own.

I went to school a week ago with your letter at the fore-front of my thoughts. I tried to emit your invisible "dolphin-waves" of happiness as I crossed the concrete courtyard of Bernholdt-Regen. I held my head straight. Tucked my hair behind my ears. For once, my goggles and forehead were exposed.

No one took notice. The students around me carried on chewing their cheeks in the oily halls and cramped class-rooms. Idiotic as usual. I saw Lenz Monk leaning against a toilet door. Doubtless trapping some unfortunate soul inside. I *waved* to him. He blinked at me but let me pass without a whimper.

During athletics hour, I was eliminated early from a game of dodgeball and took a seat along the sweat-stenched bleachers beside my fallen comrades. I *could* easily win at dodgeball if I chose to. MBV allows me to see the trajectory of a ball the moment it leaves someone's fingertips. Especially in a noisy *Hauptschule* gymnasium. I *could* win.

I dislike drawing that sort of attention. I am no longer anyone's experiment.

Small steps. I nodded to the person sitting beside me—a notoriously quiet boy: Owen Abend. I notice him for the sake of his silence. When I sit alone in the cafeteria, I can pick him out of a crowd. He appears as a dip in my sight. Not a hole, but the slightest dent of a body perpetually quieter.

Owen blinked at me. Quietly, of course. But he didn't flinch.

Lenz got eliminated with the smack of a ball to his chest. My teammates patted him on the shoulder.

I raised my voice alongside the rest. "Perhaps next time."

His eyes narrowed. Soon he loomed over me.

Allow me to describe Lenz Monk. He smells of cigarettes and sweet pumpernickel bread. He is large. Far larger than me. (I am short for my age, and about as thick as the combined flimsy pages of the letter you urged me to hit myself with.) His shoulders are rounded. One of his eyes moves more slowly than the other. He is ugly. But who am I to say so?

I forced a smile. "A valiant effort."

He tried to shove me in the chest. Likely just to push past me. He does not usually act when many people are present. He torments in private. I should have been safe.

Had I not reacted.

Understand that I have the quickest reflexes, Ollie. When every minuscule movement made by another person is apparent to your brain the very *instant* it occurs and sometimes the moment before it occurs, your natural impulse is simply to respond. Without conscious thought.

The moment he raised his hand, I was bending my torso out of his way. He hit only empty air. Tripped forward a step or two. One boy laughed. Owen Abend put his hand over his mouth.

It was, to quote your Liz, "no biggie."

Lenz Monk disagreed. He punched me in the face.

MBV meant I could have ducked under his fist. I could have countered him with one of my own punches before he realized he had swung past me into the wide-eyed bunches of students watching from the bleachers behind me. I might have slipped from the meaty fingers that clutched at my collarbone. Darted in, quick and close. Left a demeaning kiss on his nose tip.

So why did I take the punch right under my right lens? Why did I let his heavy fist dislodge my goggles? Set my nose to spitting blood, my cheekbones to creaking?

Because. In that precise moment, I remembered you. You ran straight at that power line.

And no demeaning peck could do the damage to him that

my sudden unveiling could. The punch landed me on the polished floor. I peeled my goggles away. Pushed them over my forehead until they pulled my long bangs up and away. Held my bloody nose to my sleeve and lifted my head high enough for Lenz to see the nothingness.

Because you told me to, Ollie. Because that could be my superpower, yes?

Under my breath I was click, clicking. But I did not replace my goggles.

MBV revealed Lenz's expression in excruciating detail. His face nearly curdled. His disgust crept down from his brow and coagulated around his nose before slipping down to pull the corners of his mouth away from his teeth. Teeth fell open so that he could let sound slip out between them. Sound that made his horror so clear to me.

Behind us the crowd craned forward in a synchronized motion not unlike the wave audiences form during sports matches—but everyone recoiled twice as quickly. I saw one girl actually trip over the bleachers backward, but while she caught the heel of her foot on the step, I was also seeing Lenz's horrified face, twisted in high-definition, and I was also seeing my gym teacher, Herr Gebor, stomping toward us from the locker room with one of his shoelaces untied, and I was also seeing a moth flitter about high, high above us, and I was also seeing a million dust motes collect on the rafters, and seeing how Owen Abend's eyes widened, and seeing how the stream of warm blood caught and pooled in the pocket between my bottom lip and my gums, and seeing the aimless patterns in the polished wood grain beneath my feet and tailbone, and very nearly almost seeing straight through Lenz's pores to his gaping skull underneath—

The scientists were not completely wrong about my brain. When I am upset, I cannot focus my MBV on any single thing. The sound and fury of everything simply pours into my head from all directions while I click, click my confounded tongue. Seeing everything at once makes my head hurt and my heart flutter. This is the worst possible thing. My simpleminded heart. My struggling pacemaker.

For an instant, Lenz was motionless.

Then he smashed my face into the floor. It hurt so much I could hardly feel it. As if my body turned my pain receptors to ice. My goggles broke against my forehead; the right lens popped free from the frames. They slipped from my head, scratching and tearing my face in stinging lines as they peeled away.

People shouted. Cheering Lenz on? It was so noisy with their words. I could see the drool in the backs of their throats when they hollered. They rooted to see my face caved in. Watching a live freak/fag/retard's face avalanche is quality entertainment. Regardless of whether you've got MBV or 20/20 vision, or you have to squint through glasses.

"*Freak*," Lenz spat.

A great yanking at my upper arm: Herr Gebor pulled us apart. He glanced at my face and swore beneath his breath before releasing me, Ollie.

Deprived of my goggles, I scratched my hair down over my eyes. Scratched and clicked and scratched and clicked.

One person kept her head. One of the few people I

somehow lost sight of in my frantic, haphazard MBV. She grabbed me beneath the arms. Hoisted me to my feet. Frau Pruwitt looked me dead in the face as if I had eyes she could meet.

I know that there's a customary cliché about librarians being what crass people might call "hard-asses." Frau Pruwitt is granite. Had I tentacles underneath my goggles, she would not have batted one eyelash. She must have heard the fuss from the hallway. She unceremoniously shoved a wad of tissues right under my gory nose. Pursed her lips.

"A *tussle*, Mr. Farber?" She sighed. "Come along, then."

I was still seeing too much while I was dragged to the headmaster's office through throngs of pupils who parted like Moses's sea before us. Seeing so much, I felt as if my head would divide itself just as the crowd did. My jerking heart might do the same. Imbecilic thing.

At some point I was deposited in the headmaster's office. I understood, through the haze, that I had been suspended. I was left to wait and catch my breath and brain and heart rate on an uncomfortable sofa in the hallway outside the main office. Left to hear the sound of mites in the brown carpet clicking away in time with my own clicking, click-clicking. On the opposite side of a glass wall behind me, I could see/hear men and women in the office whispering. One man, my history instructor, clutched his rumbling stomach. As if the sight of me made him downright unwell.

"But he *must* be blind."

"He's still making that sound. What is that? A tic?"

"Why don't we have more information about this? He should have accommodations in place."

"His guardian only told us he was photosensitive. When he was enrolled. That was all."

My physics teacher: "I thought the goggles were a harmless affectation. He doesn't have many friends; if he wanted to use 'photosensitivity' as an excuse, I couldn't blame him. I had no inkling that he was actually . . ."

"We'll be held accountable. A plan should have been in place. Aside from all the rest, he has a pacemaker! Of course he'll be at a disadvantage among normal students."

Oh. *Normal* students, Ollie.

I finally despised you then, Ollie. My head was tearing itself asunder. I could not filter a single whispering thing out. The thing about having no eyes is that you can never close them.

I clamped my hands over my ears. Tried to hear only my irregular heartbeat. The gentle buzzing of my pacemaker. The air whooshing through my lungs. The blood pulsing through my veins and arteries. The sounds of my skeleton. The sounds that I am never rid of.

In my lap were my battered goggles. Frau Pruwitt waited beside me, arms folded.

"Cheer up, son," she said gruffly, without looking at me. "Soon be Christmas."

It is February.

It was only after I sent you the enraged letter that I remembered something vital.

There were too many stimuli in that gym that day, Ollie. Too much noise. It took me until late that night to think clearly about all that I'd witnessed and experienced.

But the goggles.

I couldn't remember picking up the goggles. They were torn from me. How did I end up clutching them again?

After Herr Gebor pulled Lenz off me, something miraculous occurred. Something wondrous. My appreciation for language rarely has need of the word *wondrous*.

Before I was dragged to the office with the fearsome librarian, someone stopped me in the doorway.

Owen Abend. A poke on the shoulder. He shoved my goggles into my hand. He had taken the time to pop the dislodged lens back into place.

Perhaps school will not be so unbearable when I return. When my suspension ends. Or is this only your optimism tainting me again?

In any case, it is not the worst thing I have felt.

Please do write me soon.

Sincerely,

Moritz

chapter nine
THE WOODS

Please don't apologize to me. It makes me downright squeamish. Yuck, man. Yuck. I agree with you that I don't deserve it, really, so enough of that nonsense. And I already told you to call me Ollie!

I got your very angry letter on a Wednesday. I may have mentioned that Wednesdays used to be the days that Liz came over after she was done with school. I'm always a bit cantankerous on Wednesday evenings when she doesn't show, so when Mom came in dripping with snow with the mail dangling from her mittens, and I saw your letter on top of her hospital bills, I was really hoping for a Super Pen Pal Self-Esteem Boost . . . which I'm not sure being screamed at in German is, exactly. (I can guess what *fick dich* means. I read that line aloud and Mom nearly stabbed herself with her sewing needle.)

I can tell that you're not telling me everything about yourself, but that's not the same as lying to me. I don't know why I expect everyone to be like me. If that were reality, there'd be an awful lot of noise pollution clogging the air. Probably wouldn't even need MBV to see it!

Maybe I do Fake the Happy. I sort of assumed a pen pal was some imaginary person who wanted to hear all about skipping and joyful times and eating bacon, especially if that pen pal seemed to be a manically depressed German kid. (No offense, Captain Mopes-a-Lot.) You're going to be sorry for calling me on this one, though!

Gird your loins! Prepare for an influx of *honest* ANGST in your mailbox!

Your showdown with Ugly-Face Monk (I don't have to be nice) read like the panels of a pretty decent action comic, even though you got your ass whooped. I imagined "POW!" sounds. I really don't regret telling you to take off your goggles, because in my head you did it in slow motion, pausing for dramatic effect. You said some girl tripped when she saw your true identity, right? In my version, she screamed and fainted, and her hair turned white, too.

I'm sorry you were in pain, though. It sounds like when you can't filter your MBV—that's like when I'm surrounded by electricity and wishing I could stop a seizure that doesn't give two tiny craps about my wishes.

Also, I think you've revealed your love interest at last: Frau Pruwitt and her figurative titanium bum! I look forward to hearing about your awesome attempts to woo your librarian. (But not really. Because that would be gross, man. What are you even *thinking*, Moritz?)

As for those teachers you overheard in the office—are you sure that a portal to hell hasn't opened in a boiler room in your school? They sound slightly evil. Exorcise them, or ignore them. They're just *Tyrannen* of a different kind.

Have you seen Owen? You should thank him. Then you can magically begin hanging out!

Wait, how *do* most people make friends? I've only done it once. There has to be an easier way of going about it than getting thrown around and bleeding all over the place. But both of us went through that. So maybe . . .

Nosebleeds = Friendship. Maybe friends are drawn to bloodshed. You know. Like sharks.

And hey! Speaking of scary friends, it's really funny that you called Liz intimidating, because she's way shorter than me and has, like, baby hands. But I get what you mean. Maybe if I talk more about one of my wonderful and totally terrifying acquaintances, you won't have to think about yours for a while?

I stood up and tried not to glare too hard at the power line. Berry juice stained my palm and blood dribbled down to my T-shirt, and Liz stared at me with bulging eyes, like she was going to grab me and shake me just to see if I jingled.

"You look like an extra in a horror movie." The berries had vanished, probably shoved into her pockets again. "And maybe you are! That looked almost like an invisible hand shoved you away. Wicked."

"Wicked . . . ?"

"That's what English kids say. In Harry Potter. I think it's cool."

"You think it's wicked."

"Yep." Liz frowned. "So you're the Amish cabin kid. I thought you'd be grosser. Have crooked teeth and a hunchback. You know, like your mom's married to your uncle or something. Not that I'm judging you, if that's the case. You can't control who your parents were."

She was giving me whiplash. "Wha . . . ?"

"Hey!" She stood close, too close. "You're injured, right? So how about we go back to your place to clean you up." Her eyes sparkled. "No one will believe me when I say I went to your house! Mikayla will tell me I'm bullshitting her again."

Although Auburn-Stache had the strange habit of hissing "Pissing Nora!" whenever he dropped something, Mom never cussed. I made a conscious effort to close my mouth.

(Oh, man. Mom had to be wondering where I was. I'd run out on her while she was drawing water for a bath. She must be raiding the nearby woods by now, or in the long grass of the backyard, standing on tiptoe and shielding her eyes from the sun and calling my name.)

"Well?"

I blinked. "Maybe . . . maybe not. No. Don't."

She snorted. "Did I get it right? *Is* your uncle your daddy?"

"That's not it." I stared at my feet. Things like this weren't allowed to happen to me. I couldn't just have conversations with normal kids in the woods.

Liz was crouched over my fishbowl, sniffing it. Poking it, for whatever reason. She may have licked the glass.

Well, *abnormal* kids in the woods, even.

"You're the first kid I've ever talked to," I said.

"No way." She rubbed her chin, smearing juice along it. "Wanna come back to my uncle's place? He's got gauze. Or toilet paper, at least. And he definitely isn't my daddy, so don't worry about that."

I looked back at the driveway, at my bike lying on its side. I could probably make it to the bike before she could grab me. Then again, she looked pretty spry and she'd already caught me off guard once.

She seemed just as likely to tackle me to the ground as the power line was. I looked back at her. Behind her the tassels on the silver cable wriggled in my direction, teasing me.

You haven't won this one yet.

Finally I nodded.

Liz hefted my bike upright and began to push it into the woods for me. "Come on," she called over her shoulder. "We can follow the deer trails."

I followed her, Mo.

Dream-walking.

It was a short hike through the forest to Junkyard Joe's, and the afternoon sky was visible above the pines. Even so, the path was mottled with shadows, and it wasn't a path I was used to taking, so I should have been watching my beaten Timberlands and trying hard not to trip in front of her again or drop the fishbowl. But I kept watching the way she moved.

People all have different ways of moving around. This is something you definitely notice when you've only ever seen a few people. Auburn-Stache is twitchy, Mom is careful and deliberate, and Liz . . . well, she moved like she had springs on the bottom of her feet. I kept waiting for her to jump into the sky and just keep going, like an astronaut in zero gravity.

Liz clambered noisily over logs I chose to walk around. She was dragging the bike along the leafy ground as if she didn't even remember she was holding it, stopping every now and then to pick berries from bushes or acorns from the ground and shove them down into her apparently ocean-deep pockets. Other times she would stop and point out random plants or rocks or marks in the forest, with exclamations like "No way! A pudding stone!" and "There's probably salamanders under that log." She hefted the log up and, sure enough, there amid little writhing centipedes sat a yellow-spotted salamander, trying to bury itself and hide from her.

I could relate a bit. I was nearly scurrying away up a tree anyhow, because centipedes aren't my favorite things. (If you've ever had one bite you, you'll understand.)

Liz leaned forward and plucked the salamander from the ground as easily as she'd picked all those berries, as easily as she'd crept up on me. I thought she was going to shove it in her pocket with all the rest and I winced. No creature deserves death by overalls.

But Liz just lifted it up to her face and stared it in the eyes. It wriggled at first, whippet tail smacking against her wrist. It must have grown bored, or else it couldn't handle that stare of hers any better than I could, because it stopped and looked back at her instead.

I wanted to tell her that holding a salamander is pretty much the worst thing you can do for one, since they breathe through pores in their skin and the oils on human hands are damaging enough to them without the additional grime from the juice of unwashed blackberries. But all I did was watch her like that salamander did.

She put it back down exactly where she'd found it and set the log down on top of it, gentle as anything. She didn't say a word about it; we just started walking again.

Are you starting to see it, Mo? A little, at least?

When I could see the outlines of Joe's trailer and garage, the ghostly silhouettes of busted cars, Liz stopped suddenly in front of me. I nearly ran into her back. She grabbed me by the sleeve and pointed to a strange dent in the forest floor beneath the boughs of a jack pine.

"Wow!" She was whispering. "Have you seen these before? It's a bed for a white-tailed doe and her babies, probably. Let's not go in. We'll scare them away if they're around here somewhere and they smell us. But look—you can see where they curl up and sleep, because the pine needles are all crushed. And you can see hoof-prints here, so you know that's what it is."

"And you can smell the urine."

Liz didn't reply. She let me go and started going forward again. I wished I'd kept my mouth shut.

"Welcome to Junkyard Joe's!" Liz said, and held her arms out to the car graveyard.

It had gotten some new additions since I'd last been there—between the silver trailer's wooden porch and the garage were a decrepit pontoon boat with only one pontoon, someone's parked motor home in storage, a battered dirt bike without handlebars.

I tried to pretend I'd never seen the place before. She kicked at the grass as we stepped between lanes of pickups rusted straight through, disembodied truck beds, the remains of station wagons picked clean.

"Uncle Joe won't be home from the shop yet."

I stopped in my tracks. "You're allowed to be out here by yourself?"

"I'm *twelve*."

We stood in front of Joe's trailer.

"I should go . . ."

"Look, Uncle Joe won't care that you're here. But lemme warn

you, it's really messy inside. And Uncle Joe's got lots of stuffed animals in his trailer."

"Um . . . teddy bears?"

"No, dead ones."

"Dead teddy bears?"

At least her exasperated expression was familiar. I got that from
Mom every time I asked about the laboratory. But I didn't want to
think about that, because thinking about Mom reminded me that I
shouldn't have left her alone to worry.

"No, I mean like he shoots things with his rifle and then goes
down to Bob's on East Higgins Road, and Bob fills the dead things
with polyester and coats them in formaldehyde or whatever, and
gives them marbles for eyes, and then Uncle Joe hangs the dead
things on his walls."

"You mean taxidermy. You should have said."

Her cheeks twitched, just shy of dimpling. "No, I shouldn't have,
you dork. Now, come on. I promise there aren't dead teddy bears
waiting for us. Or dead real bears, actually. It seems like Uncle Joe
just shoots a lot of rabbits and squirrels and deer."

"Death unto all things cuddly!" I was still mumbling, but she
heard me.

I could hear the wind whistling through all the automobile skeletons around us, could feel it drying the sweat on my forehead and
blood on my chin while she stared at me. Then she laughed. You
might have thought she'd bark, but instead, her laughter was much
softer than she was—like a shock of faintly cold air when you open
a chimney flue after wintertime.

"Come on."

She leaned my bike against the porch railing and trudged up the steps. This was the same porch I'd stared at previously, when she was a little girl with a laptop and I didn't know her yet.

But I didn't even reach the first step before I felt my stomach turning over. I could see faint colors bleeding out through the crevices between the porch floorboards. Joe probably had a generator under there. Or it could have been a phone line. That the wisps of color were greenish made me think the latter. It didn't matter what it was, really.

"I'll wait out here."

"What, you're worried about your allergies?"

I nodded.

"Well, lemme go in first. I'll unplug the TV and the radio and the microwave, even."

I shook my head. "That won't be enough."

"Fine, I'll unplug the fridge, too. But the pop won't taste good if it's warm."

"There are power sockets. Wires in the walls." I shuffled my feet. "I better just go home."

Liz grabbed my arm as I turned away, smearing warm blackberry juice along my forearm.

"You're serious? It's that bad for you?"

"Why would I lie about it?"

"Man, that sucks," she said. "Look, hold these." She emptied pockets full of berries into my fishbowl. "I'll get the goods. Toilet paper works just as well outside as it does inside."

She ran inside, easy as anything, and those little bleeds of color didn't even sway in her passing. Or, if they did, they just gently caressed her, friendly to her like they never were to me. A few of them seemed to be itching to prick me, stretching toward me and away again. She kicked off her sandals on the welcome mat. The screen door slammed shut behind her.

Birds chirped in the branches overhead. The berries leaked purple into the bowl in my hands, hot in the sun. I took a deep breath. What if she was just going to leave me here?

Oh god. What if she wants to just leave me here looking stupid with a fishbowl of berries?

What else could she want from me?

I was thinking about making a break for it again, but she was already back, holding a can of red pop in each hand. I wondered where the promised toilet paper was for maybe a millisecond before I resigned myself to seeing her whip it out of one of her mystical pockets in a minute or so.

I remembered the last time I'd stood out there staring at the porch. The time when I'd seen her staring so intently at a computer screen.

This time, she was staring at me.

Liz brushed away some pine needles so we could sit on the roof of an old green minivan that she referred to as the "Ghettomobile." I've never asked about its namesake. Again, let's leave some mysteries in my life.

"It looked like you bled a lot, but at least you aren't a swooner. Some of my mom's clients are swooners. She isn't supposed to say so, because she isn't supposed to talk about her clients at all. But some of those schizophrenics and stuff have narcolepsy brought on by cato—catoplexiglas or something."

"So your mom tells you secrets?"

Liz shrugged. "If I bug her enough."

Liz was a needler, too. Maybe she could give me some tips.

It was late afternoon now, almost evening, and mosquitoes were nipping at our legs and alighting on my bloodied shirt. I was holding a big tangle of t.p. under my nose, but the blood had long since dried; my nose had stopped spewing even before we came across that pudding stone on the trail. I felt a little light-headed, and I wasn't sure it was from only blood loss.

We'd been sitting there for an hour while Liz told me all about her parents and her mom trying to stop this one guy from committing suicide by hanging himself from Christmas lights, and about a nameless teenager with borderline personality disorder who was convinced she didn't need any treatment so long as she drank a mixture of mouthwash and Tabasco sauce every morning before school. About some alcoholic who drank the antiseptic hand sanitizer right from the wall.

Man, Liz was proud of her parents. She thought they were superheroes or something. She could have been talking about anything, though. I was so desperate to hear a new voice.

"What were you doing out there, wearing a fishbowl on your head?"

"Oh. Well . . . I wanted out. I was trying to find something that I can wear. Something that'll stop it."

Liz scratched her chin again.

"Why don't you try running really, really fast? Just kind of long-jumping to the other side? Don't give it time to toss you!"

"I don't think that would work. If anything, it would throw me back farther. And . . . never mind."

"What?" She stopped kicking her feet against the luggage rack.

"Even if I got to the other side, I maybe couldn't cross back again. And I want to be able to go back home."

"Why? Don't you get bored out here?"

"My mom. I need to stay here."

"Man," said Liz, "if I ran off, I think it would take my mom a few weeks to notice." I couldn't tell whether she was joking or not.

"Um . . ."

Liz sighed. "But this is just too weird. I mean, everyone knows that supposedly there's some homeschooled kid out here in the woods because everyone knows your mom and sees her grocery shopping and whatnot. No one asks her about you. Everyone thinks you're Amish."

"Oh."

"*Are* you Amish?"

"No. I'm not religious."

"But Amish people live on farms. With no electricity. You could join them! Run away and live a normal life."

"A normal life of milking goats?"

"Don't be so picky."

I coughed. "Anyhow, I couldn't. Electricity really is everywhere. Power lines are always around even when you can't see them. And cell phone towers. This is kind of a safe zone because it's right near the state park and there aren't many lines around."

"Is that why no one texts me back out here? I figured it was because everyone has more important things to do than text Liz Becker."

She pulled a device out of one of her back pockets; it was black and rectangular, and there was a little charm of a Japanese lucky cat hanging from it. The phone was infused with enough of a tiny turquoise glow that I almost winced my way right off the edge of the Ghettomobile.

"Whoa, Ollie. It's dead. The battery's dead. Look."

She held it aloft again. Now that I looked at it properly, it really was only the lightest shadow of teal mist.

I inched back onto the roof.

Her forehead wrinkled. "Maybe you can try holding it? Come on. It's a dead battery. Bet it's hardly electric at all. It won't bite you."

I shook my head.

She dangled it by its charm. "Face your fears, Oliver! How else will you get better?"

And she pushed it against my hand, and it nipped me.

"No!" I stood up. "It's not something I can get better from. If you want to be good at helping people like your parents are, you shouldn't be so—so domineering!"

"Oh." She tucked the phone into her pocket again.

"Sorry. Please—I'm sorry. I don't really . . . I don't know how to talk to people." I swallowed. "Sorry."

She stood up suddenly and craned her neck as if looking over the horizon, into the trees. I couldn't see her face. "So you live at the end of the driveway, right? I've never been all the way down. Can I come visit you?"

"You really want to?"

"Yep."

I couldn't stop myself from grinning like an idiot. "You'll be disappointed, though. It's not very horrific. We don't even have dead teddy bears."

"You know, people have called me bossy before. People don't

always like me. I'm a know-it-all. But no one's ever called me domineering. That sounds way cooler." She snickered. "You're pretty funny, Ollie Ollie UpandFree."

"My last name is Paulot. . . ."

"Don't you know the children's rhyme? 'Olly Olly Oxen Free'?"

"No. What does it mean?"

"You know," she said, "I don't know. It's just something kids say. When I was in elementary school we had all sorts of rhymes."

"Do you have rhymes in, um . . . middling school?"

"*Middle* school." She frowned. "Not really. None that anyone tells *me* about." Her face brightened. "But we used to have all sorts on the playground. Like 'Miss Susie's Tugboat' and the K-I-S-S-I-N-G rhyme."

"I don't know those, either."

She laughed again. "Well, maybe I can teach you all the basics. I'm here until Memorial Day weekend's over. No one would miss me if I stayed a little longer. I'll come by tomorrow afternoon to begin your education!"

She hopped down to the ground.

"I'm going in. See you tomorrow. Tell your mom I'm coming, okay?"

"Wh—oh—okay! I will!" I was trying hard not to bite my tongue.

And she, toting the fishbowl of berries inside with her, left me standing there.

A visitor. Someone wanted to *visit* me. What would Mom say?

Oh no. Mom.

I dragged my bike back through the woods, stumbling through bracken as twilight arrived. It was almost too dark to ride my bike by the time I got back to the driveway, so I dropped it there on the path and began sprinting as fast as my legs could carry me.

How many hours had I been gone for?

Four? Seven?

Oh no, oh no.

The sky was heavy with dusk by the time the familiar silhouette of our triangular cabin appeared before me. There were no lanterns in the windows and when I ran into the breezeway, my footsteps echoed.

"Mom? I'm home!"

The lanterns hadn't been lit since the previous evening. It felt unusually cold in the hallway. I tiptoed into the kitchen to find it in disarray. All the bowls were torn from the shelves, cutlery was on the floor. In the living room all the couch cushions were scattered about as if a tornado had whipped them around. Books were splayed open all over the room, their spines abused. The hand-carved coffee table was overturned. I knew that my bedroom would be in a similar state of chaos, so I didn't bother going upstairs to check.

I used to wonder why she looks everywhere, even in all the places I could never be.

I went out the back door and into the long grass. The crickets were screeching something awful. I stood on the edge of the overgrown clearing that separates our house from the allergenic garage. Mom can't be the hermit that I am. Sometimes she needs to call for appointments. She needs somewhere to park her truck, and maybe to hide from me, Moritz.

Even though the garage is insulated, it glows softly crimson some evenings and at sunset the solar panels on the roof gleam silver. The generator near the rear is hidden by a hundred hues. This evening I could see the silver blush of the fluorescent bulbs inside it through the sole window near the top of the concrete-block build-ing, and I nearly collapsed with relief.

At least she wasn't driving around town this time, hollering my name in the neighborhoods. At least this time it wouldn't be the police bringing her home. At least she was here.

I waited outside for a long time for her to come out. Once or twice I tried to get closer to the garage, but the crimson light was strong enough that it made my skin feel prickly even from this far away. The closer I got, the more the long grass against my shins felt sharp enough to cut me.

I thought about calling for her. But what could I say when "sorry" couldn't be enough? It's not as though this was the first time. It's not as though I did not know better.

And something else, something small and sharp: I was afraid to see her face. Afraid of what her eyes might look like.

"I'm sorry," I told my knees.

After the night started getting cold and the stars painted every-thing in white and the crickets' songs were accompanied by the rustling of night animals and the cooing of things in the dark, I was roused from uneasy sleep.

Dr. Auburn-Stache, crouched beside me, was nudging me with his elbow. His profile was cast in orange light and black shadows when he held the lantern up to get a good look at my face.

I wondered when she'd called him. How quickly did he drive to get here? Usually Auburn-Stache came by only every other weekend. Did he leave another patient waiting on a table just so he could tend to the woodland invalid again?

"Ollie, sometimes you are an idiot."

"It was only a few hours."

He sighed. "Ah. But try to think about it from her perspective, kiddo."

I put my head on my arms. "Can you please go get her?"

"I can try. What the blazes happened to your nose?"

"I met a girl."

"Mm. Sounds about right, actually."

"She's coming over tomorrow." I wiped my eyes on my forearm.

"Then you'd better get some beauty rest, Prince Charming. Up you get." He prodded me with his red leather oxfords. "I'll talk to your mum."

"What if she won't come out?"

He squeezed my shoulder. "Shush, you. Go inside and go to bed."

I watched him scurry to the garage, the orange bobbing light of his lantern tracing the long grass of the field. A brief burst of red electricity and yellow light seeped out into the night before he closed the door behind him.

Those crickets just wouldn't shut up. I could still hear them even after hours of lying in the wreckage of my bedroom on the broken wings of a model airplane or four.

I hope you knock it out of the park when you go back to school. It's really crappy that the dinguses of Bernholdt-Regen suspended you when you were the one who got your face turned to potaters.

They can't expel you for being eyeless! Isn't that discrimination? Or are the rules different in Germany? I don't know what *Hauptschule* means, really, and Mom threw out what was left of my English-German dictionary last Wednesday after I, um, angrily tore it to pieces.

Please tell me about more of your superpowered shenanigans.

If my autobiography is starting to bore you, I'll stop before we get to the bad parts.

I can write about chromatic scales and what a pain it is to tune my glock on warm days when metal instruments go flat due to humidity.

~ Ollie

P.S. Heh—you're superpowered, I'm powerless. We're two ends of a freak magnet!

P.P.S. Apologies. I'm really sleepy, and I've started to speak fluent Stupid.

P.P.P.S. Hey, I just sat up in bed to write this, but what if it isn't a laboratory that connects us? What if we're actually related in a different way? I mean, aren't you a little curious?

I mean, wouldn't it be amazing if we were somehow brothers?

chapter ten

THE PIERCINGS

Ollie, I don't need a brother.

I can see why Liz is so alluring to you. Yet I stand by my previous deduction, Mr. Holmes. She sounds something like the girls who giggle in the cafeteria, who toss their hair in the hallways. Why do they want to be looked at?

Of course, you, too, wish to be seen. Perhaps two similarly poled magnets don't always push each other away. This isn't the same equation as Oliver Paulot versus the Driveway Power Line. Perhaps you and Liz make sense. Given your circumstances. She is not as confident as she seems. You have that in common also.

I wonder what happened to leave you lovesick and without her, Ollie. But I appreciate your attempts at linear storytelling. You've begun to hone your focus. It is not a laser beam yet. A wide laser ray. Small steps.

The state of affairs in Kreiszig: since I have returned to

Bernholdt-Regen, some aspects of my daily life have improved in ways I never hoped for.

Others leave me deeply uneasy.

After my suspension ended, I dared not step out of the *Strasse* into Bernholdt-Regen's open campus until I was certain no one was waiting in ambush inside the school gates. Lenz Monk might be just beyond the threshold, fists at the ready.

I listened with all my might through the open gates, trying to still my shaking hands and heart. Straightened my tie. Clenched my hands tightly around the cane. Father had handed it to me that morning. He does not say much, my father. His movements speak for him.

In the tiny kitchen, I could see the anxious tilt of his head. Could see/hear how his breath caught when he handed the stick to me. My breath caught as well.

My face is still swollen. Sometimes the bridge of my nose experiences twinges. Acupuncture inside my nostrils. The stick I had always refused to hold had more weight than ever before. I understood it to be my armor.

The cane was the stipulation that allowed me to attend public school once more.

My new mask, Oliver?

The morning my suspension began, I ate cereal by the crunchy handful. I focused on the noisy insides of my mouth and nothing more. But Father, home from the factory that day, ushered me away from the table and alongside him to Bernholdt-Regen. He strode me right into the headmaster's office. Most of my "peers" were in the cafeteria. We stood in front of the glass wall. He stared at the headmaster, Herr Haydn, from between the blinds. They couldn't just leave my father there. Haydn and several loitering faculty members agreed to discuss my future studies.

Father spoke. He began by convincing the unsettled staff that I am legally blind. That I had refused to use my cane out of a misplaced sense of pride. I nodded in time with his words. I tried my hardest to look unfortunate. It was not very difficult.

You are correct to mention discrimination. If I was blind, they were on thin ice. They had been less than accommodating.

The wondrous thing? I wanted to return, Ollie. I wanted to speak to Owen Abend. To thank him.

When I strapped on my goggles this morning, I tried to smile.

You've made me reconsider my surroundings. You've made me hopeful.

If that means using the cane, so be it.

From the street, campus sounded as disorderly as ever. It overflowed with the cacophony of those idiotic *Jugendlichen*. They spoke as if they were Sirens hoping to drown out the sound of the school bell. There was a great deal of movement. Students pushed and jostled and smacked against one another. MBV informed me that no one was lurking by the wall. Somewhere on the right side of the courtyard, a boy was being lambasted for his choice of trainers. Near the front steps a girl was getting her hair pulled from the roots by an envious friend. Hair-pulling and footwear-lambasting are standard fare at Bernholdt-Regen.

You asked about German schooling. In *Deutschland*, our futures are decided early. After *Grundschule* (elementary school), we are separated into three possible groups. The students who excel academically, who cross their *t*'s and double-dot their umlauts, end up at a *Gymnasium*. *Gymnasium* is preparatory school for those who wish to attend university. Students who wish to become technicians—those who wish to be mechanics, say—must qualify for *Realschule*, but may join a *Gymnasium* later.

For everyone else—for those who don't excel, those who are indifferent, or those who are *problem students*—there are *Hauptschulen*.

Ollie, I am certainly problematic. Bernholdt-Regen is for the unwanted and unworthy. I deserve nothing better.

The boy in unpopular shoes was trying to claw his way out of a headlock by the time I stepped into the courtyard. I bit my tongue to keep from clicking. I crossed the campus threshold. The earth did not crack. Hellfire didn't bother raining from the sky. Nowhere was the bulky outline of Lenz Monk.

I let the air out of my lungs. Perhaps it was safe to enter after all. Perhaps I would not whimper today.

But as I made my way forward, students made a noticeable effort to step out of my path. I am often ignored. This was something worse. It was just as when I left the gym bloodied: the seas of body odor and cheap cologne and cigarette smoke parted before me.

I am used to whispers, but there were none. People went silent when I passed. And the quieter they were, the less I could see. The hazier their faces. The blinder I became.

My pacemaker was straining as my heart rate increased. My chest ached. Sweat beaded on my brow. I bit my tongue harder. Picked up my pace. It was the strangest sensation, being the focal point of so much attention. I had to restrain myself from thwapping the spectators with my cane in an effort to see them properly. It was as though I were walking through a layer of static. Trying to catch movements obscured by cuts of nothing. Soon all I could hear was my own heart straining.

I became self-conscious about the cane. Surely none of them were buying the charade. Is there a certain tempo at which the visually impaired tap their canes? I kept falling into musical patterns. Tapping the beat of Grandmaster Flash's "The Message" against the sidewalk. At least in the cane's resonance I could see.

When I reached the stone steps at the front of the building, a girl was sitting on the top of the banister. Smoking a cigarette. There are smoking areas on some German *Hauptschule* campuses. Our school is pathetic enough that it seems to be the entire campus.

Her hair was an unruly, stringy nest on top of sides shaved down. Perhaps not so different from your enforced rooster cut. Her boots looked heavy enough to leave dents in concrete. She had more piercings than I could count, cluttered together in her lips and nose and ears; when she wrapped her lips around her cigarette, they clinked together.

The sound of them illuminated her face: a sharp nose and eyes set in deep, dramatic hollows. I could hear the wheezing in her chest even from the bottom of the stairs.

She was so vivid after the silence, Ollie.

What she was wearing was against dress code. She had a skirt hiked up very high, her socks yanked past her knees. Her sleeveless shirt untucked and spiked chains hanging across her chest. But I wouldn't begrudge any teacher for choosing not to confront that awful glare.

She shared it with me the entire time I clacked up the stairs. I wanted to retreat, even into the static behind me. Doubtless she was plotting to twist her cigarette into my ear. When I was level with her, I fought the urge to sprint beyond her reach.

I stepped inside the school. Unharmed.

And then my heart all but stopped:

"Hey," she said, turning as I passed. "You."

She tossed a paper airplane at me. I clicked my tongue and caught it at face level.

"Read it."

I tucked the plane into my satchel. I did not tell her I could not read.

"Fffrt." She narrowed her eyes. Leapt off the banister and stomped away in her boots. The echoes around her feet made waves of clarity wherever she laid her heels down, Ollie. I could see the dust in the air wherever she stepped. Could see the fibers of her tights and the way they hardly seemed to contain the strength of the legs beneath them.

*   *   *

Herr Haydn had suggested I drop out of the athletics course to avoid further entanglements with Lenz and the others. I was tempted. I am not brave.

But Athletics is the only course I share with Owen Abend, who is one year my junior. I could have sought him out at other times. Perhaps in the cafeteria or in the courtyard in the morning. But that would require a lot more gall. In the past, whenever I wandered away from the eyes of teachers I was inevitably taunted. I could not recall the last time I spoke to any of my peers outside a classroom.

When I entered the sour-smelling locker room, another hush fell. There was enough noise from the water running down from showerheads, from lockers slamming, for me to see everyone avert their gazes. I pulled my gym clothes from my bag. Changed as quickly as possible. Waited for Lenz Monk to appear behind me and shove my head against the tiles.

But neither Owen nor Lenz appeared.

I traipsed into the gymnasium with my head down. I could hear the smack of basketballs lessen for a beat as I entered. Herr Gebor, standing on the sidelines, spared a moment to bench me before telling the others to get back to their dribbling drills.

I had barely settled into the bench when Gebor approached me.

"I hope you appreciate all we're doing for you," he told me. "All the allowances we're making. If you'd told us sooner, this might have been sorted sooner. You need to *talk* to us, Farber. So that we can help you."

"Beg pardon," I said. "What allowances?"

"We had an assembly while you were . . . recovering. Every student here has been told about your circumstances, lectured about bullying. So don't you worry, Farber."

I clenched my fists. This explained the silence. The non-looking. "Tell me—have all my classmates been told that I am disabled?"

"That's . . . just know that you're safe. You're safe and you can talk to us. Understood?"

"Of course. Thank you."

In my absence, there'd been an assembly about bullying "disabled" students. In my absence, I'd become a label. Less than wondrous, Ollie.

I watched my peers bounce basketballs back and forth to one another. Watched how their faces creased when they laughed or grimaced in the echoes of the smacking. I experienced a dark moment there on the bench. A dark moment where I realized that I never leave the sidelines. Perhaps I never would.

The door at the back of the gymnasium creaked open. The volume of the room's activity revealed the face that peered through the doorway.

Owen Abend, all but tiptoeing into the gymnasium. Willing himself invisible. He was so quiet. He nearly succeeded. Something was slightly different about the shape of his face.

I was irrationally pleased to see him, Ollie.

I raised a hand. He caught sight of it. His eyes bulged. Spinning on his heel, he left the way he'd come.

What did I expect? That moment had been nothing to him. Nosebleeds may not always be enough to create friendship.

Doubtless he hardly remembered handing me my goggles. Hardly remembered that he didn't recoil as though soullessness was infectious.

Basketballs slammed around me and my breath was loud in my ears, and once again I was seeing more than I wished to, seeing wood grain and the tension in my own face.

Was that all? Was this it?

We have talked about standing up. I hadn't come back not to speak to him.

I got up and ran the length of the gym. A ball bounced toward me. I thrust it away without pausing. Followed him into the hallway. I saw him pushing his way outside into the courtyard. I sprinted after him, using MBV to dart around obstacles before me. Doors opened; I skidded sideways. A boy put his foot out and I leapt over it. I did not have time to feel foolish.

"Owen!" I shoved the door open and burst out onto the steps. "Um, hallo!"

I often experience disorientation when I move from indoors to outdoors, because of the sudden shifting of echoes. This time it cost me dearly. I ran directly into someone standing outside the door. This someone shoved me back against the wall.

It was the piercing girl. Baring her teeth at me.

(Ollie, this girl is fond of profanity. To spare your retinas repeated scarring by the notorious F-word, I have substituted it with a less vulgar word. You're very welcome.)

"Hey, didn't you read the fluffing note I gave you this morning, freak show?"

"I can't read," I gasped.

"Don't try the blind card. You forgot your fluffin' cane. And you caught the paper airplane."

"Even so. I can't read."

"Look, stay the hell away from Owen. He's been through enough. Or are you going to pretend you didn't see the bruises?"

"I did not," I said, which was true. I cannot see blotches or bruises, although I can see swelling. Which explained why his face had appeared misshapen. "What happened?"

She took four steps back. Aimed a kick at my face.

She tried to kick me *in the face.*

It happened very quickly. There was simply no thread in my body that did not tell me to avoid those heavy feet. I had no say. I could not take that boot to the face.

I ducked.

"Pissing Nora!" I cried. "Are you psychopathic?"

"I knew it," she said, and she looked likely to try it again. "You complete ass. You could have beaten the shit out of him. And you didn't."

"Beg pardon?"

"Fluff off," she said. "I don't want to see you. *You could have stopped him*, but you haven't. You didn't! Fluffin' unbelievable. Coward."

"I know what I am. Why do you think I'm here?"

She stomped away. There I stood on the steps for the second time that day. I considered collapsing atop them.

To think I had looked forward to returning to school.

I am so unsettled by the piercing girl's rage. Will she be a second Lenz in my life? My hands are unsteady as I type this. My father is waiting for me to walk to school again. I do not want to.

She has been watching me for the past few days. I dodge into closets or around corners whenever I hear her boot steps. She sits atop the stairs and glares me into school. I haven't approached Owen, but I have seen him in the cafeteria. Sitting alone, silent and half-vanished. Always looking away from me.

Rumor has it that Lenz will return from his extended suspension at the start of the new term.

Hoping you and yours are well.

Best,

Moritz

P.S. I needs must tell you that *glock* is not the shorthand version of *glockenspiel*, but of a rather nefarious pistol, weapon of choice for many inner-city gangsters.

chapter eleven

THE PUDDLES

Did you really just type "needs must tell you," Mo? *Really?* New pompous low, man. I know you like using *wondrous language* to sound ULTRAFANCY. But we've got to draw a line somewhere before your nose gets perma-stuck in the air.

And holy crap! You, with your bangs in your face, going for the scary Goth girl? It's like *Johnny the Homicidal Maniac*! Well, not really (you don't nail stuffed animals to your wall, right?). I can't wait to hear more. You know it's love when a girl throws a plane at your face and says she'd like to beat you to a pulp. *Tch.*

If she *isn't* your love interest, tell me who actually is. If you're also lovesick, I won't feel like such a loser for telling you about my romantic pining. In most stories, love is kind of a big deal. Even freakin' *Charles Dickens* wrote a romantic alternate ending to *Great Expectations*! He was even more cynical than you are. And Pip was a complete dork. If he deserved love, so do you.

Which reminds me—again with the whole "I'm not worthy"

shtick, Moritz? Why don't you deserve a nice school? You're still singing that song and it sounds like Grade A bullpucky.

You deserve as much as any "normal kid." We've been through this. Do you still have your homemade letter-bat handy?

Don't let the anti-rubberneckers get you down. Let them not-stare. Like you said, you can totally thwap them with your cane. You're Dolphin-Man! Anything is possible! You leap feet in hall-ways! You duck Goth kicks! Kapow!

As for wondering why Liz ditched me, why I'm plagued by anti-appetite for tuna sandwiches, why Mom basically drags me to the bath after she fills it, and why she actually locks me *outside* now to make sure I get "daylight"—well, we're getting there. It's sort of inevitable. Like the driveway being empty is inevitable.

I got to have a few awesome years with Liz before I ruined our friendship. Let's keep this mask on for a little while, all right? It's not about faking optimism, I swear. It's just . . . I still can't really think about the camping trip without freaking out. Mom's not the only one who tears things off shelves around here.

She wanted me to write so that I could work through what hap-pened, but it's a *lot* of work.

Let me write a little longer about happy things, okay?

The day after I met Liz at the power line, the sky spat giant dollops of rainwater down onto the trees and rooftop. Mom was pale when she brought me toast and marmalade, and she had this sort of fake grin on her face. She came into my room, set down the tray, and started picking up all the things she'd thrown on the floor.

I couldn't meet her eyes.

"So Greg told me you went out and met a girlfriend."

My stomach felt so tangled up that I wondered if she had stashed a battery in my toast. "Not a girlfriend. And his name's Auburn-Stache. Don't be weird."

"Was it Joe's niece? I heard she was visiting for the holiday. She's about your age, you know."

"Mm."

"Whatever happened to my loquacious brat?" Mom forced a chuckle. She was holding the broken wing of a model Boeing 747, squeezing it too tightly. "Don't you want to talk to me?"

I choked down my toast.

Ugh. That morning, Mo.

After we'd put the house back together and dusted all the surfaces we could think of, I kept picking up books to read and slamming them shut again after staring at paragraphs without digesting them. I had pages lying all over the bedroom floor—I'd persuaded Mom to pick up gentlemen's clothing magazines years ago, when she told me that paisley was an Auburn-Stache thing, not an Everyman thing. She told me not to wear a suit, but I did it anyway.

"It says a host dresses to impress. And there's nothing so classy as a suit and tails," I said, straightening my fedora. "I don't wanna blow it."

"You look like you're dressed for a Mafia funeral," said Mom. "Should I be looking for concrete blocks and skeletons in the fishpond?"

She herself was wearing a nice floral-print dress she usually saved for going to town. I might have called her a hypocrite, except for the fact that every time I spoke I sounded like I was gagging on dismembered frog bits.

I changed my outfits three more times and ended up in corduroys before Liz arrived. I wondered if other kids did things like this, or if this sort of habit was specific to cabin-dwelling electro-sensitive hermits. I even spiked my rooster hair up a little.

"Not a freak," I told the mirror. My nose was bruised a bit purple near my eyes. *"Wicked."*

Mom couldn't sit still. She kept getting up from the table and walking over to the kitchen window to pull back the curtains and look at the rain-drenched lawn, only to close them again, and then sit down and repeat the whole cycle after seven minutes. She definitely hadn't slept enough. She was doing this thing she does where she plucks the hairs from her eyebrows without realizing it.

"I hope she likes mashed potatoes," I said. A shepherd's pie was in the oven. "What if she hates mashed potaters with a deep, loathing passion?"

"Don't be silly," said Mom, biting her lip. "Every child likes mashed potatoes. Every child ever."

"Is that written down somewhere?"

"Some laws of the universe go unspoken." Suddenly she pulled the curtain open and closed again and gasped. She turned her back to the window, hands splayed behind her on the pinewood counter.

"What? What is it? Is the sky falling?"

She shook her head. "Someone's here. Ollie. Should I chase her away? I have a rolling pin. A variety of rolling pins."

"Mom."

We don't have a doorbell. We never really have any callers except Auburn-Stache, who just waltzes in. All the same, I felt as though I was waiting for a bell to ring. A death knell. I'd been reading John Donne and, before that, *Macbeth*. Not the world's best idea.

"You'll be fine." Mom's smile was pasted on. "*We'll* be fine."

"I'm sorry about yesterday," I blurted.

Mom blinked. Her smile slipped a little. But she nodded.

"Don't make a fuss. I'm happy for you."

I tried to smile. Milliseconds later, it became a grimace as I stared down at the brown corduroy nightmare I had resigned myself to.

What the hell was I wearing?

I tried to run upstairs to change once more, but Mom grabbed my arm and held it.

"This time I'm the kickstand, then."

I think my hair deflated.

I couldn't help but think that it would be better if one day in the junkyard was all Liz and I ever had, you know, Mo? I'd already almost blown it; surely if I spent more time with her I'd end up revealing my total lameness as a human being.

"Ollie Ollie UpandFree?" I jolted back from the door. "Non-Amish boy? Helllllllooooo."

"Just answer it!"

At last I opened it and gaped at what appeared before me.

A dirt-colored monster, all pointed teeth and shining black eyes, was looming on the steps. From head to foot it was an absence of color. It dripped sludge from elbow tips and braid ends, from chin and nose.

"Hey," said Liz. The shining coat of grime that covered her obscured her freckles. "I've been puddle-hopping." Her teeth glowed like stars in the mucky ether. "Wanna join me?"

Mom, behind me, laughed out loud like a crazed thing. Like what I imagine a hyena must sound like, or the Joker from *Batman*.

"Mom?!"

"Go." She shooed me forward. "Puddle-hopping!" She wiped her eyes on her hands. "Honestly—I don't know why I was so worried. Go!"

She didn't even make me change out of my cords. She just shoved me out the door, umbrella-less.

Are you starting to see it, Mo? Why it's Liz, why even then it was Liz?

I'd seen puddles pooling in the driveway my whole life and never thought to go out and jump in them.

By the time we got back inside, Mom had a soapy bath and hot chocolate waiting. Once we were clean, we sat at the kitchen table and blew on the surface of our mugs, warmed by the stove that housed the shepherd's pie.

"Man, your mom really looks after you."

I nodded guiltily. Mom was probably scrubbing the bathtub even as we sat there.

Liz stretched her arms across the table and sighed. "I haven't had a bath in years."

"Well, that explains the awful odor."

"Yeah, yeah." She elbowed me. "But we only have a shower at my place."

"What, your parents didn't have money to buy the whole tub?" I joked.

Liz scooted her chair back and glared daggers at me. "Oh, yeah, because *that's* hilarious. Social workers don't actually get paid all that well, you know. Especially when they get laid off like Dad was."

Once again I was blowing it. "Why are you getting angry with me?"

"You're terrible!"

"I am?"

"You shouldn't make jokes like that!"

"Why not? I wasn't trying to be rude. I didn't know that you didn't have money."

"Are you serious?!" She was standing up now. "You didn't know. Yeah, right."

"I'm serious! How was I supposed to know anything like that? Am I breaking another stupid real-world rule? Is that something I'm supposed to care about when I meet someone? How much money you have?"

"Yes, you're supposed to care about that," she said. "Most people definitely care about that."

And she gave me the biggest smile.

Never ask me for advice on girls, Mo.

She was quiet for maybe three seconds. "Welp, enough sitting around. What do you do indoors all day, without a computer?"

"My parents love cripples. Weirdos, too," Liz informed me. We were playing with building blocks in my room. I kept dropping pieces.

We were sticking turrets onto ships, constructing floating castles. Liz couldn't move without causing a fuss. When she came in my room, she knocked over three stacks of books and a pile of scrolls, and stepped on a model airplane. She prodded my model skeleton with her shoe, tapped my glockenspiel with her fingernails.

"Why do you play the xylophone?"

"It's a glockenspiel. And why not?"

She shrugged. "I feel like you should play the piano or something. Something cooler. More dramatic."

"If you think that playing 'Ride of the Valkyries' on the glock isn't dramatic, you don't know what you're missing."

"Weirdo."

You imagine that I'm loud? Whenever she called me "weirdo," she did it at something that felt like ten thousand decibels.

"Weirdo?" My pirate stabbed her tower. It fell into her frigate's sail. "Is that a real word, even?"

Liz twirled the sail between her fingers. "Hey, I've been called worse. But you're the biggest weirdo I've ever met. You say whatever you're thinking. You don't go to school. You've never used the Internet."

"But I can't."

"You're hopeless, when I think about it. You've never texted anyone. You've never seen . . . I dunno. Bathroom hand dryers or a vending machine—"

"But—I told you! I *can't*!" I dropped my pirate.

Blowing it, blowing it.

"*Hopeless*. You've never seen a movie or a train, or heard *music* or—"

"Shut up!" I kicked her frigate over. "I know music! I play the glockenspiel!"

Liz terrified me with her smile again. "You didn't say 'I can't!' that time. That means I can help you."

Her social worker parents had really done a number on her.

"What do you mean by that?"

"You'll see," she said. "Next time I come over."

"There's going to be a next time? You really want to come back over sometime?"

"There you go again, saying whatever you're thinking right when you think it. Yes, if that's okay with you. I had fun. More fun than at home, for sure."

"Or at school?"

"People aren't like you at school. They don't listen to me."

"What? I didn't hear you."

Liz didn't laugh. "But you *did*."

It didn't matter that the sky was dark outside, that we needed four lanterns to see by.

She was lighting up the room for me.

It's kind of strange to be talking about how things used to be, knowing that they're so different now. I thought at first it was because of the weather. There's so much snow outside and on the house, on the branches, that it feels like the weight of it all is pushing our cabin slowly into the ground. The window in this room— when the frost creeps across it, it may as well not exist, Moritz.

There are a few more golden moments to tell you about before I get to the meat of what went so wrong between me and the girl I fell in lovesickness over.

Man, you wanted me to stop faking the happy, but even writing about the happier times has started to feel kind of unhappy. Maybe you should stop getting to know me right now. Before it becomes a shitshow.

Then again, I don't even notice what day of the week it is anymore! So it really shouldn't bother me when Wednesday passes. No matter what, I lie in bed a lot and I never get up in the afternoon to go stand in the driveway nowadays. Maybe I'm getting better, Moritz.

Mom keeps staring at me. She doesn't look exasperated anymore. She looks really tired.

Moritz, tell me some good news. Would that be okay?

Sincerely,

Oliver

chapter twelve
THE BOOKS

I think this is the first time you did not needle me about the lab. This, more than anything, tells me how unhappy you must be.

I am the one who told you to be honest with yourself. Never feel as though I do not wish to hear about it. Between the two of us, perhaps we can spread the misery a bit thinner. You need no masks with me, Ollie.

I hear loud and clear your plea for good news. I can oblige. It does not do to dwell on things that upset us. Dwelling can make things fester. It is better to bury dark thoughts.

Let me tell you a wondrous story. For once, let me be the shining one. It is springtime. Birds are noisiest now. I can almost see the shape of the sky.

Bernholdt-Regen offers basic courses in all major subject areas, but the school is heavily focused on home economics.

Finance. Safety courses. Courses that will be most useful for students destined for jobs that demand no university degrees.

Because I love literature and my school does not, I despise *Literatur* with Frau Melmann. Frau Melmann is a woman whose nostrils are eternally flaring. Whose eyes are forever narrowed as if she is sucking the bitterest of pills. And she is—she chose a career that she both loathes and is terrible at. Bitterness makes sense. When she reads the works of great poets, words turn to fire and brimstone on her scorching breath. Even when we are not reading Dante.

I sit beside the window in the second desk from the back of her classroom. As far from her cheek-sucking as possible. I told Frau Melmann on my first day in her class that being closer to the board would not facilitate my "learning disabilities." I told her my frequent "blind panic attacks" would distract my peers from paying attention to her melodic voice. *Melodic* as phlegm.

I spend silent reading hour with my headphones on, listening to audiobooks that the other students move their lips to in paper format. Before my suspension, we were reading Hermann Hesse's *Siddhartha*. God knows why. Concepts of self-actualization are beyond most of my classmates. They are too busy with concerns about who may be romancing their girlfriends. Or how soon they can read a summary of *Siddhartha* on the Internet.

Headphones shrink my world. When sound waves are pressed directly against my head, my field of vision is restricted. I can see only the insides of my ears. The outline of my skeleton. The hazy buzz of whatever leaks through the soundproofing. This can be very therapeutic—I sit in my so-called *Literaturkurs* with the Beastie Boys' *Paul's Boutique* strapped to my head, seeing nothing but a field of numbing, finite sound.

Having *officially* declared blindness after my suspension, I saw no reason for this routine to change. I entered the classroom on my second day back to the static hush that was becoming familiar. It had followed me from the courtyard to my locker, from my locker to the classroom on the second floor. Followed me alongside the footsteps of that Goth girl. I tapped my cane when I walked to my desk. Scuffed my shoe against a bookshelf for effect.

Frau Melmann entered the classroom after I sat down. She looked disheveled, as if she had just been engaging in fisticuffs with a gale. Her eyes homed in on me like one of your laser beams.

"Why are you here?"

"Are you speaking to me, Frau Melmann?"

"Yes." My classmates did not look at me. "Why are you here?"

I cleared my throat. "You need to be more specific."

"Excuse me?"

"Why am I here, in this classroom? Or why am I here on this miserable planet? Why are any of us here, for that matter? What's the *point* of our poisonous species?"

"You'll be completing your *Literaturkurs* in the *Bibliothek* from now on."

"My headphones are just as effective here." I tapped them to demonstrate.

In the echoes of someone's snigger, I saw her show her teeth. Was that why she was always unhappy? Because she could not smile properly? "There are more resources for the visually handicapped there."

"How nice. But I am *not* handicapped." Again, my impulses are too fast, Oliver. I did not mean to refute being blind. I meant to express my loathing of the term *handicapped*. "*Behindert*," as it reads in German.

"There's no sense denying it, dear," she said. Then I really was grateful to leave, Oliver. Before I succumbed to thwapping someone—this time, a teacher—with my cane.

I deposited my headphones in my satchel. Walked to the front of the classroom, dragging that useless stick behind me.

This story will become a happy one soon. At least by my low standards.

The *Bibliothek*, or library, of Bernholdt-Regen is a spacious room. A smattering of shelves in front of very large windows. The *Bibliothek* is forever in a state of disrepair. God only knows when anyone last checked out a book for leisure. Yet despite the decrepit state of the library's visitors, the library's contents are meticulously maintained.

"*Guten Morgen*, Frau Pruwitt," I told her. She loomed behind the checkout counter. Standing as straight as you please. Watching me tap my way halfheartedly down the threadbare stairs into the main reading room. "I am here for the wondrous array of materials for *behindert* students."

Frau Pruwitt raised an eyebrow. Exhaled loudly enough to illuminate her wrinkles. "Don't say '*behindert*.' It's a hideous word."

She and your Liz are the ones who may be related, Ollie.

"You know that I am." I tilted my head away. "You pulled me from Athletics. You saw what is beneath my goggles. Or rather, what isn't."

Pruwitt the Impenetrable raised that eyebrow once more at the cane I was tapping against the foot of the checkout counter.

"You don't need this." She tore it from my fingers.

You recall, Ollie, how MBV enables my reflexes? Even so, I doubt I could have stopped Frau Pruwitt from taking that cane from me. Even if I'd had hours to prepare. Titanium indeed.

"As far as I see it, Mr. Farber, this cane is no more than a toy. This isn't kindergarten. We don't bring toys to school. If you would like your plaything back in the future, and you would not like me to snap it in two over my knee, please take your seat."

"My seat?"

She gestured to a revolving chair behind the counter. I sat cautiously. That eyebrow of hers was impressive. How could she hold it so high for so long?

"There will be no headphones permitted in here," she told me as I yanked them free of my satchel.

"But—I truly can't read—"

"You're illiterate?"

I bristled. "Not in the least."

"Then learn to learn more, Mr. Farber."

Frau Pruwitt handed me a book from among the pile on her desk. Of course, it looked blank to me, apart from the embossed cover. I struggle to read even that sort of thing; letters become so jumbled inside my head.

"Read this."

"I'm not illiterate. But I do have something of a learning, ah . . ."

That eyebrow derailed me once more.

"I mean to say, as much as I would like to, I can't." I frowned. "Mock me if you must."

She made a *tch!* sound, Oliver!

"Mock yourself. I don't tolerate laziness. I don't know how it's possible, but you see just fine. So click all you need to until you can read the book."

I pursed my lips. "I can *attempt* to read the title because I can see the raised outline of the letters. It's embossed. But images on a flat surface . . ."

It was so strange to be talking about this with a severe old librarian, but even stranger that it did not feel strange. Perhaps this was similar to being scolded by a grandparent.

"Well, well! Whatever is the matter with your generation? *Try* harder!" Frau Pruwitt slapped her hand on the table. "What about the space between the ink and the paper? Surely printed font is slightly raised or indented on the pages! The font wasn't grown on the trees, now, was it? The printed letters are either thicker or thinner."

"On a nearly microscopic level . . ."

"You're saying that isn't enough for you to work with? I drag you down the hallway, bleeding and mumbling about how bothersome the individual *dust motes* clogging your vision are—"

I had been mumbling?

"—but now, when you're in a completely reasonable state

of mind, you won't even *try* to read a damn book because it might possibly require the slightest bit of effort? Shame on you, son. Your mother should be ashamed!"

"You don't know anything about my mother."

"Do. Not. Shout. In. My. Library." With each word, she tapped her long-nailed fingers on my wrist. "I know your mother isn't here. Who is? I am."

I swallowed. "Undeniably."

"Start with the title, Mr. Farber."

I leaned forward. Tried to focus my MBV on the letters. They shifted before my ears.

"Click if you need to. Don't be shy!" And she clicked her nails against the book, illuminating the letters for me.

"I'll be damned," I said.

It was a copy of *Daredevil Visionaries, Volume 1*, by Frank Miller.

Her eyebrow was still up near her hairline.

"Sit yourself down and clickity-clack until you can read comics like any other boy."

I picked up the book.

Oliver, what if people apart from you could see me as something, someone, deserving of happiness? Not as a hero, mind. Just as "any other boy."

The idea frightens me. Coward that I am. Me, born of science and ambition gone wrong. I felt that wrongness every day, until you wrote to me. Until you infected me with wondrous, hopeful nonsense.

Frau Pruwitt has given me a book about a certain blind

superhero. And now I am feeling something other than despicable.

What have you done to me, Oliver Paulot?

Initially, nothing came of our exercises. Frau Pruwitt was right. There is the most microscopic layer of space between pages and the ink on them. Like you, I struggled with focus. I tried to narrow my MBV. Tried to aim the clicks precisely.

That was the only noise Frau Pruwitt would allow me to make in the library. Not that there were many students to disturb in the high-windowed room.

I gave myself headaches. A more violent person might have tossed that book down on the floor. Frau Pruwitt made no point of watching me work; she went about her business among the shelves, chasing out any pupils who dared giggle in the aisles. At the end of the day, she'd ask me to tell her what I'd read.

At first, I only shook my head.

"Tomorrow, Mr. Farber."

After a week, I started to grasp how to see the panels. How to aim the sound so that the words and pictures appeared in my head. Just barely. I began to see shapes. *Letters.*

Ollie, if I could write like you do, I could describe how I felt when I read my first page. When I clearly saw those first images. It was only an introduction page, featuring little more than Daredevil's billy club–toting silhouette. But it was enough to make me proud.

Matt Murdock disguises his weapon as a cane. You must have known that. And he is blind but not blind, Ollie!

Of course I'd seen letters. I'd memorized the spellings of

things, just so no one could ever call me illiterate. But I'd never truly stared at words on a page and strung the shapes together within my head.

The librarian handed me another book when I read the first page to her. A book with intimidating heft.

"It's a start. Later, read this one."

I focused. Clicked. *"Der Herr der Ringe?"* I said. *"The Lord of the Rings?"*

"I'm an old hippie. So sue me."

Here is my grand news, Oliver.

I am learning to read. Frau Pruwitt is assisting me. Not in Braille, but in text. One day, perhaps even very soon, I'll be able to read your letters on my own. Without Father's accent. I'll see your abhorrent handwriting for myself and scrawl back at you in my own.

And here is one last bit of news. I unfolded the piercing girl's paper airplane at long last in the library, while the air turned warm outside.

Here is what it said:

If you're a decent fluffing human being, stay away from Owen. —Fieke

Could I actually be such a thing?

Mo

P.S. Send me an extensive booklist, please. I want to read all the books that made you, Ollie Ollie UpandFree.

chapter thirteen
THE BOOK LIGHT

That last letter was like staring at the sun, Moritz! Glorious burns on my corneas! I never thought I'd see you that happy, and now I feel like the blind one. I'll tell my keepers I got my dose of daylight. Don't worry about me being unhappy!

But which lady do you go for? There's Fieke the Goth Wonder (what kind of name is Fieke? I mean, maybe it's kind of awesome, but I don't think I'm pronouncing it right: "FEEEEEEEK"), Frau Pru-witt of "steel buns," and sourpuss Frau Melmann, the underdog no one's rooting for.

Seriously, I keep teasing you about these dames (that's the polite way to address a group of women, right?), but I'm still wait-ing on your love story. If that sounds dolphin-wavy, so be it! But if we're such good friends, I don't see why you're so closemouthed. I mean, you don't think I'd be weird about it or something, right?

No matter what you said.

Anyhow, I would ask you to send some of that love my way, but

I think I'm finally coming around to the idea of perpetual hermit bachelorhood. Hermit Bachelors are gentlemen. I have to move on from Liz.

It's so cold here for spring. We've still got slush and snow beneath the low boughs of the pines. I spend most days under my comforter. Dorian Gray spends all day sleeping, too, and no one wonders if *he's* depressed. I mean, I can fold paper just fine without standing up. I can do calligraphy in bed. All my boring hobbies can be bed hobbies, so why bother?

Auburn-Stache wasn't too pleased during my last checkup. He was really gentle when he took my blood pressure, like he was worried he was going to crush my arm in the constricting sleeve.

"You need more sun."

"I'm a vampire now. Didn't you hear?"

"You need to eat properly."

"Haf thee blood for thif night creature?"

He grabbed my chin and made me meet his eyes. "Do you see me smiling, Oliver?"

"I can never tell with that mustache of yours, Major Armstrong."

"Major—?"

"Alex Louis Armstrong? From *Fullmetal Alchemist*? Why does nobody read manga? Never mind."

Dr. Auburn-Stache released my chin and the armband at the same time. "Maybe I need to move out here for a while. You aren't recovering well, or at all. And where do you think your mum is right now?"

"Over the moon?"

"Don't be cute. She's downstairs resting. Do you know why?"

"She had three Popsicles and now she's feeling a comedown from the sugar high."

"She's *exhausted*. And you're lazing about like a dead boy."

I scowled. "Hey, I didn't ask her to worry."

"Everything she does is for your sake."

"But I'm not the one who wants to marry her."

His eyes flashed. For the first time in my life, I wondered if Auburn-Stache might hit me. It shut me up, at least.

"Oliver, I know you're still, ah, *recuperating*—"

"I'm just dandy, Doc."

"I *know* you're still in pain, but your mum needs you. And you need her. You've only got each other."

"She's got you, too."

Auburn-Stache sighed, plied his goatee with his fingers. "She doesn't have me in the way you're implying. She never will."

It sucked just hearing him say that. You know what I mean, Moritz? It sucked knowing that all of us Idiotic Lovesick Cabin People were romantically doomed. Even Auburn-Stache wasn't laughing anymore.

"I'll try harder," I said. "Please don't leave your other patients high and dry or low and wet or anything else."

He ruffled my hair. "Ollie. You don't really think I'm here because you're a *patient*? You're family. I could never be grateful enough, really, to have known the Paulots. You and your parents took me from a very dark place . . . to a better one. "

"Are you about to tell me about the laboratory? About my dad? I promise to eat like a king if you tell me something new. I'll get a *tan*. Honest."

He paused. "What a *bribe*, Oliver. But it's not my place to tell you such things."

"Wait. You *want* to, don't you?" I couldn't believe it. He looked even twitchier than usual; his leg was shaking. "You think she's wrong to keep things from me?"

"Not exactly, Oliver. I understand your mum's perspective."

"Well, that's one of us." I coughed. "Is she really that sick?"

"She'll be better if you get out of *your* dark place. It's been months now, Ollie."

"But who's counting."

He sighed and leaned forward. "But you *must* know that it really wasn't your fau—"

"You should go check on her. This vampire needs some shut-eye."

He opened his mouth and closed it again, eyes shining behind his glasses. I pretended to be fascinated by the loose threads in my sheets until he got the point.

After he was gone, I pulled the blinds down and kicked away enough of my books and models to shut the door. It was nighttime inside again.

Maybe I could climb out of dark places, if someone pulled me out. It can't be you, Moritz, because you'll never meet me.

And maybe it can't be Liz, either, but it used to be.

Liz began trying to treat my incurable illness—in secret, of course. If Mom had known what Liz and I were up to, she wouldn't have let the girl within a fifty-foot radius of me. I remembered how she'd flipped out at Auburn-Stache after the house fire because she thought he might be "experimenting" on me. If she realized what Liz and I were doing, she might have chased her with more than a variety of rolling pins. There might suddenly have been bodies in the fishpond after all.

But because Mom had no idea, because she saw that I was a

happier kid and I didn't try running away from home anymore, we had some fun before Liz started going to high school.

Liz explained my circumstances to her parents, who were exactly the sort of accepting people she had described them to be. Her father wrote Mom a letter that made her teary-eyed, made her run around opening windows and singing. Despite the locked doors, I think Mom always wanted me to have friends, but it was pretty hard to persuade people to send their kids to a cabin in the woods to spend time with someone they presumed was a young delinquent and his basket-case caretaker.

Starting the fall I turned eleven, every Wednesday afternoon Liz's dad dropped Liz and her bicycle off at the end of our long driveway. She rode up to our porch, usually wearing a plaid skirt and white tights coated in mud.

She always shouted "I'M HERE!" at the top of her lungs, even before she was within sight of the cabin.

I was always already in the driveway.

"And I'm HERE!"

Where else could I be?

The second time Liz came over, she came to my room carrying her dad's "borrowed" book light inside her raincoat. The book light had a tiny electric battery in it that I could practically smell on her.

"Why would you bring that?" I snapped.

"Calm your jets, UpandFree. It's turned off. It's *tiny*."

"Yeah, well, so are particles of Hebenon. They'll still curdle your blood."

"What's Heb—oh, forget it. Look, Ollie, don't pretend to be a sissy. Because you aren't."

"Oh! So you've noticed I'm not a girl?"

"Sheesh, Ollie. You'd have a hard time making friends even if you could go to school!"

"You're a charmer."

She actually punched my bedspread in annoyance. "Gah! This is what I'm saying! You're never serious about anything!"

"I'm serious about being afraid of that book light."

"No."

"What?" I blinked.

She didn't look away. "You're not. You can't be. I watched you run straight at that power line. You let it tackle you without even hesitating. Don't pretend to be a sissy!"

And she pressed it into my hand.

"I *like* you because you don't pretend."

It was the most precious thing I'd ever held—imagine being able to read at night without a lantern!

Every week, she handed that book light to me. And I would hold it, even though it buzzed oddly against my skin and flared in my aura, gave me the pre-seizure wooziness. I held it tight.

Because she asked me to.

But before she started "helping" me, she began each afternoon by listing off things I'd never done until I was crazy annoyed. No one could rile me like Liz. Even if I met all the other people in the world.

"You've never sat in a massage chair, or seen a sitcom!"

"I hear they aren't funny anyway!"

"You've never seen a tollbooth!"

"Why would I want to?!"

"Or a humidifier."

"Hey, low blow! I'd love to see a humidifier!"

"Or even a *lamp*."

"I've seen lamps, damn it!"

Once I was angry, she would toss the light to me.

I shivered when I caught it, my head throbbing, but I wouldn't fall in front of her again.

I held it for as long as I could. My palm sizzled.

She grinned. "See? No biggie."

Over the several months' worth of Wednesdays, we got up to a lot of shenanigans in the woods, climbing trees and looking for frogs, building forts and digging disgusting, muddied swimming "pools" that always ended up filled with earthworms and leaves and deer piss after a day or so.

We spent a lot of days at the junkyard, too. We had scavenger hunts orchestrated by Uncle Joe, who mostly liked to sit on the porch with a beer and, weirdly, Noam Chomsky books in hand, hollering instructions at us from his lawn chair. He also liked to take photos of birds; the batteries in his camera were small and far enough away that they didn't bother me. We used to lie on the roof of the Ghettomobile and count stars, which sounds hammy but was actually nice. Or we'd set up a tent in one of our backyards and have a campfire and catch fireflies and shout "rabbit!" whenever smoke wafted into our faces.

I never challenged the power line, although we passed close to it when we were walking the trails. We were always quiet when we were near it. It was like an unspoken rule. I was biding my time; so was the power line. But I didn't really want to leave home as much anymore. Home was where Liz came to find me, where I shouted, "I'm here!"

Liz brought the book light all the time, for what good it did. The one time she tried switching it on before tossing it to me, I started shaking and it somehow got flung against the far wall of my room. I hadn't thrown it. It just buzzed and jolted and got as far from me as possible, like it had a mind of its own. Like it couldn't bear the bizarre charge of me.

That electromagnetic repulsion effect had happened again, and I was panting.

"Maybe next week," she said. "Don't let it get you down."

It made me queasy. Not the electricity. The way she said that. Maybe she was starting to believe what I'd told her from the start: there was no getting better.

But let's stave off the darkness a little longer, okay?

I've saved the best day for last.

Moritz—I don't know why I didn't say it clearly. Caught up in my own crap, I guess—but it's *awesome* that you're learning to read. I'm going to send you the best reading list I can think of, and purposely tuck some crappy books between the good ones to keep you on your toes.

I'm evil. It's funny imagining you reading, oh-so-slowly, oh-so-clickity, just to realize that you've read a "bodice-buster" romance about a lusty pirate and a blushing damsel. (Don't ask me why I have those books. I have broad tastes, okay. Are you interested in space cats?)

I'm not going to say that you could be "any other boy," though, Moritz. Because I still think you should be aiming for total badass superhero type. Yeah, I knew about Matt Murdock's darn echolocation. I was being *cunning*, see. I am waggling my eyebrows and nudging you with my elbow. MBV is worthy of comics.

All those times I told you to have confidence and you finally get it from a disgruntled librarian? Are you shitting me? You are *a decent human being* (again, I despise the way you despise yourself!), and if you really want to talk to Owen Abend, you should go for it anyhow! Fieke the Fierce can't stop you.

Maybe that's why Liz left me behind. I never threw an airplane at her face.

Ha, ha.

~ Ollie

P.S. I guess I haven't been needling you so much lately because I'm sick of getting needled myself. Seriously, if people keep tiptoeing around me like I'm on my deathbed, I'm going to go from troubled Jekyll to apeshit Hyde. I may throw battle-ready Dorian at their faces. He may be a cuddlesome lump, but he's got the teeth of a piranha, my deadly Persian cat!

chapter fourteen
THE CIGARETTE

I am irritated that you're trying to, ah, "set me up" with three different ladies that I am acquainted with. I know you think yourself quite the comedian. I want no part of your speculation. You snickering fiend.

You may not be needling about the lab. But allow me to silence your newest needles: I don't wish to discuss my romantic inclinations. This has nothing to do with you and everything to do with me, Oliver. I trust you. But this issue is not one I trust myself to speak about.

As for Fearsome Fieke (that's pronounced "FEE-kuh"), there have been unusual developments in that area. Calm yourself: they are of an unromantic nature.

I did not know how to approach Fieke. It was not that I could not find her. I saw her every morning before school started. Fieke is always easy to find. She jangles. Thumps. She announces her every movement with an arrogance that would terrify lesser men than you.

I am a lesser man. But I had to brave an attempt. Thanking Owen has become a fixation. After he was absent from school for several consecutive days, I resolved to confront her.

On a brisk April morning I heard her stomping on the far side of the school. She was looming by the recycling bins. There was her slight wheezing. Her noisome piercings. She was tapping away on the keypad of an outdated, battered phone. She has taken to jabbing her cigarettes into a long, sharp cigarette-holder.

I had carefully considered what I would say. How I would describe the debt I owed to Owen. I wanted to tell her, as thoroughly as possible, that—

"Fluff off."

Like a hissing viper.

"Yo." My disarming introduction.

"I told you to fluff off. Never say 'yo' again."

"Duly noted." I coughed. "An American boy sometimes encourages me to use outdated slang. And I am fond of eighties hip-hop music."

She flicked her cigarette to the ground. Stomped on it. "God, I wish I could *beat* you. Spit out what you want."

"It's regarding—beg pardon. Were you chewing tobacco and smoking *simultaneously*?"

"Do I have to answer that? You can see what's inside my mouth." She tucked her hands into her pockets. "You still forget to use your cane half the time, you know. And real blind people don't tap them like that. You look fluffin' spastic."

"I'm sure I would know more about that. Being the blind one."

This time she aimed a punch at my nose. I twisted my head away.

"Are you done?"

"You've made your point." I breathed deep. "I read your note."

The bell rang overhead, but she began walking away from the school building, toward the back entrance and the street.

"Took you long enough."

"There's no call for rudeness."

"Wow. That means a whole lot, coming from you."

"Tell me why I have to stay away from Owen Abend."

"What, you gonna beat me up if I don't? Oh, wait. You're a pussy."

"I am not. And yes, theoretically—I *could* beat you. I'm capable."

She was still scowling. "Yeah, you could. But you fluffing didn't. You let Lenz smash your face in. Then he bashed in Owen's face for helping you, you mopey bastard. But you don't give a shit about that."

"I do. I want to thank him. You and your confounded boots won't allow me to."

" 'Confounded boots'?"

"Or whatever you call them."

She eyed me in silence. Then: "Owen's thinking of dropping out of school, you know."

"Let me speak to him."

Trying to be heroic, Ollie.

She coughed into her hand. "Fluff it. Come on."

And she walked right out of the schoolyard and into the street.

"What are you doing? The final bell has rung!"

She kept walking. Loud as a rampaging elephant.

What could I do? Soon she would be lost in the early morning crowds. Lost to my sight despite the volume of her.

I followed her into the chilly morning.

Fieke led me to a *Kneipe* I hadn't known existed, a pub of sorts called *Der Kränklicher Dichter* ("The Sickly Poet"). It was tucked away behind a city plaza, not far from the *Städtisches Kaufhaus*, a multistoried shopping mall. Halfway there, while we were passing through a flower market that smelled so strongly of blossoms that I imagined I could almost see colors in the scents, she yanked the cane from my hands.

"I'll show you how it's done."

Fieke waved the cane in huge arcs. People scurried left and right to avoid her blows. She closed her eyes and mimed a look of utmost concentration. Old women covered their mouths and tittered with concern.

"Stop that," I said.

Fieke smirked. "But I'm *blind*."

"It's distasteful!"

She thrust the cane against my chest. "Isn't it, though?"

I was relieved when we escaped the stares of stallholders, but my face was still burning. We entered the cool dark of the *Kneipe*, the smell of smoke and damp.

The barman, wearing a beret of all things, nodded at

Fieke like they were old friends. We sat down in a corner booth removed from the weekday morning patrons. I noticed a stage in the center of the room. A circular space where a man was crouched beside a microphone.

She nodded at it. "Look."

"What is he doing?"

She pursed her lips. "You didn't even turn around. You can see what's behind you, even?"

"Well. Yes." I often forget to turn my head when people say "look."

"How does it work, exactly?"

"It isn't dinner conversation." Here we were, casually discussing the ailment that usually made young ladies trip backward over things, Oliver.

"Why not? I'm not ordering a damn thing."

"I can 'see' anything that I can hear. A crude way to describe it. Are you familiar with echolocation? Although the comparison, ah . . ."

She chewed her cheek. Didn't blink.

"I know it can be unsettling. Let me appease you." I intentionally turned around in my seat. I mimed *looking* at the stage, as if I had not been able to hear its location since I'd stepped in. As if I were normal. "My, what is he doing?"

"Man, you're a freak."

"Do not call me that."

"I can call you anything I want. You owe me."

"Why should I owe you anything?"

She sighed, rasping on smoke. "Owen is my little brother. I had to bandage his fluffing wounds after Lenz knocked his head against the bleachers. I had to sit next to him when he got his stitches and he got two teeth pulled. After he helped you."

The blood left my face. I had not realized the extent of Lenz's handiwork. "When was it?"

"Right after he handed you your goggles. Gebor turned his back to calm the masses—the idiot—and the moment he wasn't looking, Lenz went apeshit on Owen. He *always* goes apeshit on Owen. Why do you think he's still suspended?"

"Is Owen . . . is he all right?"

"What's it to you?" She watched me for a moment. Shrugged. "Well, his face isn't a fluffing purple blood cake anymore." She nodded at the stage. "Shut up. This guy's about to perform."

On the stage, the man stood up straight, nodded at his minuscule morning crowd, cleared his throat, and began reciting into the microphone. It was a torrent of melancholy sound, Oliver, and it carried across the room, illuminating every crevice until I was almost blinded by the pocks and scrapes in the bar.

"Wir sind für nichts mehr erreichbar, nicht für Gutes noch Schlechtes. Wir stehen hoch, hoch über dem Irdischen—jeder für sich allein. Wir verkehren nicht miteinander, weil uns das zu langweilig ist. Keiner von uns hegt noch etwas, das ihm abhanden kommen könnte. Über Jammer oder Jubel sind wir gleich unermesslich erhaben. Wir sind mit uns zufrieden, und das ist alles!—Die Lebenden verachten wir unsagbar, kaum dass wir sie bemitleiden. Sie erheitern uns mit ihrem Getue. Wir lächeln bei ihren Tragödien."

Roughly:

"We are touched by nothing, no longer responsible for good and evil. We stand high, high above earthly concerns—every man for himself. We do not speak to each other, because that is boring. None of us cherishes anything, and so we have nothing to lose. We are as content to be miserable as we are to be happy. We are satisfied, and that is everything!—We pity the living, just as we despise them. Their fuss is amusing. We smile at their tragedies."

"What is this?" I whispered.

"You're a fan of performance speaking?"

"I'm not."

"Well, you suck. That monologue—it's from a Frank Wedekind play. Spoken originally by a character named—"

"Moritz." I swallowed. "The ghost of a boy named Moritz, who took his own life earlier in the play. He was doing poorly in school. Because he could not sleep." I stood. "I'm leaving."

"Moritz, wait."

"Oh, yes. My *cane*. I have to be distasteful."

"No. Sit down. Look—"

"Do *not* ask me to look. I am *always* looking."

She bit her lip. *Clink*. "I mean, come here. Sit. You want to meet up with Owen? Fine. I can arrange that. But not at school. Not where Lenz would hear about it."

I sat back down. "Then where?"

She smiled. "First, why don't you go on up and perform. To show you're a dedicated little gerbil."

"I would prefer not to."

"Go on up, or I'll never let you see him. Ever."

If I could scowl properly! "You can't be serious. You bring me here and—then you demand— You simply cannot be serious."

She blinked. Clicked her piercings, so that I could see the smallest of sardonic dimples. "Can I not be?"

"Infuriating wretch." I stood up once more.

"Get your cane."

"No." I pointed my finger in her face. "I am going to silence you, you rackety girl."

She blinked in shock. Then broke into an enormous grin, the first I had ever seen on her face. It was a coiled thing. Not precisely pleasant.

I walked to the stage. Bowed. Took the microphone. And I "owned" the stage with my personal rendition of Dr. Dre's immortal masterpiece, "Nuthin' but a 'G' Thang."

I sat myself carefully in my chair. The morning crowd was still applauding. Beverages of an alcoholic nature appeared at our table. Old Swiss men slapped me on the back.

"Allow me to meet with Owen, please."

"At this point I would let you impregnate me!" Fieke cackled.

"That would be unnecessary. And undesirable."

"Hah! Fluffin' unreal! I thought you were taking the piss earlier, but what the hell? How does someone like you get into *rap, Brille*?"

(*Brille* translates as "glasses." Or "goggles.")

I folded my hands on my lap. "I suppose . . . I've often felt like a public enemy."

After a beat, she laughed once again, grabbing my shoulder and shaking it. "Unreal. Fine. *Look.* Ten PM next Friday. He'll be looking for you in the *Partygänger Diskothek.*"

"I'm not one for the *Diskothek.*"

"Really, *Brille*? After what you just pulled?"

"A fit of passion."

"Again—you're a freak. If you wanna see him, you've gotta meet him in a crowd. Lenz can't get into that club. It's a safe zone. And here's the good news: I'll be coming with you, looking sickening as always."

"Perhaps we have opposing definitions of the phrase 'good news'?"

"Shut up. Was that a joke? Shut up."

"I can manage by myself."

"As if. I'm coming. And don't bother bringing your cane."

What on earth, Ollie. What on earth.

Tell me of your final happy memory. Next week I can tell you about meeting Owen Abend, another boy who is making me a decent human being.

Moritz

P.S. You've asked me not to needle. Don't fling a cat at my face (I would only dodge Mr. Gray), but know that I am worrying. That is all.

chapter fifteen
THE LIVING ROOM

So I want to tell you about the best day of my life. Simply, without fuss or hoopla. Except that isn't really possible—because fuss and hoopla were both present on the day in question.

And this was the day when I realized what Liz was to me. I mean, really realized it (I know I've blabbed about being lovesick, but it wasn't always like that in my head). Liz and I were friends, and really good friends, but here was the day that upped the stakes.

Now it just sounds all dolphin-wavy up in here, but please have mercy again.

The party was for my thirteenth birthday. It wasn't actually on my thirteenth birthday, but a few days before it, because normal kids usually have to go to school on Tuesdays.

My birthdays were always nice enough before. Mom would usually give me some new model fossils or miniature-sarcophagi-making kits, and make me an awesome, multilayered cake (she went through a wedding-cake-hobbyist phase), and Auburn-Stache would come over and join us for a night of stuffing our faces with almond chicken and playing board games (I kick royal ass at Clue, if you're wondering). Pretty tame, by all accounts.

But my thirteenth birthday became a bigger deal, maybe because I'd become a teenager. I don't think Mom was convinced I'd make it to adulthood, but I was getting closer and she was getting hopeful. In the weeks before October 11, she kept dropping all these fond little hints that she was bursting on the inside (and not with grand mal seizures). Like, sometimes she would let her face relax and she'd just drape her arms around my neck without warning.

"You've grown so much! Who's this man in the house?"

It was downright creepy. Like a very loving leech had possessed her. She meant well, I think. But it was like she was trying to sap the aging right out of me with statements like:

"What happened to my little kickstand?"

And:

"God, I can't believe how much you look like your father!"

Catchphrases, Moritz. She developed *catchphrases*. And she was mentioning Dad, which was even freakier.

I started hiding out in the woods more, clambering up into our old tree forts or visiting the pond and dipping my feet in for the hell of it. Mom was way more lenient nowadays, and had been ever since Liz started coming around. Over the past few years she'd only locked herself in the garage seven times or so. Another reason to be grateful for Liz.

(And another reason to miss her, now that Mom is locked inside the garage every other day.)

Anyhow, she and Liz plotted and schemed behind my back to throw me a party. I knew they were planning something on account of all the obvious whispering and winking, so I was mentally prepared for them to jump out from behind trees and throw confetti in my eyes.

On that Saturday, I followed the deer trail to the junkyard not remotely at unawares. After all, Liz wasn't stopping to scope out things on the forest floor. She was way too eager to get to Joe's. She couldn't keep a secret without it basically leaking out her ears, and she dragged me right through the trees as if we were being chased.

They had constructed an enormous white tent—a pavilion of sorts—near the center of the yard, in an open space of thirty feet or so.

"You made me a circus! There had better be juggling bears. Juggling dead teddy bears."

"It's not a circus."

I grinned. "Of course not. It's a birthday tent!"

"You could have at least pretended to be surprised."

"You like me because I don't pretend."

"Ugh. Just come inside, doofus."

"Nope. I hate to disappoint. Let me try again." I blinked and rubbed my eyes with my fists. "Whoa! What could that be? Surely not a surprise party."

"Shut up, doofus."

"You don't have to finish every sentence with 'doofus,' you know. A boy has feelings, you know."

"You don't have to finish every sentence with 'you know,' you know."

"I know."

She pulled me into the tent.

*   *   *

What I stepped into was a living room. Not like the living room in our cabin, which is full of lanterns and bookshelves and a fireplace and Mom's handmade furniture and paintings.

I stepped into a modern living room. A television, a stereo with speakers, phones on the coffee table, power sockets and plugs and wires, wires everywhere tucked behind couches. There were so many electronic devices in there that I jumped backward and trod on Liz's foot before I realized that not one of them was giving off seizure-inducing color. Before I realized that every object was an imitation or had been gutted.

I could never have hoped to see so many people in one place. I heard later that Liz, Mom, and Joe had checked the pockets of and patted down every person who arrived. If anyone resented that, they didn't tell me. Most of the guests were Liz's extended family: her muddy cousins, perfumed aunts, and baseball-capped uncles. I spotted the local state park guy who keeps an eye on wildlife and plays poker with Mom sometimes, too, and Lucy, Mom's pharmacist, whose glasses sparkled with rhinestones. But Liz had also persuaded two friends from school to stop by and meet me, friends I'd heard about in passing with increasing regularity over the past few months: a blond boy named Tommy, a red-haired girl named Mikayla. (I remember just staring at her, half convinced she was wearing a wig, just like Mom has started doing. I'd never seen curly hair in person before.)

"Surprise!" cried the crowd. Just like in a story. And it was a crowd. At least thirty people were gathered there in my mock living room, standing beside the television and a vacuum cleaner and a laptop and a—*oh my fluffing god a humidifier.*

"Welcome home," said Liz.

I stared and stared and said nothing.

"Oliver," said Mom. "Say something."

"You remembered. I can't believe you remembered the *humidifier.*"

I almost burst into manly tears. (Of course they would have been manly; I was thirteen now.) I'm pretty sure the deformed face I made to fight back those manly tears convinced all the people at the party who didn't know me already that I was a nutjob, but that was okay. They didn't have to understand. Liz did, and she put her arm around me until I could stop sniffling, laughing her light laugh. Mom looked teary, too, so I smiled and said, "Give me a tour!"

"Eat your cake first."

After we massacred the towering skyscraper of a cake (Mom had shaped it into a fondant-coated amplifier) and the other guests started meandering, beers in hand, Liz and her friends took me around the living room to show me how all the illusions were created. There was dry ice in the humidifier, emitting clouds of white fog. There was a windup music box inside the gutted boom box. The speakers were really strange because they were made of cardboard.

"Where did you get all this fake stuff? Why would anyone ever make cardboard televisions? Not just for me, I mean." I blinked. "This wasn't made just for me, was it?"

"Tommy's dad owns a furniture shop. They put out cardboard appliances and stuff so people can imagine what the furniture would look like in their own houses better."

"That is so weird. People are so weird. Thanks, Tommy . . . ?"

Tommy nodded at me. *"Mmmph."*

"Well, I'm glad I'm not the only one feeling speechless."

"Tact, Ollie. Where has it gone? He's *shy*."

"Oh. I've never met a shy person before. What's that like for you?"

Mikayla burst into high-pitched giggles while Tommy stared at his feet.

"Omigod, Ollie. You're just *too* funny!" Mikayla put her hand on my arm, which was weird. Liz gave her a look and steered me away from them, dragging me over to the bookshelf.

There were some books, presents from Auburn-Stache and Mom. (Mom knew I was getting really into medieval folklore, so she had some books on King Arthur, and Auburn-Stache has a sense of humor, so there were also copies of *The Adrian Mole Diaries* and some Terry Pratchett books.) But scattered among the books were some framed photographs—

My mouth fell open. "Whoa—wait, are these photos of us? Of me?"

"Yep! Happy birthday, Ollie UpandFree."

There was one of us lying on the roof of the Ghettomobile, one of us up in the tree branches, one of us just standing in the woods: Liz crouching over something, me just watching her with this bemused expression on my face. I'd never seen a photograph of myself before; I didn't know I was that gangly.

And Liz. No matter what, she looked pretty, even in the pictures where she was caked in mud and her hair was in disarray. It was like she was always lit up from the inside.

"But—how?"

Someone cackled behind me. Junkyard Joe cracked a grin. "You didn't really think I was just sittin' there on the porch takin' pictures of birds, now, didja?"

"I did, actually! You said you were an ornithologist!"

Joe cackled again and took a swig of beer. "Hell no. I can't tell a duck from a chicken. But I ain't a bad photographer. I figured I was sitting far enough away, and there's a helluva zoom on those lenses."

I swallowed. "Thanks, Mr. Fay."

"Ain't no thing. It's nice havin' folks in the yard. You gave her a reason to come visit, you know." He looked a bit sad for a moment. "You ain't the only one who gets bored in the woods."

I turned around and there was Mikayla again.

"Your hair is crazy. Why is it so curly?"

"Oh, stop it!" Again, she put her hand on my arm. It bothered me, though I couldn't say why. "Your hair is crazy, too. I wish I had a Mohawk."

"It wasn't my idea," I told her. "Where's Liz?"

"Oliver! Come sit down!"

I left her standing there and joined Mom on the couch in front of the massive cardboard wide-screen television.

"You had better watch out," Mom said, raising an eyebrow at Mikayla.

"What? Why?"

"How are you liking your party?"

"It's awesome, Mom. Thank you. Was it your idea?"

She smiled. "Nope. It was all Liz. But you know, I wish I could really give you this."

"You give me enough, Mom." I tried to laugh. "I'm sorry I took all this away from you."

"*Tch!* Up-shut."

"I mean it, Mom. Sometimes I feel like— I mean. No humidifiers for either of us."

"Meh. I never owned one anyhow." She paused. "But I do have to admit something."

"What?" Was she about to tell me something about my birth? An untold story about Dad and Auburn-Stache? About the mysterious laboratory?

"I do miss shit-coms sometimes."

I sighed. "Yeah, sorry about that."

"Let's see what's on TV, hey?"

She handed me a plastic remote devoid of batteries.

"Press the on button."

"Won't that shatter the illuuuuusion?" I wiggled my fingers. "When it doesn't switch on, I mean?"

"Just do it!" came the muffled voice of Auburn-Stache, from the direction of the television. The tent canvas was trembling there.

"Um . . . sure, Possessed Cardboard Television Set. Why not?"

"Wait! First ask what we're watching!" Liz's voice.

"What are we watching?" I cried.

"A live concert," Mom said.

I pressed the little red on button.

Someone popped the front of the box out, and who should be sitting there but Auburn-Stache, holding a harmonica. Squeezed in beside him and leaning on the frame of the screen was Liz with a toy microphone.

"Welcome to the inaugural Oliver Ages Hoopla!" said Liz. "I'm your announcer, Awesome Person. Please welcome the talented Lady Paulot to the stage."

Mom stood up and left the tent, bowing at the whooping, slightly buzzed crowd of the Fay and Becker families. Moments later, I saw her edging into the screen from behind, holding an acoustic guitar.

I laughed. "You play the guitar?"

"I birthed you! I can do *anything*!"

I knew there was a guitar in the house, tucked away under Mom's bed. I'd never seen her play it.

"Pay good attention, kiddo," said Auburn-Stache. "We went to all this expense and you're zoning out."

"Auburn-Stache, you're a harmonicist?"

"Nope. Never. But you don't know any better, yes?"

Liz snorted. "It's your first live show, UpandFree, so deal with it."

She counted them off. They began to play.

I dealt with it, more or less, although my eyes kept welling up for some stupid reason, and my nose got runny. I couldn't tell you what they played, there in my makeshift living room. They played folk songs, rock songs—songs I'd never hear otherwise, songs that weren't ideal for glocking to. Liz wasn't much of a singer—she may have been a bit tone-deaf, even. But that didn't matter. The crowd of partygoers gathered around, holding bowls of popcorn and singing along as if they'd heard the songs their whole lives. They probably had. And today, I could pretend that I had, too.

Eventually Liz stopped screeching long enough to say, "We now interrupt our programming to bring you a message from our sponsors!"

At which point Mikayla pushed her way on-screen and advertised red pop by chugging an entire can of it.

Liz shoved Mikayla away again and leaned out of the TV, extending a hand toward me.

I reached out to take it, but instead she passed me something.

Not a paper airplane, Moritz.

It was that book light again, and I didn't feel a thing but the warmth of her palm even though it was glowing white. I slipped it into my pocket. The buzz of it there no longer made me queasy; if anything, it seemed to charge me up, wake me up, fill my bones with the same glow Liz had.

As night fell, Junkyard Joe demanded we all "pop a squat" on some of the busted old cars and wait for some sort of "grand finale." Liz was off helping him get something ready, so I leaned against an old Dodge truck beside Auburn-Stache. You would have loved this night, Moritz—everyone was being so noisy, so rambunctious.

"What do you think of your 'dream life,' Oliver?" For some reason, he spoke carefully.

"I think it's the coolest thing anyone's ever done for me."

"You do seem to be enjoying yourself. I am happy to see you looking so well."

"Hey, I always pass my health checks."

"There are different kinds of wellness, kiddo."

I noticed that his goatee was streaked with strands of white, and some of the crinkles around his eyes weren't from smiling. "How about you?"

"What about me?"

"Well, how's your wellness?"

"Why bother about me when that young lady is waiting for you to join her?"

"Good point, 'Stache. And you can join Mom." I nodded to where she was standing on the other side of a bonfire. "She really cares about you, you know. Even if she hollers. Don't just loiter on your lonesome."

"You're your father's son."

"I am?"

Was my needling finally paying off? But right then, Liz ran forward and grabbed my hand.

"Come on, come on." I thought she'd drag me to the Ghetto-mobile, but she dragged me instead to the empty, pseudo living room and we sat on the couch. A rip in the canvas overhead gave us a view of the sky. We began counting down. Before long, the fireworks started. I had never seen those before, either. Junkyard Joe got them illegally somewhere; when I asked him about it later, he just tapped his nose all mischievously.

Hey, what do you see when you look at fireworks, Moritz? I bet you can see them a little bit, since they're so loud. Or do you see the smoke? The ash? The gray debris?

As amazing as they were, I stopped looking pretty fast. I couldn't get over sitting in that homemade living room.

"What's up, Ollie?"

"This is just too . . . Look, I never thought I could have all these things, even for pretend. I didn't bother dreaming of it, you know?"

In the sky overhead, the fireworks crackled and burst. Liz's face was lit in purple and pink flashes. Like she was sunbathing in electricity, but there was no pressure at my temples. Only her, looking at me.

"You're being too honest again."

"No, because I'm lying. I *did* bother dreaming about it. I do dream about it. All the freakin' time."

Liz was *never* as quiet as she was in that mock living room. Then:

"I dream about that, too, Ollie. All the freakin' time." She laid her head on my shoulder.

So I guess that was the moment, the final moment, that sealed it for me.

It's really cold in my room still, and my fingers are numb. I'm not ready to write about the terrible things that happened yet. Next time, I guess. I can't stall forever. It's been eating me up. Maybe that's why I'm losing weight and it has nothing to do with not having tuna sandwiches.

I look forward to your letter, Mo. I want to postpone my next few.

~ Ollie

P.S. I still can't shake that weird notion. I mean, maybe my dad didn't die. And your mom didn't, either. Maybe our parents are actually—well, our parents. And maybe that's why I get you, and you get me. Wouldn't that be *wondrous*?

Bro?

chapter sixteen

THE OUTFIT

How can I express my growing concern?

You wanted to share your story with me. But if doing so will be detrimental to your health, stop it now, Ollie.

Do you remember when you first began writing me? You used to babble. You used to be curious. Used to wonder. Ask me any number of frivolous questions about television and the Internet. My thoughts on cartoons. You asked about my personal life. Nudged and pestered and needled. I thought that if ever I met you, I'd want to smack you in the face with an electronic device. Perhaps a video game console. To hush you and your illumination.

That was you. That was the same Ollie who was impossible to ignore. Who took me, for once, out of myself. The first one to make me smile in . . . I shiver to think how long. I shudder to recall the afternoons before I could await your letters. The afternoons spent in this dank apartment we struggle to pay for. Above this city of people who could not care less whether or not I listened to them before you began writing to me.

Before you.

I can no longer ignore that you haven't seen the sun. You? The boy who used to climb trees and run away from home? *You* can't get out of bed?

And now you write your story as if into emptiness?

I am here. I am not a void, Ollie. I am reading. I can't take you from dark places, but I am listening.

If writing your biography is sinking you, stop writing. I *would* rather you told me about the humidity's effects on your glockenspiel. Or the birds outside your window. The fibers in your T-shirt. The wrinkles in your face. Rather that than write a history that racks you with pain and guilt.

You speak of the best day of your life as if you don't anticipate ever having another good one. Your fondest memory is of being shoved into a cheap imitation of things you can never have? Why weren't you insulted by Liz's display? That party was a mockery. The "living room" you could never live in? Why would anyone want to show you what others find necessary to life? Why would anyone want to change you? To "correct" you like that?

Why not celebrate what you *do* love? What you have accomplished? Your glockenspieling. Your calligraphy. Your burgeoning origami skills. Your storytelling!

Why not celebrate that you are a wonderful, funny, irritating, talented young man anyone would be gratified to know? Someone I would die to meet?

I am not kicking you while you are down, Ollie. I am telling you to celebrate what is real in your life. Celebrate who you are. Not who Liz wishes you to be. Claw your way out of this nostalgic hole you are digging.

Get out of bed.

For the last time, abandon the idea that we might be blood relatives. Nonsense. I spent a lot of time with my mother, even if I never understood her. My birth father was nobody. Nothing more than the person who impregnated my mother. He made a bastard and vanished. There is no sense in romanticizing it. Herr Farber is my father now. There is no sense in seeking the past.

The past is never any better than the present, and it is not what you have to look forward to.

We don't have to be related in order to be close. Sometimes you are not as amusing as you think you are. Sometimes I think you are a child, Oliver.

Perhaps I should be kinder to you in your sadness. But nothing makes me so angry as the idea that you are letting yourself wither away. For the sake of a girl who does not appreciate you.

I will imagine that you asked about me in your last letter. Wrote a passage such as this:

I hope you enjoy your totally wacky trip to the Diskothek with Fieke! I think you made her swoon with your amazing rapping skillz. It sounds like she might maybe somehow be the right kind of girl to whip your goofy, pompous head into the proper shape! You realize this trip is probably a date, don'tcha?!

How kind of you to ask.

I don't know how to dress for a *Diskothek* in general, let alone how to dress when meeting a boy under strange circumstances at a *Diskothek*. Under the watchful eye of his imposing sister. And her equally imposing boots.

"Who gives a crap how you dress," Fieke said. "You're still pretending to be blind, right? Wear a fluffing tutu. It's not like you usually dress well anyhow."

"Beg *pardon*."

"Well, you're color-blind. It shows. Puce pants and a mustard-yellow shirt? Please, Moritz. Have you ever considered that people don't avoid you just because of your goggles?"

It was the weekend. We were at the *Kneipe* again. I am half convinced Fieke lives there. The only time she doesn't look irritated is when she is listening to the local performers reading their poetry. Singing their songs. Performing their irksome scatting. That's the only time she doesn't jingle and spit. She is quiet then, apart from the slight wheeze in her chest.

She accompanies me home some evenings, however, so she must not live there. We both live in Ostzig. The watchful eye she's been keeping on me is peculiar. She must not entirely hate my company. I would say we were friends. She would snort derisively and stomp away from me if I said anything of the sort.

"Well, won't you help me pick something out? Something that isn't a tutu?"

"*Fff*. No. I didn't even dress my Barbies as a kid."

"Your Barbies were nude?"

"I tattooed them with permanent markers. They weren't nude. They were *art*."

That was unhelpful. I resigned myself to asking Frau Pruwitt for her advice. Pruwitt seemed intent on actually giving me work to do in the library, now that I could read all the book titles.

"What can you tell me about the customs of *Diskothek* attire?" I hazarded.

"I can tell you that it's irrelevant to alphabetizing self-help guides, Moritz."

"Ah."

She sniffed down at me from up on the footstool. "Did someone ask you to go?"

"Not precisely. But . . ."

"Well, don't let your newfound love life interfere with your studies."

She climbed down. Shoved the step over one meter.

"Why should my studies matter here? It's Bernholdt-Regen."

"They matter if you ever want to get out of here."

I had no intention of asking Frau Melmann.

I recalled your tale of dressing for Liz. There are no fedoras in my house. Father owns only two ties; usually he wears his workman's clothes, suitable for welding. Although I have heard that some *Diskotheken* favor industrial music, I doubt I could pull off a full-body jumpsuit. Even if it was color-coordinated.

I decided to match Fieke. Yesterday I purchased an outfit

from the secondhand shop. The salesclerk assured me it was entirely black. Black pants. Black shirt. Black boots for the rain.

I hope that will suffice.

Gott in Himmel, I am uneasy. And not only because of the *Diskothek*.

Lenz Monk returned to school this week. In some part of my heart, perhaps in the weak left ventricle, I had prayed he would not be returning to Bernholdt-Regen at all. But this morning in the courtyard I sensed him there, clearly visible in the resounding waves of the rainfall. He cracked his knuckles. I could hear it from meters away.

He quieted when I passed. His eyes followed me all the way into the school. The stare of someone who would not hesitate to shove me off a bridge. Would not hesitate to pummel a boy as small as Owen into nothingness. Would the threat of expulsion spare me his attentions?

Fieke said his father held some sort of sway. Lenz's father and Headmaster Haydn were old friends, or so she'd heard. That was why Lenz was not locked away in a juvenile detention center.

I broke into the iciest of sweats once inside. My pacemaker labored. My chest twinged. I nearly shrieked when Fieke leapt down from the banister in front of me.

"You look uglier than usual."

"Lenz has returned."

"Nothing's going to happen, pussycat."

"Because of the school assembly."

She sighed. Tobacco breath wafted into my nostrils.

"Because I won't let him fluffing touch anyone here. He won't hurt anyone again."

"Did he hurt you as well, Fieke?"

It took half a glare to silence me.

Last Friday, while I was fulfilling my duties in the *Bibliothek*, Frau Pruwitt handed me a many-paged, stapled document.

"Must I read this?" I clicked in apprehension.

"You don't have to. But you'd be a fool not to."

I listened well. " 'Application . . . Application for *Gymnasium* Transfer.' Wait."

She nodded.

"But it *can't* be allowed."

"And why not? You accepted no accommodations for your visual impairment during the placement assessment, correct?"

"That's not why I failed. I didn't even take the test."

"And why not, Moritz?"

I took a deep breath. Only to bite my tongue. "The timing was terrible. There were other, ah, distractions. And . . ."

Nice schools are for nicer people, Oliver.

"But you're willing to transfer now that your head's on straight, yes?" Of course her eyebrow slipped upward.

I stared at the books lining the shelves on either side of us. Books I once thought I could never read. Until I spent time in the *Bibliothek*, books were something I had never considered myself worthy of enjoying. Being who and what I am. Coming from the place I came from.

There are many things I never allowed myself, Ollie.

But you've told me to be brave.

"Yes," I said. "Yes, I am willing."

"Good. Because I told them that you didn't apply because you were disgruntled by their lack of accommodations."

"But—"

She raised a hand. I winced. She rested it on my shoulder. "You belong in a slightly classier hellhole than this. Fill out the forms. Show up for the test."

"I'll need references."

"You've got them. Fear not. Herr Haydn still owes me for the dinner party fiasco of twenty-eleven. And I happen to know something nefarious about Frau Melmann and her online gambling."

I had to clear my throat. "Thank you."

"I don't want your thanks. I want you to read *War and Peace*. Every last word."

"Right."

For a brief instant, that application was the best thing I'd ever read, Oliver. Even better than *The Catcher in the Rye*. Even better than *Fahrenheit 451*.

I cannot speak for fireworks. Rain increases my vision more than you can imagine, in concentric rings of sound. But snow is silent. Difficult for me to see at all. Yet I can always feel it on my nose and cheeks. It is cold but soft. To me it smells like salt. Understand that even when I lecture you, even when I am cold, I am trying to be soft as well.

I should write more. But it is Friday at last. Fieke is

knocking her fists against the door of my apartment. Scaring the living organs out of Father. I have some sense of what you felt when Liz came to your door. Fieke is more likely to be caked in cigarette smoke than muck. But she is another person who makes me human.

You were first, Ollie.

I wish I could phone you. I'm not teasing you for what you cannot have. I'm trying to express my deepening concern.

Anxiously yours,

Moritz

chapter seventeen
THE FENCE

I don't even know what you want from me anymore.

First we agree to be honest with each other and ourselves, or whatever, and then you tell me not to tell you things that will be upsetting! Well, guess what? Sometimes things are really damn upsetting. Make up your mind. You told me not to pretend to be happy.

It's not like I've stopped wondering about you, you know. You wanted me to *stop* asking about you. I can't believe you never told me about your parents. All I know about my dad is that he was a nice guy and a scientist, and my mom is either smiling or crying whenever she thinks about him, but I still talk about him sometimes. But I didn't even realize that you were adopted! So can you blame me for filling in the blanks myself?

Would being my brother really be so terrible?

But that's not why I'm angry. Why'd you spit all over the best memory I have? You're so determined to think the worst of Liz! Didn't I tell you that she didn't do anything wrong?

Maybe I should wait to write this. Maybe I should wait until Auburn-Stache drags Mom out of the garage for the first time in a week. But now I've got a pen and now I've got time (I've always got time, right? I don't go on adventures to *Diskotheks*), so I'm writing anyhow.

Because you're wrong. I need to talk to you about this, even if it hurts.

I don't think I can handle it on my own anymore. Sometimes I stare at the window and I punch the wall and I pinch the skin at my wrists, and it doesn't feel like anything.

Even if you are an abyss that can't make its mind up, even if you think I don't give a shit about you anymore (hit yourself, damn it!), I'm going to tell you, finally, why Liz won't come to visit me.

It started with a camping trip.

It happened around a year after that thirteenth birthday party, a few months before I started talking to you, but who's counting. Junkyard Joe had a deer blind—sort of like a tree house for game hunters—a few miles into the forest, near Marl Lake. The weekend of my fourteenth birthday was a good time to set up his gear for the upcoming hunting season, which begins in November. Besides, he just about spit out his beer when I told him I had never actually seen the lake in our woods, the lake that borders the forest and constitutes the state park.

"You ain't seen Marl?"

"Well, it's just a lot of water, right? I've seen water before. . . ."

"Jegus, boy."

When Liz asked me to come along, we were in my bedroom passing the book light back and forth.

"I don't know if Mom would like it. A few days isn't the same as a few hours."

I tossed the light back to her before my hands went numb. Liz caught it; she had cut her hair short the previous month after she started high school, and it bobbed when she swung her arms out. "Just tell her you're staying at the junkyard again. Camping in the Ghettomobile, like old times."

"Why don't we do that anymore?" I was only half joking.

"We might be too old for the Ghettomobile."

"Blasphemy!" I snickered, and caught the light again, but it wasn't my hands that were aching this time.

Things were getting weird between us. Liz still came over all the time, but we didn't seem to laugh as much. Sometimes we'd both go quiet, and it got really hard to look her in the eyes without coughing on those imaginary frog bits again.

"Why don't you ask Tommy and Mikayla to come, too?"

She looked at her feet. "I'm sure they're busy with other things."

I nearly dropped the light. "So you only asked me?"

She nodded. Didn't say anything snarky. Just nodded and held out her hands to catch the light again.

I tossed it back, and I felt like it weighed more all of a sudden.

"Well, yeah, I'll come," I said. "Sounds like shenanigans."

She smirked; some of the aching went away. Maybe I was imagining it to begin with. Maybe Liz asked me not as a last resort but as something else.

Maybe it was a good thing that things were changing.

"Yeah."

* * *

We left early on a Thursday morning. We'd packed up some basic camping gear—two tents and hiking backpacks full of venison jerky and s'more-making materials—as well as a cooler full of hot dogs to eat that evening. Junkyard Joe's backpack was this giant green lump of, well, junk. Cooking utensils like tongs and pokers dangled from his back; rope was all but wrapped around his neck.

"Shame we can't bring a fridge with us," he said as we laced up our boots. "Keep the drinks cold."

"My bad," I mumbled.

Liz rolled her eyes. "Um, I don't know about you guys, but I wouldn't want to strap a fridge to my back anyhow."

Joe grinned, revealing more gaps than teeth. "You ain't wrong, Beth. You sure ain't wrong."

It took us ages to get our act together enough to set out. After a few hours of scrabbling around looking for stray socks and pie pans, we were finally trudging out into a warm October afternoon. The leaves underfoot were hardly damp at all and crunched enough to be satisfying. The air had that awesome scent of decay. If only all dead things smelled like musty autumn.

"So you brought an oil lantern, right?" Liz asked me.

"Yes, yes. It's tucked alongside my monocle and collapsible velocipede, Jekyll."

"Oh, ha-ha, Hyde. I don't care if we're living in the past, so long as you don't expect me to manage without toilet paper. I'm a modern lady."

For some reason, I did not laugh. I blushed and dragged my feet.

"You kids," said Joe from behind us. "Wait up for your packhorse."

"I can carry more—"

"Shut yer yap, Birthday Boy, and keep marching. Who wants to sing the first camp song?"

"Oh, man, we have to go back. You need glock accompaniment!"

Liz prodded me in the back. "Don't encourage him, Ollie."

And balance was restored. Why was it suddenly hard to be ourselves?

After an hour of hiking, we arrived at the fence that surrounds Mom's property. I'd never actually seen the fence before, though I'd known it existed.

I stopped walking the moment I sensed it: a twinge in my temples, a blade in my nostrils.

"Pick it up, Slowpo—Ollie?!"

I blinked. "This . . ."

"Your nose is bleeding!"

"What *is* this?"

Up ahead I could see a band of tangerine light bulging and shrinking in orange humps, not dissimilar to the tendrils of the power line. But these strings of electricity were a bit narrower, and they rose and fell in pulses, like looping vines jutting from the ferns at waist level, almost like loose stitches in fabric. When they were present, they were downright intimidating: the orange strands outlined the entire length of the horizon, visible as far left and as far right as I could see, spitting and retreating between the branches and the trees. There was no way around it. I felt like I was reddening, like I was sunburnt from head to toe in an instant.

My head felt like two heads, three, splitting in all directions. I gritted my teeth before speaking: "There's something . . . I need to sit down. Mind if I . . . pop a squat?"

And my legs folded under me. Good thing I have experience with collapsing or I might have smacked my head.

"Ollie!" God, I hated seeing her look like that, like she didn't know what to do with me. Like I wasn't even a salamander she could study.

"Whoa there. What's up with your boy?"

"Did you bring your damn walkie-talkies, Uncle Joe?!"

"Heh. Walkies." My speech was slurred, tongue heavy. "Walkies, talkies."

I could feel the beginnings of the pre-seizure aura fogging up my vision. I thought I could smell cinnamon, which is something that sometimes happens beforehand. At least it isn't sulfur for me.

"Hell, he's havin' a reaction?"

I decided at that moment to put all my fingers in my mouth.

"No, he always tries to cannibalize himself! Yes, he's having a reaction! What's causing it?"

"Well, obviously it's the property line."

Liz was pulling me to my feet, yanking me back the way we'd come. I was biting my lip, trying to stall the seizure that was creeping into me as she dragged me away.

"His family property line. It's an electric fence, like most folks put up to keep deer out of gardens. Didn't you know?"

The sudden chill in my chest helped clear my head. I tried to take some of my weight off Liz's shoulders.

"She put up an electric fence," I said. "But she *promised* him."

"What?"

I felt like something from a zoo, Mo.

"She promised my dad. She tries to keep me at home, but one day . . . let me leave . . . so why—?"

"Ollie . . . maybe we should go camping at the Ghettomobile after all." That look was still on her face. I could see it clearly now that I had one head again. "Or a little ways back, even. I mean, the lake's just water, like you said."

"Yeah, I s'pose s'mores would taste just as good there. I can check on the site next week instead," Joe added.

"No. No, I want to see the water. The lake of water." I shook off Liz's grasp. "I can ask Mom about it later. I can needle later."

"But you can't cross it—"

"It's pulsing. I can try!" But even as I spoke, even as I strode forward, Moritz, my vision was getting cloudy. I know I told you that we should aim for superheroism, but maybe you're right. Maybe we have to aim for normalcy first. Too bad normalcy is an impossible thing.

"Sheesh, you kids are dramatic." Joe was peeling his hiking boots and socks from his feet. He dumped his massive backpack into my arms, and I nearly fell over again. "Let me deal with this, eh? Hold my purse, Barbra Streisand."

"Who?"

"An actress. I'm sayin' you're a dramatic woman."

And here's what Junkyard Joe did: he strolled barefoot right up to the single electrified wire buried in the light—right into what I could only see as swooping arcs of orange, could feel as sizzling warmth on my neck and ears especially—and slammed a boot down on top of it, pinning it to the leafy ground. He wedged the other one beside it lengthwise, so that the electric current was entirely blocked.

The pressure lessened at my temples.

Half the fence went out. On the left, the pulses kept bursting out, but beyond the boot to the right the fence was no more than a silver wire, suspended almost invisibly in the air at waist height. I wondered if that silver wire wound entirely around the property. I wondered whether she would have put one around our house if she thought that would keep me in better than the padlocks.

Placing a hand on the toe of one boot, Joe pressed the wire into the leaves on the muted side. "How's it looking, Oliver? Rubber boots. They don't conduct electricity."

"It's genius, Joe. You made a gate for me."

"Why does ever'one assume that all rednecks are idiots?"

"Maybe it's the inbreeding." I tried to smile.

"Hey, I'm the one who makes the inbreeding jokes, Amish," said Liz. But I didn't want to look at her.

"Don't thank me, Streisand." Joe reclaimed his pack. "Just hurry up and get to leaping."

I turned and eyed the tendrils still dancing on the left side of the boots.

"Ready or not, here I come." I sprinted forward.

I leapt the wire near the low part where he had pinned it down. For the briefest moment while I was in the air, I thought I felt those tendrils bowing out sideways to net me, but I was already past them.

I landed in the leaves beyond the electric fence, and in doing so left my family property for the first time in a decade or longer.

The air was fine, but I wondered whether the air back home wasn't as fresh. I looked back. Joe was giving me a dorky thumbs-up and grin, but Liz . . .

Liz watched me from a distance.

* * *

Not far beyond the fence, the forest switched from new growth to old growth. Suddenly the trees were towering beasts, century-old pines and beeches that loomed overhead like dinosaurs. The forest paths below became clearer but darker; the foliage overhead was thick enough to block the light and discourage even ferns from growing at the foot of the trees.

"I can't believe I've never seen this before." I was leaning back so far that I thought my head would scrape the ground. Joe was leading the way. Liz lagged behind us. I could feel her eyes on my back.

"Well, now you have. And wait till we get to the lake. You almost always see deer drinking along the east side, so long as fudgies haven't spooked them all."

"Fudgies?"

"Tourists. Flatlanders. They come north for the trees and the chocolate fudge."

I leapt a puddle in his wake. The ground was moister here, a bit colder.

"I've never had fudge."

"How on earth d'you live?"

"I wonder about that, too," said Liz quietly.

This wasn't nearly as fun as my last birthday, Mo.

Joe scratched his chin. "Well, it's October, so there shouldn't be too many tourists around, apart from a few prospective game hunters like meself. But they tend to stay near the plains on the east banks. Just how sensitive are you, Ollie? Will you start twitchin' and biting your toes if they've got their RVs parked along the opposite side of the lake?"

"Um, no. I don't think so. I'll be able to see the electricity from pretty far away, and I should be able to tell how strong it is. Whether it's just a phone, or a mini-fridge or a car or whatever. Don't worry about me."

"So—you're almost psychic? You can tell what sort of electrical object it is from far away? Get outta town!"

"I've never been to town. And I never . . . I mean, no. I don't think of it that way. It's really mostly useless."

"Stop stuttering, you idiot. Nobody thinks you're weird anymore. You're old news." I did not know whether Liz was joking with this little outburst, but at least she was talking, walking abreast with us.

"I'm old hat, huh?"

"The oldest hat."

"Like bowler hats, Dickens."

"Like Grecian diadems, Homer."

"Like Egyptian headdresses . . . erm, Ra?"

"Whatever, dork." But her lips curled upward, and before long she was far ahead of us, hopping over puddles, cheeks flushed pink.

When she was very nearly out of sight, Joe inched closer.

"Hey, I think this weekend's your shot, buddy. Go for it! I give you permission. Heh."

I felt the blood rush to my face. "I don't know what you—"

"Oh, come on. You're a hermit, yes, but you're also a teenage boy and she's a beautiful girl, my niece. Some people don't 'preciate that, maybe. But don't tell me you ain't got your hopes up."

"I wouldn't even—I don't even know—"

"You'll get your chance, Ollie. I'll be sure to wander off at the perfect moment. Probably sometime this evening, after we set up camp. I'll give you a signal, right? You'll know it when you see it!"

I waved my hands. "No, please don't—"

"What are you so afraid of, Oliver?"

I stopped walking. The wind blew the scent of pine up my nose, twigs against my ankles. I looked at the lantern dangling from the side of my backpack.

"Why would someone like Liz want anything like that from someone like me?"

" 'Cause *you* have the decency to even wonder about that, you eejit. Now, let's catch up. She's probably halfway to China by now."

But she was only several yards ahead, hiding behind low pine boughs.

"Boo!" she cried, leaping out in front of us, kicking up the leaves.

"Gorram, girl!" Joe clutched his chest. "How old are you?"

I worried she'd overheard us. I thought she was blushing, but that could have been the October air nipping her. She was laughing breezes.

And then I was, too, and so was he.

"I wanna get there before sunset. Come on."

We spotted Marl Lake in the late afternoon. We could see it sparkling up ahead from between the trees. More than that, we could smell it, taste it in the way the air grew soggier. I was glad that it was autumn, or else the mosquitoes would have been sucking us something awful.

Finally we stepped out of the forest and almost right into the dark water. I could see pines lining the opposite bank a few hundred yards away. The sun was rippling along the soft black waves, and skippers darted across the surface of the water by the shore. Frogs were rustling the long grass. We stepped onto moist ground that gave beneath our feet.

"Wow," I said. "That is slightly better than your average puddle."

"A little bigger," said Liz. "Nice to know there are bigger things in the world."

"You think it's purty now? Jist wait until sunset."

And then he did something terrible, Junkyard Joe:

"Yeah, *sunset*!" he shouted, giving me two thumbs up and heartily winking. "That's when I'll be at the deer blind, don't you know. At. *Sunset*."

"My uncle's a crackpot," said Liz.

Before we made camp, Joe led us north along a thin trail through the cattails beside the lakeside and then into the woods a little ways to point out his deer blind. It was essentially a large green tree fort decked out in camouflage flock and layered in plastic tarps for the off-season. We clambered up the wooden ladder behind him—he had a cozy setup in there, with a couple of chairs and space for a sleeping bag, although he was right about needing to patch it up a bit. Water had been leaking through and rotting the plywood by the ladder, the floor was coated in pine needles and leaves, and a robin had left the debris of a nest in an upper corner of the wall. We got a good sense of why he was so proud of the blind: the vantage point from up there was vast. We could see the lakeshore, where deer were likely to drink, and the long grass, where they were likely to graze.

We set up the tents a little ways away from the water and the blind, on the most level ground we could find and not too close to the lake; we didn't want to get flooded out if it rained. Joe had been right about other campers: I could see a faint electric haze—the smog made it look like three large vehicles at least—across the water, but we were far enough away that I wasn't worried.

It took some time to sort out the tent poles and dig a pit for the campfire and gather kindling. It was my job to dig two holes far away from camp: one for doing our business in, and another for burying food scrap in. All this was fun because we worked together on it.

Before long, we'd cooked our hot dogs and eaten them, too, and then, as it was starting to get sunset-y out, Joe waggled his eyebrows at me and announced that he was "OFF TO THE BLIND FOR A LONG BIT OF TIME SO DON'T WORRY ABOUT ME COMING BACK RIGHT AWAY AND PLEASE ENJOY YOURSELVES."

Is there a name for the action of putting your head in your hands? There should be, Moritz.

Because once Liz and I were left alone, it seemed like neither of us knew exactly what to say.

"Nice fire, eh?" I said anyway. "Very fiery, isn't it?"

"Actually, it's getting too hot." Liz stood up. "Wanna go down to the lake?"

"Why not."

I'll tell you why not. Because I had been thinking, while we were eating hot dogs and I was digging poop holes and climbing the ladder to the deer blind and looking out across my first-ever lake, I wasn't seeing much but the way Liz couldn't seem to look at me and I couldn't seem to look at her, either.

All that time I was thinking about what Junkyard Joe had told me about this being my chance.

And I was thinking that he was right, and I was going to take it.

So we had only been standing awkwardly by the water, watching dragonflies flutter around and shine in the last few golden minutes of daylight as the sun was sinking just oh-so-perfectly down into the horizon, when I said:

"People in novels like to confess love at sunset, you know."

Liz stared at me. "Yeah, it's the same in movies. Like seeing the sun go away makes people want to make out because they're afraid to be alone once it's dark."

"Well, the dark can be scary, Liz."

"*Hmmph.*" She tucked her bangs behind her ear, but they fell right back into her face again. "I don't know. Maybe it's better when you can't see what you're doing. And other people can't see you or—anyhow, sunset confessions are totally lame, Ollie."

"Yeah, totally. The worst."

"*Mmmm.*"

The light was fading, and so was the promised chance. Or it felt like it. Maybe people confess at sunset because it feels like time is running out.

"Except, well. Okay, can I say something?"

She chuckled. "Since when do you ever ask that?"

"Well, regardless of the sunset. I mean, it's just a coincidence. Um, I think I may kind of love you? Just so you know. Not to be weird or whatever. But anyway."

I waited. Water lapped at the edges of our boots.

"Well, it's not like you have other options, is it?"

"Well, no. That's true."

She smacked me on the arm.

"Ow!"

"Well, thanks, Captain Tact!" She spun on her heel and began clambering up the muddy shore toward the trees.

"Wait—why does that matter? Why are you freaking out?"

I didn't follow her, but she stopped. "What?"

"Why does it matter whether or not you're the only girl I know, if I think I sort of love you or whatever?"

"Ugh. God, I wish you'd seen a romantic comedy at some point in your life, Ollie."

"No, I mean it. Explain why you hit me."

She clambered back down the shore again. "What you're saying is that you might have 'maybe fallen in love' with anyone who happened to meet you at the power line and offer you blackberries. That it didn't have to be me."

"Yeah, well. Maybe. So?"

"*Gah!*" This time she shoved me, and I fell back enough to put one foot into the cold water.

I squeaked like an unmanly mouse and she couldn't help but laugh. You would have laughed, too.

"I'm sorry!"

She took my hand and yanked me back out. I tried kicking the worst of the water from my boot, but it was already creeping icily between my toes.

"Freakin' cold!"

"Sorry, sorry. We'll go back to the campfire. Sorry!"

It was finally dark out as we stumbled into the forest hand in hand.

"I still don't get why what I said was wrong, though."

"Oh, shut up about it, Ollie!" She pushed a branch out of her way, and it smacked me in the shoulder when it snapped back. We came to a hollow dip in the forest floor, a circular indentation in the soil where the leaves were flattened. And suddenly we were standing in a deer hollow and this felt more like the place to do it than any sunset-y lake.

"I mean, *you* were the one who was there asking me about deep-sea diving, not someone else. It *was* you. And now it can never be anyone else, because it already happened and that's it. I mean, you're already *it* for me. All hypothetical, other girls already missed their chance with the local hermit."

"You total idiot." She let me go. "You don't know anything about other girls! I go to school with people—people way better than me, you know? I know so many people, Ollie, and I can't compete with some of them. I know people who are beautiful. People with talents and charm and money." She smiled sadly. "People with bathtubs, okay? So for you to just say something like this is just . . . it's not fair to you. There are so many people you haven't met. I'm no one."

"Yeah. But I *haven't met them*. I met you. Basically to me you're everything, you know?"

Without warning, she leaned forward and pushed her mouth against mine.

There, when I was about fourteen, I had my first kiss with the girl who makes me lovesick. It was a sloppy, tooth-mashing affair that didn't do much for either of us.

And I wouldn't have traded it for the entire Internet or all the humidifiers in the world.

*   *   *

I wish, Moritz, that I could stop my story here. I wish I could say that this was the last of it. I wish that I could say we had many more kisses and they weren't as terrible as that one.

But we didn't.

I can't face writing this now. I'm just really tired again.

So why not just go ahead and tell me about Owen Abend. Or scold me some more. Whatever. Give me the snowfall.

~ O

chapter eighteen
THE DEAD MOUSE

Oliver.

I don't *want* to scold you. You are my truest friend.

Do you understand that?

I apologize for making you think otherwise. Like you, I am trying.

Tell me whatever you need to. I will not discourage you. I don't know what possessed me. Please, speak if you must.

I know how valuable speech is. Especially after the night at the *Diskothek*. It was the strangest of nights. It reminded me that perhaps silence really doesn't help either of us. I will find the strength to confide in you when I can. Truly.

For now, let me tell you about my meeting with Owen Abend.

I appeared in the entranceway to our cramped apartment in my carefully selected outfit. Fieke raised her eyebrows. She didn't offer commentary.

Father scratched the back of his head. I had never had any guests over before. Perhaps he wondered whether Fieke was a nightmarish apparition.

She was still wearing lace-up boots, but these had heels like knives. Stilettos, yes? I worried that she would not be as illuminating, given her change of footwear. Then she took a step forward. Those heels clicked piercing visions into my head.

"Um. Shall we?"

She sniggered. Jingle. "We shall."

Dad stopped scratching his head. He put his hand on my shoulder as I followed her out.

I waited for him to say, "Fly! Fly, you fool!"

But he said only: "Be kind."

I asked whether we could walk there. Fieke pointed word-lessly to her feet. Walking on knifepoint pains the sole. She led me to the train station. I swallowed hard. Plunged down the stairs after her.

We stood on the echoing platform.

"What's the matter with you?" she said.

"People are staring. Rude, isn't it?"

"That's because you're clicking like a mad thing on steroids."

"They can rot. But yes. I'm anxious."

She elbowed me. "About your hot date with Owen."

I shook my head. "I don't do well with public transpor-tation."

"Is it to do with the shrieking?" she shrieked. The train pulled in, shrieking.

"I am used to shrieking. Unfortunately."

The doors hissed open. Expunged steamy air. How many bodies were in that car?

"But I am very unbalanced."

"No kidding."

"I mean—"

"Then hold me, baby."

She took my hand and led me into the smothering walls of the train car.

It was only three stops to the nightclub district. The train was weaving and clacking as we rode through the city. I was disoriented. I couldn't tell where we were headed. I couldn't stand alone without falling over. This wasn't fun.

Transportation of any kind all but cripples me. I can't hear properly with the background noise of motion. The constant movement jars any potential echoes into nebulousness. Everything outside the windows is invisible to me. In cars I can sit down at least. But the trains in Kreiszig are overcrowded. Seats are never guaranteed. So I stood there, queasy and unbalanced. Many of the other passengers were anticipating a fine night out. They laughed and chattered as the train rattled onward.

I held Fieke's hand. I could smell the smoke on her and it did not ground me.

She needed to trim her nails. Were they painted black as well?

Black is the only color I am certain I have seen. That's a story for another never.

We took the subway to Kreiszig Central. When we

climbed the stairs and reached the respite of open air, I wished I had visited before. I did not despise it yet. *Party-gänger* was not even close to being the only *Diskothek* in the city. This was an entire block smattered with them.

We left Grühl Street and wandered south toward the *Disko* itself. We passed a *Marktplatz* that smelled of roasted chicken, teriyaki, and incense. The air was full of noise. People eating. Tumultuous movement and shouting and music from each and every direction. A great number of people dressed exuberantly for the night out. Wearing leather and spikes and all manner of strange attire. My goggles were hardly remarkable alongside those chains and Mohawks. Ollie, you said walking in the woods with Liz felt wonderful, like dream-walking? Perhaps this was what I was doing. I was light-headed from the train journey, but this made it all the more vibrant: the popping of greasy meat on spits illuminated stall-holders' faces, the buzz of bulbs overhead caught moths in the night, the clip-clop of footsteps showed me the cobbles in wondrous detail. From somewhere nearby, bass was pounding the earth, jolting everyone in and out of clarity with dizzying effect.

I stopped in the street, Ollie. Simply to listen to it all.

Fieke, ahead of me as always, stopped as well. She did not ask me what I was doing. She looked back at my face, smirked, and took my hand once more.

"Come on. He's waiting for you."

As much as I love hip-hop concerts, I have never been enough of a dancer to visit a *Diskothek*. The world should be grateful. But even while we waited in line, it became apparent that I had been missing out on a novel experience. The noise! I saw the world in bass tremors.

"Maybe if you looked this excited at school, people would want to talk to you rather than beat your face in." She couldn't be smiling? Happy dolphin-waves, Oliver.

"I appreciate loud music."

"I gathered that, *Brille*."

Before we reached the door, two young men a few places ahead of us were ousted by a bouncer. He hoisted them up by their belt loops. Dropped them off the sidewalk. He pocketed their false identification cards.

"Fieke. I'm underage."

She raised a pierced eyebrow. "No shit."

I hunched my shoulders. Attempted to sidle from the queue. Fieke grabbed me.

"Now, this is more like you."

"But—"

"Shut it."

We reached the door. The bouncer, large and awkwardly haircutted as one might expect, clapped Fieke on the back.

"Fee! Where've you been hiding? Who's your date?"

"Mel, Mel. He's Owen's, not mine."

"Really?" He scanned me. I did not squirm. Much. "Nice goggles, kid."

He held open a palm.

"Thank you." I reached out to shake his hand, but he pointed to my goggles.

"*'Thek* policy and city regulation. I can't allow any guests to obscure their faces."

"Oh, come on. He's too short to be a criminal."

Mel cracked his knuckles much as Lenz does. His fists appeared before me in sharp detail. They were large fists.

"Fair enough. Owen will have to meet us outside."

I tried slinking backward. Fieke clutched my arm tighter.

"Aw, come on, Mel. For me?"

He shook his meaty head. "Bad enough I let you in as it is. But I'm not getting fired over a Cyclops visor."

"So you're acquainted with the X-Men?" My second comics series, Oliver. "We have that in common. But there are no lasers in my eyes. This isn't science fiction."

"Where did you find this kid?"

"Fine. Sorry, *Brille*."

"Why are—"

She yanked my arm down with one hand. Shoved my goggles up with the other.

Mel cursed. "You didn't say he's blind!"

"Tragic, right?"

"I'm *not* blind."

Mel recovered with noteworthy speed. "Oh. Well, I guess I'm acquainted with one of Xavier's rejects now. Go on in. Owen's at the tables."

I was likely a furious shade of red. Whatever red looks like. I held my chin high to reclaim my dignity. Replaced my goggles. Mel snapped his fingers when I passed. I tilted my head toward the sound.

"*Wahnsinnig*," he said. Crazy.

*　*　*

A wall of sound. A wall of sight. Bass beating through the soles of my feet. Even in the recoil the buzzing world was clear in there. When the bass boomed, I saw follicles.

Electronic music, Oliver, is something else I wish you could experience. I say this without mockery. It imitates life. Crashes and peaks. The rise and fall of tension! I might call it wondrous.

So much motion. So much sweat. So much detail. It was overwhelming. I felt I could see the veins of people, the very tissues of them. Almost down to their bone marrow. They basked in what the DJ was spinning out. It was as if I almost understood them.

"Don't stand in the doorway." Fieke dragged me across the floor, squeezing us between writhing torsos and jumping feet. Not for the first time I wished I could see lights.

"WHERE ARE THE TABLES?"

"OVER THERE!" She pointed upward, toward a stage.

"WHY ARE WE SHOUTING?"

"IT'S A CLUB!"

I focused on the stage. She meant "turntables."

There was Owen Abend. Performing in a vest and a flat cap. "Jamming" with a laptop before him. Perhaps it reflected him as he reflected it. The quietest student in Bernholdt-Regen, making more noise than anyone in the room. Transferring all the sound and volume he could want through the speakers.

Owen Abend looked up. Caught sight of us. Somehow. Perhaps because we were standing still. Perhaps because *Schicksal* (fate) is strange.

This time he did not retreat. He waved and mouthed "Hallo!" at us.

Behind me, Fieke's face curled into a smile. A real one.

Owen Abend opened his mouth wide. The noise showed me his teeth when it echoed inside his cheeks. Showed me his gums and two empty sockets where Lenz had knocked his teeth out. And showed me one more thing:

Owen Abend had no tongue.

At the bar after his DJ set, Owen Abend blinked at me. Moved his mouth. No sound came out. Moved his fingers in signing. His sister translated for him.

"HE WANTS TO KNOW IF YOU'D LIKE TO GO SOMEWHERE QUIETER?"

"Not in particular."

He laughed at me, a laugh much stronger than a tongue-less boy had any right to. I'd thought he was shy.

I didn't feel like laughing now. I did not want to think of why he was tongueless. I did not want to think of my mother. We weakhearted fools. People are born without things all the time. Really. It probably had nothing to do with her. Nothing to do with the place that raised me. With that damned laboratory, Ollie.

Fieke cussed. Grabbed the hands of Owen and me. She led us to the ladies' room, much to our mutual humiliation. There was a line as long as any I'd ever seen. Fieke stomped her way through it. A few girls whistled and jeered as she shoved us all into a bathroom stall.

"Yeah, yeah. And one of them's my brother!" Fieke cackled evilly.

"*Ewwww.*"

"Well, get on with it, *Brille*." She folded her arms. Leaned against the door. "Here's that golden opportunity you rapped for."

And so it was while we two were standing on either side of a toilet that I finally thanked Owen Abend for handing me my goggles before my suspension:

"Thank you for handing me my goggles before my suspension."

He blinked at me. Moved his hands.

"He says 'no biggie.'"

I shook my head. "I'm grateful to you. And sorry he hurt you after."

"He doesn't want an apology or gratitude."

"What do you want?"

Owen stared at me. Slowly, carefully, he moved his hands.

"He just wants it to stop. Lenz to stop."

Stop, Owen mouthed. Holding up his palm.

Owen Abend's story is not unique. Apart from his tongue-lessness. His muteness has always been part of him. Some people are born without things. There's not always a laboratory to blame. There's no reason for me to recall my mother and the scars I have.

Lenz Monk has hated Owen for as long a time as the Abends can remember.

Of course I was never Lenz's only whimpering target. Of course not.

Although Owen spent much of his youth in sign language

camps, he is not deaf. Just as I am not blind. He attended
public school. Became accustomed to writing his thoughts
out on a whiteboard he carried with him. He has forsaken
this board for silence at Bernholdt-Regen. Silence is harder
to mock.

At the age of seven, Owen attended the same *Grundschule*
as Lenz Monk. Not far from our homes in Ostzig. I was elsewhere then.

One of Owen Abend's earliest childhood memories: Lenz
Monk pushing him down a playground staircase. Pressing
his face into gravel. Not a "biggie." Children push. Fieke
helped him up. Pushed Lenz in return. The way they speak
of it, Lenz Monk was a bulky boy. Shiny with grease. Notorious for bowling kids over. Unaccustomed to being shoved
back. Fieke was already a kid to be reckoned with, despite
her pigtails. I can be fanciful: I imagine she already wore
black boots.

Fieke's resistance only encouraged Lenz's brutishness.
Owen could not so easily defend himself.

Another memory Owen shared in that bathroom stall
retold the day that Lenz Monk discovered that Owen
Abend was not *only* quiet. Owen Abend could not cry out
for help.

Lenz was old enough to be punished for his more worri-
some delinquent acts. He was nearly expelled for pouring
bleach into a goldfish tank. And again, for vomiting inside
another student's desk during snacktime. Lenz had taken to
plucking dead mice from his father's traps and force-feeding
his classmates "fuzz sandwiches." I suppose wedgies were

growing dull. Though I've so far avoided sandwiches from Lenz, this is no stretch to believe.

On this day, Fieke had stayed home sick. (Where home was, she neglected to say; the Abends are quieter about the past than even I am. I do not needle.) What choice had Owen but to walk back alone with Lenz pattering behind him? Spitting on his back without Fieke to cuss him away?

Under a bridge by the canal, Lenz waited. When no one else was around to see, he yanked Owen up by his backpack. Pried open his jaws and jammed a dead baby mouse between them before clamping his mouth shut.

Most people would have shoved such a repulsive thing out with their tongues. They would have screamed. Called attention to their plight.

Owen could not. His tonguelessness meant he could not spit, and Lenz held his arms behind his back so he could not pull the mouse out with his fingers.

Owen could either choke or swallow. He swallowed.

Lenz released him. He forced Owen's mouth open. He saw neither mouse nor tongue inside. He gagged and threw Owen down against the pavement.

After that, Owen became a primary target. Lenz sought him out on a daily basis. He waited in the street outside Owen's home. Waited with pockets full of stones and glass and decaying mice. Waited with no expression. Waited for Owen to whimper.

I looked at Owen. Delicate features. Wide eyes. "You may drop out of school?"

He nodded.

"You should not. I've been reading a great deal of late. About, ah, heroism. Dropping out won't help the others he's tormenting. And what good could it do you? He knows where you live. He will wait."

We hung our heads. Listened to the sounds of a girl in the next stall vomiting the entire contents of her stomach into the porcelain toilet.

"Why do you care?" shot Fieke, suddenly.

Owen stared. I restrained a click.

"I . . . well, it is only . . . it is only that I feel responsible for you."

Hands and faces moving.

"This was going on for ages before you got punched in the gym. You don't owe us crap, Owen says."

"I feel indebted to you."

He frowned. Fieke sniggered.

"Don't mock me. Let me help. Few people have been . . . so kind to me."

Owen stared. Nodded.

Fieke slammed her fist against the wall. Someone in line squeaked in surprise.

"*Look*, if you're really looking to prove you're thankful, there *is* something you can do."

Owen blinked at her; I lifted my head.

"You can use your supersonic hearing. Stand up to him and scare him off for good."

Like a superhero, Oliver?

"You're suggesting that I, ah, confront him?"

"No," she said. "I'm suggesting you beat the living shit out of him."

Owen Abend is sitting across from me in the Sickly Poet. This is my first handwritten letter, Oliver. Owen is not wearing his flat cap today. He sips water, not coffee. Perhaps he is only halfway pretentious.

You were my first friend, Ollie. Could this be another?

He smiles rarely, but those smiles are bright. He may not speak, but he laughs in waterfalls, dolphin-wavy as that may sound. I can't read his hands. I *can* read the notes he writes me. Read the rhythm of his feet and fingertips against floors and tables.

Owen hasn't returned to Bernholdt-Regen, because Lenz is on the prowl once more, pushing faces into urinals. I see Owen elsewhere. He is always pleased to see me. He does not care that I have no eyes, just as I do not care that he has no tongue. Perhaps we could both forget ourselves in not caring. I am as human as he is.

Outside school, he is constantly fiddling with things. Picking up pens and tossing them or doodling on napkins. He redeems his silence with perpetual motion.

Often we go to the *Kneipe* to watch Fieke spout poetry. He taps a foot in annoyance. I *tsk* in my teeth, and then we smirk at each other. For once I am grateful not to have eyes. I do not think I could make proper eye contact with Owen Abend.

Now he taps his feet against the floor. Just from the way he is going heel-to-toe with his shoes I can tell he is getting impatient.

Owen has an uncanny sense of rhythm. I knew this the moment I saw him manning those turntables at *Partygänger*. His wondrous musicality would probably extend to his pitch. If he could enunciate, I believe he would have a beautiful voice.

Owen is sighing now. Looking at me pointedly.

"Almost, almost," I tell him.

I'll finish writing later. Fieke is performing soon. I do not want to face her glare while she rattles off Radiohead or Deerhunter lyrics. She does not realize she is a cliché. She gets offended.

I embody your old optimism, Ollie Ollie UpandFree.

My friends and I—friends, Ollie?—are going to prevent Lenz from hurting anyone else.

Fiecke is onstage glaring at me. Giving me the finger. Owen looks at me with hope. Perhaps that is what friendship is. Spending time with people who aren't repulsed by you. Even when they should be.

I will not fail them. I am not my mother. I am better than she was.

I used to dislike everyone. Even now I don't know what to expect from the people around me, Oliver. Alone in a crowd. Now the crowd is unfolding before me, and it is full of life and terror and wonder.

All this, because you told me to stand up, Oliver Paulot.

I am more than nothing because of you. If you are swallowed in grief or in pain, please know this: my life is forever improving.

Please. Whatever you are about to tell me, don't ever doubt your worth. Don't worry that I will turn away from you.

You made me real, Ollie.

Your dearest friend,

Mo

chapter nineteen
THE PHONE

Let's get the needling out of the way:

Why do you keep mentioning your mother all of a sudden? Who was she? I want to know, Moritz, even if I stopped asking.

It's cool that you think so highly of me, but you've got me on a pedestal. You may be my best friend, but you can never *be* here. And sometimes it just sucks. I'm happy for you but sad for me, and then guilty for feeling sad for me when I should just be happy for you, and then I feel like an ass in general.

It's also cool that you've found friends and more in Kreiszig. And now I have some idea about why you didn't want to talk romance. Owen means a *lot* to you, doesn't he? I get it. Are you guys really planning on beating up Lenz? I'm glad you're feeling more heroic, but . . . well, that seems like a weird thing to bond over. Then again, it's been nosebleeds all along.

I really could use a friend out here in the woods. I wish I could meet you. Really. Mom's back in the house again today, but she's white as snow. Did you know her hair's been falling out? I've seen it on the floor, on couch cushions—strands of blond that catch the light and look almost like electricity. Before, I thought she wore hand-woven wigs for fun. . . .

I keep thinking about the medical bills that arrive at the mailbox. Her trips to the pharmacy. Maybe I've been ignoring it all this time. It's been here all along, her being sick. But somehow it's getting deeper and darker in the woods.

I wrote the remainder of our camping trip. I'm sending it to you today.

Maybe it'll explain why I've been so haphazard and stupid up until now. Or maybe not.

Is it really summer already? I should go write in the living room, where it's warmer, but I can hear Mom wheezing down there. It's quieter up here.

Here's the last part of my autobiography, Moritz.

Here's what Mom wanted to distract me from.

"Do you know what some kids at school started calling me when I first moved out here?"

I shook my head. I felt paralyzed after that face-mashing session. My half-frozen foot was resting on a warm stone by the campfire, my sock and boot drying out beside it. Liz sat across from me, eyes shining in the dark.

"White trash."

"I don't get it. You're not even pale. And yeah, sometimes you're muddy. But that's not the same as being garbage."

"Oh, Ollie. Sometimes I think it's awesome that you don't know about things like this. Other times I think . . ."

"You think what?"

But right then we both almost jumped out of our skins when a huge *crack!* broke the night air.

"Maybe they're lighting off fireworks across the lake?"

"That was only one sound."

"Someone's started hunting season early? Hope they've got a license."

Liz frowned in the firelight. "It's too dark to be hunting. I mean, sometimes hunters wear night-vision goggles because deer get pretty active early in the morning. But it's not morning."

"Maybe Uncle Joe is trying to get a lead on the competition. That's *his* venison, damn it."

"Maybe . . ." She pulled up the hood on her sweatshirt. "I'm going to go ask him if he heard it. Hand me that lantern."

"My foot isn't dry yet."

"Wait here, then."

But I was already hopping along behind her with one boot on, wincing when I stepped on acorns and pinecones barefoot. The blind felt a lot farther away in the dark. Fog had crept off the lake to curl around trees, around our waists. I huddled near Liz as she walked, still really aware of how close she was. Every few steps or so, something on the forest side of us scurried along the ground, crackling on leaves and brushing through undergrowth. Probably only squirrels, but we picked up our pace. The water seemed too dull, somehow. It wasn't reflecting the moon.

By the time we turned down the trail toward the deer blind, we were jogging.

"Man, he's going to laugh at us—"

The moment we burst into the clearing beneath the blind, Liz put her hand over her mouth. It's a good thing we'd learned our lesson years ago about buying sturdy lanterns; it didn't break when she dropped it. Liz rushed forward in the dark. When I scrabbled to lift the lantern up again, I saw why.

Junkyard Joe was sprawled at the foot of the tree like a dead thing.

I think you're the only one I could talk to about this, Moritz. I can't even describe how it felt. If my handwriting's worse, it's because my hands are shaking. And it's hard not to smear the ink. Sorry.

"Oh god, oh god."

Liz was shaking him. In her panic, she was rattling him so much that it almost looked like *he* was seizing.

"Don't shake him. If he's hurt, don't shake him. That's . . . um . . ." I couldn't think, I couldn't think. "Bad for his anatomy."

"Uncle Joe? Oh god. Uncle Joe?"

"He was shot? Has he been shot? Who shot him? Was he shot?"

"I don't know! I can't see anything! I can't really see without a damn flashlight, can I?!"

Some part of my brain registered that there wasn't any blood; I looked up the ladder to the blind. It was hard to be sure in the lantern light, but what we'd heard was the sound of one of the rotten plywood floorboards falling through. It looked like he had fallen twenty feet to the ground.

"He fell. He just fell, Liz. You can see it. You can see the boards gave out. He just fell."

"*Just?* He's not moving! I can't tell if he's breathing! Oh god, oh god!"

"He may have broken, um, broken his spine?"

"Oh god. Ollie, we need help. You need to go get help. Call someone."

I just kept shaking my head. "I can't call someone. Phones. I can't."

She was tearing at her hair, snot running out of her nose. God, I was breathing so loud! And when I blinked, I almost heard the sound of my eyelids in my ears. Almost like you. But this was nothing out of a comic book. This made no narrative sense. This was a freak accident that already I could see did nothing for any of us, didn't allow any of us—not Liz, not me, not Joe (poor motionless Joe)—to develop as characters. This was—

"Go get help! My phone!"

I don't know how I had time to be hurt, but I did. "You brought your phone?"

"Go get it! You could hold the book light, so you can hold a damn phone! In the tent! Run!"

"Let me check first. Whether he's got a pul—"

"*Go*, Oliver!"

Maybe she should have gone, but how could I ask her to leave him? How could I say anything when I couldn't think?

I couldn't think, Mo.

It felt like I was dream-walking again. Like the day I met her. But I was running instead, and it was dark and cold and I couldn't feel my foot, and when I got to the campfire, I nearly tripped and fell right into it. This was nightmare-walking?

I tore open Liz's tent, heart thumping against my ribs, grabbed her backpack, and took it out by the fire so that I could see what was inside, and then tore through her clothes and past her toiletry bag and through the pack's lining and finally something stung my hand:

The phone had been wrapped up in two Ziploc bags, rolled inside her bathing suit, but it was glowing just enough to make me nauseous. Gagging, fighting the tremors, I tried to grab it.

But I was way too hyped up, too *charged*, and when I reached for the phone it spun away from my hand and smacked against the circle of stones around the fire pit.

"Shit!" I scampered after it again, but it was repelled again, almost into the coals.

I upended the bag of extra tent poles and pulled it over my shaking hand like a glove. It made the slightest difference, and I was able to pick up the phone. I could feel the veins in my hand popping, but I held tight. After a second, it buzzed against my palm, and I squeezed tighter. After that, it didn't sting quite so much.

I ran. I ran, but I already knew.

I'd known when I first saw him there. The way his torso was twisted. The way his body was breaking so many basic anatomical rules, there was no way he wouldn't be paralyzed at the very least, no way he would walk or sit on the porch and fake bird-watching—

And I ran anyhow.

Nothing had changed at the clearing. Liz was still shaking him, still pressing her ear to his chest. Joe's eyes were closed; his face was pale, very still. And I knew again.

His spine was broken.

I was biting my tongue so hard that I was piercing flesh, and the arm that held the phone was numb all the way up to my shoulder. Dry heaves racked my chest, but all I could really think about was how I should tell her, but I couldn't tell her—

Liz looked at me with wild, hopeful eyes when I burst out of the foliage; if she realized, she was pretending she didn't. I held the phone up and felt my head clear a bit when I handed it over.

"Here! But I thought there was no signal out here—"

"That was years ago!"

She pressed a button on its side and tapped the screen. I waited for the phone to reflect her, but the screen buzzed to white for only a second before hissing back to black, to nothingness.

"It's not working—what the hell? What's wrong with it?"

She tapped ineffectually at the screen.

"Oh no." I pressed the heels of my palms into my temples, but it wasn't enough. "No no no no no NO!"

"What—did you drop it?!"

"I didn't. I swear I didn't. It just . . . I couldn't touch it."

"What's wrong with it?"

The screen was empty. I took a step back, then another.

"Electromagnetism."

"Oh god. You shorted it? He's dying and you—! Anyone else here and this wouldn't have—couldn't have—but no, I brought *you*!"

I know she was beyond upset. I know she was devastated. But I can't forget the way her face looked when she said that.

"*You* could have gone for the phone, if I'm so predictably terrible!"

Then she was standing, holding it out in front of her, up to my face. I winced and shook my head, shook my head. Blank screen, but I still felt tiny needles pricking my skin.

"What are we supposed to do?" Her face was collapsing in on itself, an imploding star. "What are we . . ."

She pushed the phone closer to me.

I put my hand in front of my eyes, but I shouldn't have. I shouldn't have, because with the sight of her and the almost-corpse of him and the volume of my breathing in my ears and everything else, of course I felt bee stings in my fingertips and suddenly I had repelled it again.

The phone smacked her in the mouth with enough force to tilt her head back slightly, enough to knock against her teeth before it fell to the forest floor. She whimpered and covered her mouth and stared at me like I was . . .

"Liz—" I reached for her, and she withdrew, eyes wide.

"Go. Get away from me!"

"Liz—I'm so sorry," I mumbled. "The campers. I'll go get the other campers. Maybe . . ."

"Anyone else and this couldn't happen." She was so quiet. But there was no way I'd miss a word of it, even as I backed away from that look in her eyes. "Anyone in the whole world, and instead it was you."

I stumbled alone in the dark, heading in the vague direction of the other campground across the lake, falling over logs and my own feet and almost falling into the water again, scraping my arms on branches and brambles all but invisible in the dark. Away from the clearing, away from the lantern, away from Joe, away from Liz.

I followed foggy gray trails of electric smog to the opposite side of the lake, trails that became tinged with color the longer I stumbled along them. I kept falling, kept eating dirt, and I couldn't figure out why, because I didn't notice that I had sliced my foot open until hours later, maybe after midnight or maybe close to dawn, what felt like eons after I left the clearing where Liz and Junkyard Joe—dead, he *must* have been dead—

—*you don't know that. She wouldn't let you check his pulse. She didn't even want you to touch him, freak.*

Freak, freak, freak.

All I could see the whole time I was wandering through the dark were the same stupid images spinning through my head: Liz's face when she told me to go, the stillness of Joe, the kiss, her face, the terrible kiss, the dark. Her face.

Firelight filled my eyes, but I didn't realize I had arrived at the campground until I walked right into some man who wore a fluorescent-orange vest.

"Help?"

"Jesus, kid, where did you come from? Aren't you freezing?"

"He's vomited all over himself—"

Fire and light and noise and, yes, lines and clouds of electric colors that were stretching out to greet me. The smog of their trucks, the buzz of their lamps, all stretching out fingers to hold me. I would be happy to meet them, happy for them to shut me off.

"I don't need help; Joe does. Except if he's dead, he doesn't need help and maybe he's dead, but he's over there, and you should go . . . go . . . help him because I'm a freak and I can't do it, okay. I can't do it and I can't do phones and I *can't.*"

"Here, son," said one of the men.

He held up something that was buzzing blue and sizzling gold-fuzzing light, and wrapped it around my shoulders.

And with the weight of the electric heating blanket on my shoulders, I was gone, gone, gone.

She was right, you know.
   If it had been anyone else, it wouldn't have happened that way.

~ 0

chapter twenty
THE CAT

Moritz, I'm sorry. I'm so sorry. If that's what it takes, I'm sorry, I'm sorry. I was an idiot, I'm always an idiot.

Why did you stop writing me?

Please. You have to talk to me. Please. I know you aren't ether. I know you feel, you think. I know you care. I never thought you were a void.

Where are you? What's happened in the weeks since we last spoke? What should I do? What would you do if you were me? How can I ever expect Liz to come hang out after all that?

I don't think I can answer any questions without your help anymore. I can't focus enough to think of answers, and if this is a laser beam, then it's getting wide enough to swallow the world or something, and that doesn't even make sense and I'm sorry for that, too.

Moritz, I don't know what's worse: that maybe you never got my last letter and I have to write it all over again, or that maybe you did get it and you're so disgusted that you don't want to speak to me anymore. Has something happened to you?

Stop writing, Mom says. Maybe it was the wrong idea to write. Stop writing. It's not therapy. Stop needling, because maybe that's all we're doing to each other. Experiments of our own? Sorry, Moritz.

But I didn't finish it; we're not fully up to date yet. Please let me finish. Please listen to me, and I'll be quick and there won't be any fuss and hoopla.

See, Joe didn't die after all; it was touch and go for a while. He was comatose for a month, and with every day that he was sleeping, I was almost wishing he would die because he was dragging out my guilt, and yeah, you can say the fall wasn't actually my fault—I've heard that from everyone, even from Liz once, when she stopped by to tell me he'd woken up and the doctors, they told him he'd be paralyzed from the hips down probably for as long as he was living, that one doctor said he broke sections of his lower spine (*vertebrae lumbales*) and tore nerve clusters on impact and that getting a medical helicopter out there sooner probably wouldn't have helped, PROBABLY, and even during the early days when I was in my sickbed half comatose myself with stitches in my foot, and Mom was there telling me "Shush" and "It's not your fault." And Auburn-Stache kept holding my hand and he wouldn't even smile his goofy smile and he said, too, "It's not your fault," even then I heard "probably."

We all heard about the doctor saying "probably." *Probably* means maybe he could have been walking now. Maybe. Probably, maybe.

And then last week, while I was waiting for you to send me a letter, when I was waiting for *anything*, Dorian Gray died. He just curled up on my bed and didn't get up again when I tried to shove him off my pillow as usual. My cat? That wasn't my fault, either, because that cat was really old, and he meowed whenever you touched his back or scratched him under the chin, didn't purr but meowed in pain when you stroked him because of arthritis, and he couldn't even really jump up on the sofa anymore, and things that are old die sometimes and there's nothing you can do about it but bury old things under a pine tree in your backyard.

Or things that are young die, too, especially when they do secretive work in laboratories and they really shouldn't, because that can ruin a family and a kid's life, I think. I'm starting to put the pieces together and maybe being a lab experiment is the *same* as being sick after all, because we don't live in colorful panels with speech bubbles and exciting noises.

Moritz, please. I don't know who else to talk to. I can't think straight. The house won't stop moaning, and my fingertips are raw from folding origami flowers because I don't know what to do or what to play or read to make this better. Maybe my fingertips will peel away, just rub away, and the bones will poke through, and then how will I hold the pen properly to write you because bones can't grip without skin, even phalange-bones, and I'd just end up bleeding all over the paper so you have to answer me soon.

To make it stop.

Moritz?

Please.

chapter twenty-one
THE FISHBOWL

It's been so long since I last heard from you, and I'm happy to report that I haven't given up on you yet! I'm still writing you pointless letters every week, even though my autobiography is pretty much up to date. It's not like things have been all that eventful here, so I'll just keep telling you about the books I'm reading and about building bike ramps and about baking cheesecakes (German double-chocolate ones, strawberry ones, and blueberry ones, but not blackberry ones), which I've been getting into. But there aren't enough people to eat the cakes, so they end up moldering a bit in the icebox, but we try to eat them anyhow.

Mom is looking younger in the summer weather. She isn't prancing around sniffing daisies or anything, but she's been sitting on the porch and teaching me to knit lately. I think maybe we're both doing better. I mean, I've come to terms with losing things, and she must have done that ages ago. I never see that lab coat. I don't even bother needling her about my dad anymore.

Anyhow, I try not to worry about you. I try really hard, just like I try to focus. I really hope you aren't dead or something, or Lenz didn't beat the crap out of you again. But if you are lying in a hospital bed somewhere, I think I'll keep writing you anyway, because it does help me and it gives me a reason to write. I can pretend. If that's okay. I know Liz wasn't into pretending, except for when she was pretending I could have a living room like any other kid who maybe wouldn't let her uncle get paralyzed out in the cold woods.

Focus, Ollie. Focus.

Who'd have thought I could miss someone I've never actually met? *Me*. I've thought that. I miss tons of things I've never seen, and now you most of all.

Something kind of miraculous happened the other day, and I need to tell you about it.

Liz rode her bike up my driveway on a Wednesday afternoon.

I wasn't waiting for her. Mom and I were actually out back dead-heading multicolored daylilies in the flower beds that border the house, so she ended up having to walk around over the uneven grass to find us.

She didn't shout "I'm here!" like she used to, but Mom still heard her coming.

"Ollie, don't freak out." Mom squeezed my arm.

I turned around, squinting in the sun, and there she was. Like she'd never left, and for a moment, I wanted to just grin at her like *of course* we were fine, but then I could see ages between us, months of standing in the driveway by myself. My throat constricted and my ears burned and I couldn't say a damn thing, because what if it came out as screaming? I dropped the shriveled yellow flower head.

She put her hand over her mouth. Her hair was growing out, and it seemed darker against the bright blue sky. She hadn't bothered with braids. Not a speck of muck on her. I almost didn't recognize her.

"Hey." More of a whisper than a scream. "How's it hangin'?"

"Oh, Ollie," she said, kneeling down and wrapping her arms around me.

I'm not going to lie, Moritz. It felt really nice to feel her arms again, and she smelled awesome, like sugar or something, but in my head she was still standing in the forest clearing, looking at me with that face, so I gently pushed her away and stood up. It was weird—I was way taller than her now.

"I could play the xylophone on your rib cage!"

"Glockenspiel, please."

"Have you both gone on a hunger strike? I want to stuff burgers down your throats. I mean . . . what happened?"

Mom smiled at her. "We're just going through some growth spurts, Elizabeth."

"What, even you, Ms. Paulot?"

"*Tch.* I'm a late bloomer. And you never really grow up." After seven seconds, she climbed to her feet. "I'll go get us some lemonade, hey? Like a good motherly stereotype."

She left us there on the sunlit lawn.

"Ollie," Liz said, "you look terrible."

"What a lovely thing to tell me on a lovely summer's day. And speaking of lovely, you look lovely."

"I mean it. You and your mom. If I'd known . . ."

"If you'd known, you could have stopped by every week to comment on how terrible we look." I laughed and began trudging toward the porch.

Freak, freak, freak.

"Oliver," she said, "why won't you look at me?"

"The sun's in my eyes."

But even when we reached the shade, I didn't really look at her.

"So, what brings you to our humble abode, Liz? Looking lovely, as already stated?"

She didn't smile. "Lovely, huh."

"Yep. I guess high school still suits you, then."

"Well. High school isn't actually that different from middle school, turns out."

"I wouldn't know, of course."

"Ollie . . ."

"Look, Liz—what do you want?"

And here I was trying for a sunny disposition, Moritz! I was trying, but it's hard. Because you told me to be honest with myself, and honestly I wasn't feeling very sunny inside. I felt like something small that was hiding in the dark until Liz lifted the log to see me squirm.

"I want to go to the junkyard, but not by myself. There are some things there in the trailer that I want to pick up. Some things Uncle Joe wants in his hospital room. I'm the only one who knows where he keeps things. I was the only one who visited him."

"Oh."

"But I wasn't really visiting *him*, you know." Did her voice crack?

"You weren't, huh."

She put her hand on her cheek and looked out at the lawn. "I wasn't. And that makes me feel worse about it. This was where I ran away to, I guess."

I shrugged. "This is all a bit too grown-up for me. I just want to go inside and play with my Legos. Like a good little hermit."

"Please, Ollie." Funny how she isn't even fazed by my sarcasm anymore. I guess she shouldn't be, since I learned half of it from her. It probably bores her.

"Lemme get my shoes on."

Liz shook her head. "No, not today. Next week, maybe."

"Why wait? It sounds so very fun."

"I have plans."

"Plans?"

She blinked at me. "You want me to say it? I'm meeting friends. For friends things. For high school things and electronic music and electric lights and all sorts of power lines. Happy?"

"Oh, wicked." This was all wrong, but I couldn't seem to stop it. "You can tell them all how terrible I look!"

She stood up. "Why are you being this way?"

"I'm Captain Tact."

"Fine. Whatever. I'll see you next week."

Maybe she used to run away to me, but now it wasn't *to* but *from*. One word, a whole world of difference, Moritz. Sometimes I don't appreciate language after all.

When I went back inside alone, Mom was standing just past the screen door in the hallway. There was no lemonade in sight, and she was looking just like she did on the day when Liz knocked on the door all caked in muck.

Well, almost like that.

You could play the glockenspiel on her rib cage now, after all.

It might have been the perfect time to needle her about Dad. A breeze could bowl her over. Probably her walls would have crumbled if I mentioned the lab.

Seeing her like that, it didn't even cross my mind.

The following Wednesday, I met Liz at the power line and we trekked through the same old trails to get to Joe's place. But Liz didn't stop to pick up a single pudding stone, and the junkyard looked more like a graveyard than ever. The trailer at the center of it was just as abandoned as the rest of it now.

"Man, this is just awful." My mutter rang against aluminum skeletons.

"You don't always have to *say* what you're thinking."

Her lip trembled, and I thought for the briefest second that I didn't know who she was anymore, that she might be the type of girl to collapse in the leaves and then I could hold her or help her up and—

Liz walked toward the trailer. "Wait here."

"Obviously."

Soon she was up on the porch and inside the trailer. Hard not to think about the first time I'd stood here waiting, and how different that was. Déjà vu is pretty common when you never leave a square mile of land.

Why did she want me here? It could have been anyone else, right?

Again, I wasn't expecting her to come out so quickly.

"I never gave you this back." She held the old fishbowl I'd worn to the power line.

I grinned. "Oh, wow! How thoughtful. You know I've been so lost without it! Wow!"

"Ollie."

"I mean, I was really hoping you'd drag me out here to remind me about the uncle I almost killed and then regift me with the symbol of our friendship!" I laughed. "You know what? You should shatter it. That would be *really* symbolic."

"I don't think you almost killed him," she whispered.

"Oh, well, that's a relief! I'm a freak but not a murderer! Great! Well, let me do the honors! I'm more used to breaking spines and phones, you know, but I can do this! I can break this!"

Her eyes were welling. "Ollie!"

I snatched the bowl from her hands and threw it against the porch.

You may wonder why I was trying so hard to make the girl I'm lovesick over bawl her eyes out. Maybe I just wanted to know whether I could still make her feel things.

Of course the bowl failed to shatter. The glass was thick, and it bounced once and rolled away along the wooden boards. I reached for it, but pulled my hand back quickly.

Those tendrils of electricity were still itching their way up from under the porch and they nipped at me. I cringed and recoiled from the buzzing heat, but when Liz tried to pull me away, I shrugged her off.

"Enough, Ollie! I just can't worry about you on top of everything else."

"You don't have to worry about me."

"Look at yourself! You look like you've got cancer, or like you've forgotten how to hold a fork, or—"

"Or like I spent months alone in a cabin in the dark, huh. Maybe I've got scurvy, hey?"

"Never mind." She was stomping away, maybe like Fieke does, arms flat against her sides, hands clenched into fists. She no longer looked remotely like she was going to cry. "We're just talking about you again."

"Who else do I know?" I threw my hands up and followed her. "I don't have all your amazingly distracting high school friends!"

She spun around to confront me and part of that terrifying expression from the clearing was there on her face again and I almost swallowed my tongue (almost but not really because we've been through that).

"He was *my* uncle. My family." Her shoulders sagged. "And he's just this stranger in a wheelchair now, and always will be, and you were there, and no matter how I try to think about it, no matter that I know it wasn't your fault, you were there—"

"Please just stop."

"No matter what, *you were there*, and when I look at you, I see him lying there, and I just can't remember you any other way than jumping out of those bushes and handing me a phone that didn't work, that wouldn't work, that can't work. Can never work with you."

We were standing in the center of the yard now, right where she'd set up my living room.

"So you're angry and sad because . . . your phone doesn't like me?"

"Try to be serious for once."

I took a few steps back and leaned against the nearest decrepit vehicle. The rust-eaten metal seemed to give beneath me.

"Okay," I said after a deep breath. "Okay. Makes sense."

"Ollie—"

"Nah, it's totally cool." I grinned; it felt wrong, but I was going for it. "Then why didn't you have one of your new friends come out here with you today? Why ask me, murderer—"

"I told you—"

"Murderer of *phones*?"

"Ollie, you're still my best friend. I just had to stop coming here. Because I'm not like you."

"Liz—" She wasn't saying "freak" but that's what I was hearing.

"*Listen* to me." She closed her eyes. "I spent so much time wishing that this was the world. I sat in school and just waited for Wednesdays, because on Wednesdays I wasn't just some piece of *trash*, some gray person that no one bothered thinking about."

"You're every color, Liz," I blurted, because my throat was burning.

"I know you think that, Ollie." Her expression softened. "But don't you see how messed up that is? That the only time I felt important was around someone who didn't know any better?"

"Ouch." I tried to laugh. She sounded like you now, Moritz.

"Don't be hurt. I'm not a hermit. I can't . . . I can't live out here in the woods. You're my best friend, but you can't be my only friend."

"We're best friends who can't look at each other." I laughed. "Maybe we should start wearing big black goggles around, too."

"What?"

But thinking about you, Moritz, just choked me up a bit, so I tried laughing again.

"Well, next time, bring the other friends along, too!"

She pursed her lips.

"Yeah, let's do it! Let's have everyone over for my next birthday.

That'll give you plenty of time to warn them not to climb into deer blinds when I'm around."

She shook her head. "I don't feel like I'm the same person out here."

"Are you a *worse* person?"

She shook her head again. "That's not what I'm saying."

"Then have 'em stop by. I bet they're curious about the local leper, too. I *can't* leave the woods. Let me meet all those people you think are more interesting than you and let me be the judge! You don't have to tell them you *kissed* me."

God, the look she gave me!

"I'm not embarrassed of you. I just don't want them to . . . be dumb about it. Not you. Them. People can be so dumb sometimes."

I drew myself up. "Yeah, you shouldn't worry. I've heard from *my* best friend that I'm pretty likable. Or I used to be. Not sure what happened. Well, maybe I'm sure. But I think at some point I wasn't always boring enough to drown in or whatever."

"I don't know what you're talking about, Ollie. You aren't making any sense."

I held my arms open wide.

"Tell them I'll show them a good time! Invite the whole damn school! The circus is open!"

Her eyes narrowed. I realized I couldn't tell what she was thinking, whether she was angry or sad or annoyed or frightened or what. She stood up and held her finger up to my face.

"Look. I'll do it. I'll ask everyone to come out for your birthday. But only if you promise me something."

"What, fair lady?"

"Start taking care of yourself, doofus." She wiped her eyes. "Eat something. Look after your mom. Start giving a crap again. Because that's what we've got to do."

"We have to start giving craps? To whom?"

"I *mean* it, weirdo." She jabbed me in the chest. "You're important to me."

"Even if you can't stand my face."

"Yes, even then."

"Okay," I said. "Okay."

"Come on. Help me sort this stuff out."

Liz spent a couple of hours going in and out of the trailer, pulling out odds and ends, cleaning out the fridge and going through the closets. It wasn't a big trailer, but it seemed Joe had filled it up with himself. She was collecting photographs and books and throwing them into her backpack alongside his camera.

"Do you want any of these?" She gestured to the collection of taxidermied birds and rabbits she'd deposited on the porch. Their glass eyes were catching the afternoon sunlight so that the animals almost looked alive again.

"My symbolic fishbowl should be enough, thanks."

The afternoon was growing chilly when we walked back to the driveway. Liz stopped beside the power line. Her bike was parked beside the post.

"Why didn't your parents come out here with you?"

She shrugged. "Mom still wasn't really feeling up to it. She and Uncle Joe were pretty close growing up. And after what happened, I think she feels guilty for growing apart or something. She's basically renting a room at the hospital."

"Oh."

"Keep your promise." She pointed that old accusatory finger at me but lowered it slowly. "Are you going to be all right, Ollie?"

And the first thing I thought was no, not now that Moritz doesn't write me. But then I remembered how I don't know how to feel about anything anymore, about Mom or you or anyone, so I opened my mouth and let my jaw hang for a second before replying.

"Just dandy. Will you be back next week?"

I wished I hadn't asked. Pathetic.

"Um, I might be busy."

"Yeah, yeah. No biggie. Well, tell your friends about the party! Tell them it'll be a real riot."

"Mmm," she said. "See you around, Oliver."

And she pedaled away through the curtain of tangerine light, and she couldn't see how the streaks lit up her skin so that when she was beyond them, she looked like an amber light going out.

Please write me.

~ Ollie

chapter twenty-two

THE DEER BLIND

Moritz,

This birthday party I made Liz promise to. I'm going to turn it out. It's going to be a party those kids will never forget! It's a month away, and that gives me a month to make it awesome.

I told Mom, and at first she was all apprehensive. But then she totally got on board, and now she's at least as excited as I am, plotting party favors and sketching out plans for how we'll rearrange the cabin. (I don't want to spoil the party for you, but it's going to kick *Arsch*.)

Also, there's something else. Liz has started visiting again. Not a lot, but every now and then. Twice since the day I failed to shatter the symbolic fishbowl.

I tried to be less ANGSTY (already sick of that word, and now it's being retired). It was kind of a struggle because I asked her to pass me the book light again. Like old times.

"Sure it won't hit me in the face?"

September. Liz is back at school now. This year she's started wearing eyeliner, like some demented Egyptian princess. And her clothes don't fit her like they used to, or else I never noticed before. They're snug, to say the least, and she's not just a tree-climbing stick insect like she used to be and I still am.

I smiled. "I wouldn't want to mess up your makeup."

She rolled her eyes, and I pulled the battered old light from the pocket of my hoodie. I handed it to her. She began our mantra:

"You'll never hear New Wave, or a dentist's drill . . . or the bell chime between classes . . . or . . ." She stared at the old book light and sighed.

What right did *she* have to be bored?

I held my hands up. "Here."

She passed it to me, but for a single moment, there was pity in her eyes. That was something I'd never seen there. It made me drop what I'd caught.

"Oh, Ollie." She frowned. "If it hurts, let's stop. It's just sorta . . . cruel."

I picked it right back up, but Liz wasn't looking at me. She was looking at my room, and the books and models and telescope and skeleton and puzzles and such. And then her eyes caught sight of the massive pile of letters on the table. Did you know you've written me half a book by now?

"What are these?"

I wanted to jump up and shove them away for some reason, but I didn't. "Letters from my pen pal. He lives in Kreiszig. That's a city in Germany."

"Really? Well, he sure is devoted."

"Yeah. He was. He was sort of my hero." I actually said that, Moritz. Because it's the truth.

" 'Sort of,' huh? I've heard writing letters can be therapeutic."

The light in my hand was building in pressure, but I didn't release it. Not after that look she gave me, Mo.

"This room feels like home."

I scratched my chin theatrically. "Profound. Yes, very profound."

She didn't laugh. "I mean it, Ollie. This was where I wanted to be, growing up. This was where I was happy."

"You love your parents. You never shut up about them."

"Yeah," she said. "But they shut up about me plenty."

She took the light from me. Her fingers brushed mine, and I remembered, suddenly, standing by Marl Lake with her. She must have remembered, too, but for us that memory was immediately followed by the one of the man who fell in the forest. She pulled her hand away.

I cleared my throat. "One month till the big day. Did you tell everyone to come? Tell them to prepare for the hermit party?"

She nodded. "I will, yeah. I will."

"Promise?" I shot for nonchalant. (Is just chalant a thing? You know more about English than I do.)

"Well, you're not looking so cancerous anymore, after all."

"All those kids will be disappointed."

"Nah, you're still plenty ugly." Her lips twitched.

"But you're looking at me now."

I wasn't sure whether she was about to say something or not, and then the way I looked at her might have changed her mind, and she left with the book light still in her hand. Like she was confiscating it.

The next time she came, she didn't bring it back.

* * *

I had a dream about you, Moritz. It was really weird. We were both crouching up in Joe's deer blind. Even though I've never met you, I knew it was you because you just had these gaping black holes where eyes should be. (I know you don't, but dreams are like that.) And we were looking out the window and you were pointing at deer and hares and things, but I just kept seeing white static, white lines, and saying, "I can't see anything. I can't see anything."

And you just smiled at me and said, "*Tch.*"

I don't know if it was a good or a bad dream.

Can I tell you what the worst thing about your silence is? I mean, one of the worst things?

It ruins your character arc. No, listen—I mean it. In a decent book, you would have been allowed to, like, grow up and get the girl (Sorry—boy, right?) and save the day before vanishing forever. Your disappearance doesn't make any narrative sense! It's been driving me crazy.

I keep thinking of stories where similar things happen—where friends or loved ones vanish. And do you know what usually happens? The ones they left behind chase after them, through hell or through gates of truth or through magic wardrobes or across oceans aflame in gasoline fires or through collapsing black holes, by magic or science or willpower and mental muscles. They go out and they *find* the lost ones.

I would do that if I could, Moritz.

But I can't. I can no more go looking for you than I can go moonwalking. Even if I found you dangling off a cliff, I couldn't pull you up without dropping you when your pacemaker triggered one of my seizures.

More than ever I'm powerless.

And so this must mean you're not gone forever. Because you've been writing to me like a fantasy character from the best books, like a kid pulling a sword from a stone. You've been writing like the underdog about to blossom into something great. Like the best of the X-Men. So you can't just leave your own story.

You'll be back. You have to be back. And you'll have a lot of reading to catch up on.

chapter twenty-three

THE CANE

Dear Mr. Paulot,

I am pleased you still write to my son. It has come to my attention that he no longer sends replies. He can read without my help now. I felt it would be invading his privacy to read the letters you have written to him. In the years that he has been under my guardianship, I have always tried to respect his privacy. He has not always had any privacy to respect.

Because of this, it was only last week that I became aware that all the letters he has written to you remain stacked on his desk in a neat pile, sealed and stamped but never sent. I was sorry to learn that he has not sent them, because I had hoped you remained his last source of solace. Watching his recent decline was bearable when I thought you were counteracting it. Now that I know that is not the case, I feel I must contact you and tell you about Moritz's behavior.

Something has happened to my son, and it is something he will not speak to me about. We have always been quiet, but this silence is different. I once looked forward to clocking out of the factory to enjoy a few hours' time with him in the evenings. Now when I return from work, our home is awash in a melancholy that is difficult to bear. I have a hard time crossing the doorway; the lights seem to flicker, the furniture looks older even than it is. If I approach Moritz's bedroom at the end of the hallway, the gloom in the air feels so heavy that my eyes water.

Moritz rarely leaves his room. He has stopped going to school. He does not bathe and does not sleep. I can hear him clicking his tongue even in the early hours of the morning.

There is a history of mental illness in his family, but Moritz will allow no medical professional near him, apart from the doctor who monitors his heart. I considered forcing him to see another, but after all he has endured, that seemed too cruel. I cannot commit that act of betrayal.

This began months ago. Moritz went out with friends in the late afternoon, and when I came home after the late shift, the gloom had moved in with us.

His friends—the girl in boots and the mute boy—have not stopped by to check on him, although Maxine Pruwitt, his librarian, has come by. She was adamant about seeing him and pounded on his bedroom door for twenty minutes straight. He did not answer. After such a long time, even she seemed to succumb to the gloom emanating from his room.

He must have heard her. We could hear him clicking. He does not stop, now.

She pushed school transfer documents under his door and left twice as angry as when she arrived.

In the early morning or late in the night, he cracks open his door; sometimes I can feel him passing in the hallway, and it wakes me from sleep as if a nightmare has slipped by.

I recall reading your "dolphin-wave" theory of Moritz's emotional transference.

I try to join him in the kitchen when he goes on these excursions. He eats in silence and mostly only uncooked oatmeal. I make coffee that he does not drink, and I sit across from him at the table and try to find words to say, but we have never communicated much in this way.

He does not wear his goggles. His hair is greasy enough that it looks as though he has been standing in the rain. His breathing is often stilted. I have been careful to check his pacemaker every time he appears, and he does not protest. So at least he is not wishing for death yet. But he will not talk to me.

He clicks.

Sometimes he writes to you at the kitchen table, by hand now. Which would make me proud in other circumstances.

I ask him what's wrong and he shakes his head. He will not face me. Of course, he does not have to, but he once chose to.

I ask him how he is and he shakes his head.

I ask him how you are and he leaves the table.

At first I thought he was angry with you. But then I read his movements more carefully; the way his ears redden, his lips curl down. It is not anger that has silenced him.

It is shame. Or fear.

I do not know what he is afraid of.

Afraid you will reject him? He underestimates you. He will never again be a trusting boy, after all he has experienced. But his past is not mine to tell you.

Forgive me for breaching your privacy and invading your correspondence. But as the closest thing to his father, I cannot remain silent any longer.

This evening I asked him to bathe, and at last he complied. While he was in the bathroom, I broke into his desk drawer and read your letters. I plucked the oldest envelope from his stack, and on my way to work, I will place it in an envelope alongside this note and send it to you.

I will take a deep breath before I enter the apartment this evening. He will notice the letter's absence. I do not doubt the gloom will deepen.

I do not want you waiting and wondering if he has become lost in a wardrobe. His narrative continues.

My son is only as flawed as any human being, but he is unwilling to accept himself. I know you are willing to accept him. When I met him long ago, I saw myself. Before I met him, I was also always alone.

Moritz and I have an understanding. I understand his silence, and he understands mine.

But you are the first person Moritz has truly communicated with. You are the first step into society that he has ever willingly taken, and I am so proud of his progress. I am grateful for your devotion; he is as well, which is perhaps why he finds it so difficult to contact you now.

I beg you, do not dismiss him. Do wait for him to explain

himself. We have not seen all that he has seen. Words are not easy for all of us.

Gerhardt Farber

Oliver, I don't know what I should do. You're telling me your story, and I can do no more than skim the contents of your letters. I cannot begin to process your words except to say:

What happened to Joe was a tragedy. In *no way* was it of your making.

Now I am the one who cannot focus. Forgive me. I don't know what to do.

I am considering going to the hospital. Not for myself. But I am alone in my kitchen again. I am frightened. I do not know whether I should turn myself in to the authorities. Or say nothing.

I don't know what to do.

It is my fault that Lenz Monk is hospitalized. I cannot hide this. It must be written all over my face. All over my soulless eye sockets.

We made a great game of it. Typically during the hours spent after school in the Sickly Poet. We'd order drinks and plot Lenz's unfortunate demise. We had a list of ludicrous schemes that read like Edward Gorey's stories about dead children.

A is for arsenic in Lenz's soup!

B is for burning him down to his shoes!

C is for cutting his heart from his chest!

D is for drowning him down with the squids!

And so on. We joked about performing it at the microphone. We were only joking.

I did not intend to kill him. Only to frighten him. To discourage him from targeting the tongueless and eyeless again.

But Fieke wanted more. She dragged on her long cigarettes. Swore under her breath that he had it coming. Her heart rate increased; she seemed almost thrilled. Instilled with a fiery drive for violence.

I should have shied away, Ollie. I have seen scientists look like that.

We resolved that the best way to confront him would be to lure him into instigating a fight. If someone witnessed the attack, it would seem he had started the altercation. We waited for him after school today. Under the bridge where he'd fed Owen a fuzz sandwich. First we met at Owen's dingy apartment. Owen and Fieke live alone. Fieke is old enough to be a legal guardian. Before that, they lived in orphanages. They don't speak about the past any more than I do. I do not needle.

Ostzig is unapologetically rough. Their apartment, huddled away in the basement of a brick building, makes the one I share with Father seem glamorous by comparison. They did not invite me inside. They asked me to wait on the sidewalk.

Fieke led the way from the pavement to old, winding cobbles that curled away beneath *Südbrücke*, a pedestrian bridge across the stinking canal. I tried to squeeze Owen's hand once as we approached. My heart beat harder when he withdrew and tucked his hands away beneath his arms.

He was still angry with me for last night. (Do not ask about it now, Oliver.)

Fieke and I hid in an alcove between two concrete support beams. Owen stood alone in the center of the pavement.
Far too exposed for my liking. The wind picked up; the sour
smell of cold canal water pricked my nostrils. There was
another scent as well: pumpernickel.

"He's coming," I said.

Sure enough, moments later, that signature slip-scrape of
Monk's uneven gait led to his appearance before us. He was
walking with his head down, looking at the cobbles. Until he
nearly trod on Owen.

"What do you want," he grunted.

Owen blinked.

There was something the matter with all of this. The
look on Fieke's face was that unpleasant smile. I could almost
hear it. So creaking. So forced.

And Lenz . . .

He looked angry, yes. But also troubled.

I didn't have time to consider this. Fieke pushed me out
into the fray.

Lenz jerked back. Showed his teeth.

"Listen." I pointed my cane at him. "You've had your
fun. Never again."

"Leave me alone," said Lenz, scowling.

He tried to push past both of us, leaving me with my
mouth agape. Fieke stepped into his path with her arms
folded over her chest.

"Away, Fieke." He pushed right past her, much like he'd
tried to push me in the gym. But she didn't dodge it. She bared
her teeth and took his palm against her sternum. She made
no effort to catch herself.

When she fell, Owen pounced.

I had thought he was meek as a lamb. But he leapt right onto Lenz's back and threw his arms around his throat. Nails out like a lion.

"Moritz, you idiot! Get him!"

"But—"

Lenz Monk grabbed Owen by the head. Pulled him over his shoulder to throw him against the cobbles. Owen landed on his back and cried out. A squawking cry that cut me to the core.

Because the moment Owen cried out in pain and coughed air from his lungs, my heart rate increased and my pacemaker strained, and I saw every scratch that had ever been made in the stones underfoot, every strand of hair in between them, the insects colonizing underneath the rock, the fungi growing on the underside of the bridge, and the minuscule portions of phlegm expelled with Owen's exhaled lungful of breath, and the tiny particles of flour in Lenz's hair and the way his eyes were crinkled with rage and hurt. Because I heard all this, I moved before the second was out. Before I knew it, I had done it.

I had done it.

MBV allowed me to aim the butt end of my cane directly into the softest pressure point in his throat and stab with as much effort as I could muster. With all the precision of a surgeon installing a pacemaker. With all the talent of an artist with a brush or a seamstress with a needle.

It took precisely one sharp thrust and then two hands shoved against his diaphragm to undo him.

Lenz didn't even raise a hand to me. He gasped for air, clutching at his throat. Tripped backward over Owen's supine form. When he fell, he smacked his head against the pavement.

Crack! And in the echoes, his head was swelling, and in his wheezes, I saw he was not rising again.

What monster am I, Ollie?

I took three steps backward. I could not escape this.

"Got him!" Fieke's eyes shone with inhuman rage. Similar to my own fury moments before. She climbed to her feet. Dusted off her knees. Relit her cigarette before helping Owen up. He was wheezing but smiling. That frightened squawking, that cry that called me to action—was it a performance?

Did I transfer my rage to them? Was this what I did to normal people? Or was this rage all their own? I did not know. I could not spare the time to care.

I could hear Lenz's pulse. But he had hit his head hard. He burbled. In his burbles I heard again how monstrous I am. I heard my nothingness.

Lenz was sprawled across the cobbles and bleeding between us. But both Owen, wheezing, and Fieke, scowling, stared at me. They were not the ones who'd wrecked him.

"Why are you looking like that? He had this coming. See if he fluffs with us again. Wait and see."

"Call an ambulance."

"Are you kidding?" she said. Owen shook his head. He was still coughing. I did not feel sorry for him.

"Your phone. Give it to me. He hit his head."

"Hell no." Perhaps she was in shock. Perhaps I should

have commiserated. Should have realized she could not be as cruel as she seemed.

I stepped forward, cold and clicking. Fieke took half a step back. I grabbed her. I could see precisely how she was going to move. Suddenly she looked alien to me—a terrified little girl who thought I might hit her—but I only took the phone from her pocket and turned away.

She replaced her mask of rage. But I had seen that little girl and she was well aware, so she spat out with more bile than before: "Coward! Just duck your head again, all right? Just leave!"

I did not reply. I called emergency services.

I hope he is not dead. I hope he has been hospitalized. Not placed under a coroner's care.

I left the scene of the crime.

What have I become? My mother's monstrous experiment and I can't pretend to be anything else. I can't hide behind goggles or masks.

Oliver . . . should I go see him?

You would. Certainly you would.

You ran directly at that power line.

I stepped outside the apartment door and into the mildew-ridden hallway. I dropped my keys onto the concrete and clutched my chest and edged back inside once more. I edged all the way backward down the hall and into my bedroom and shut myself away inside.

I cannot do it.

If Lenz were the only one, perhaps I could go. But there are others. Others all over the world who have suffered for my sake.

I can't tell whether it is my heart disease or something else that makes my ribs ache now.

But I am not so brave as you, Ollie.

How can I face you again? How can I face any soul on earth?

With all that I have seen and been.

I am no one's hero.

Moritz

chapter twenty-four
THE MUSIC

Dear Mr. Farber,

Thank you for writing. I'm glad that Moritz isn't stuck in a parallel dimension or something, and annoyed he doesn't have that kind of excuse for not answering me. I mean, at least if he were trapped in a parallel world, he could say, like, "Oh, my deepest apologies, sir! The boggiest of swamp extraterrestrials is gnawing upon my foot. While I tap inane rap music into his skull. I cannot afford to write you. I must fend him off my beloved toes! Let him rot!" or something.

Man, I miss him. Please tell him that I can't wait to hear from him again. For now, I'll try writing knowing he's on the other end. I'm relieved to know he might be there pretty soon.

Please make sure he gets this letter. Even if he doesn't write back, I don't know how to think anymore if I don't write all my thoughts down for him.

~ Oliver

MR. FARBER STOP READING THIS NOW

Just testing. I guess it doesn't matter, really.

Moritz, don't talk like that. You aren't a monster. You were scared and your friend was hurt and *fick* me for telling you to be heroic. I don't think you meant to hurt him like that. It's like you lost control, and that's something I understand pretty well.

And maybe I'm terrible, because all I feel right now is relieved. No matter how terrible a situation you're in, you're alive. So maybe you're not a hero, but you're not a villain, either. You couldn't leave him bleeding when he's left you bleeding more than once. I don't care if you came from a petri dish or Frankenstein's table. I don't care where you came from anymore, because it's enough that you exist and you keep *trying*, Moritz. That's the most human thing.

Let me say what you said to me: Get out of bed. Stand up.

I hope you can find the motivation to see Lenz. I wish I could go see Joe. Then again, I'm grateful I have an excuse not to.

I don't have excuses for everything. Sometimes I really screw up. The party was a disaster, and I wish it didn't matter.

Relieved as I am to know you're somewhere, I wish you were here, Mo.

On the day of the party, I sat on the porch and stared down the driveway, twiddling my fingers and wiping sweat from my forehead and standing up and sitting down again while Mom watched me, sipping a mug of warm cider.

I was wearing a hand-sewn "Zombie of Roderick Usher" getup,

all coated in red food coloring and dirt with painted circles under my eyes, and she was dressed as an undead version of Miss Havisham. She'd agreed to act the part after I joked that she was always single anyhow, so why the hell not take advantage of it? (Miss Havisham is this old woman from Charles Dickens's *Great Expectations*. She got left at the altar on her wedding day and stopped all the clocks in her house and never changed out of her wedding gown, even when she turned into a scary old dinosaur.) Maybe she looked the part too much. When she came out of her bedroom having exchanged her wig for a tattered bridal veil and dress, looking like a jilted widow after all, I almost asked her to change.

The party was supposed to start at noon. It was already 1:00 PM, and the long brown line of the driveway stretched before us, vanishing into trees rustling in the wind, and not a soul had come down it. By 2:00 PM, I could have sworn the driveway was more obscured by overgrown bushes than ever. I was craning my neck to see and I thought there were suddenly more trees, like maybe they were growing on the driveway and maybe people were coming down the driveway, seeing the trees, and turning back because our cabin doesn't really exist—

"You're pulling your hair, Oliver," said Mom.

"They won't come, will they? Not like it matters. It isn't a big deal. But they aren't coming."

"Calm down. You're making me wish I *were* a zombie."

"What, dead?"

"Just brain-dead, so I couldn't feel anxious. Sit down."

I tried to sit back in the rocking chair and managed it for maybe four seconds before I heard a branch snap or an animal rustle in the woods, and I was up again, leaning on the railing.

"Maybe we should wait inside."

"You used to be the one who couldn't sit still."

"No sense wasting energy," Mom said, easing her way to her feet.

"What, because they aren't coming and you knew they wouldn't and I shouldn't have bothered with this at all, because who would want to come out here anyway?"

She put her hand on my shoulder. "No, Ollie. Because I'm *tired*."

I still haven't asked her about the fence, you know. At first it was because what happened to Joe was just so much bigger than that electric fence I hadn't known about. Later, I didn't ask, because I was scared she would lie to me, or lock me inside the house for good this time. But now seemed like an opportunity, like my chance to ask her why she'd never sent me to school in a hazmat suit, why she'd never let me roll around in a bubble or something. Why she wouldn't talk about Dad. Things that used to seem important.

But I saw the lines in her face. Her red eyes. She was just as sorry as I was that no one was going to come to my stupid party.

"You should go take a nap, Mom."

She settled back into her chair. "In a bit."

Three o'clock came and went, and none of them showed up. I slumped in my seat. At four, I rubbed my palms together and Mom caved.

"This Havisham's restarting the clocks, Ollie."

"Maybe we've got the wrong day."

"Never mind. I'll go make you some hot chocolate."

"I'm not five, Mom. Chocolate won't make me forget all my woes."

"I know. I've been eating it for years. But happy birthday."

She pushed cobwebs away when she lifted her dead bride's veil to peck me on the forehead.

After she left, I put my hands over my eyes.

Of course they wouldn't want to come.

Who was I kidding?

It began to rain. I didn't consider puddle-hopping. The driveway was longer than ever and I couldn't stand looking at it anymore, so I went inside the haunted cabin to wait out the storm.

Mom stayed with me as afternoon became evening. She was over-doing it. I scowled when she came into my bedroom. I snapped anthologies closed and glared at her. Or I continued carving or fold-ing origami until she left, as if she had no more presence in my room than any of the origami litter. All the same, every seven minutes she was in the doorway again.

I finally pushed the telescope against the pinewood door until it jammed shut.

"Oliver? It's . . . dinner. Sandwiches. Not tuna."

I heard her set the plate down, but she was still standing there.

Thirty minutes later, her knocking became frenzied. "Damn it! You're scaring me! Just open up!" The door rattled. "Do I have to call Auburn-Stache?"

"Just leave me alone!" I said. "Go do something else!"

"Do *what* else?" she shouted, and her voice broke like it never had before.

"Mom?"

No reply.

I don't know how she came to be here, what exactly happened to Dad and whether she was guilty of bringing this on herself.

Maybe she wanted to start a rock band. Maybe she wanted to study astrophysics. I didn't know what she used to do on rainy days, what she used to dream about, who her friends had been. I didn't know.

I'd had one shitty day where no friends came to visit; she'd had a decade and a half. Maybe she didn't lock herself in the garage because I left her alone with a rotting brain. Maybe she really did lock herself in there to get away from me.

"Mom!"

I knocked the telescope away and opened the door.

She was on her knees on the floor. Tears streaked down her cheeks under her Havisham veil, and her shoulders shook when I held her.

"I'm sorry."

"Aren't we both? The sorriest ever. If your father could see us now."

I rested my head on her shoulder. "*Why* don't you ever talk about him? Really, Mom?"

"Needling." She took a deep breath and exhaled into my hair. "You've always loved mysteries, Oliver."

"Yeah, but . . ."

"As long as there are mysteries to solve here, you'll have a reason to stay."

You had to hand it to her. The largest, most impenetrable lock in our house, and I'd never even seen it before.

Liz showed up alone after dark. I had gone back outside after Mom went to bed; I was sitting on the porch without a coat on, even though it was damn cold. I was fuming, so I didn't really feel it.

She seemed hesitant in her raincoat as she wheeled up on her bike, nothing like how she used to be. Maybe she could see the black taffeta we'd hung in the windows, the spiders dangling from the banisters, the streamers, and the bats. Maybe she could see me sitting there. She certainly saw me when I stood up.

"Ollie," she said, hiking her backpack up onto her shoulder. "Hey. Happy birthday. Sorry I'm so late. Driver's ed."

I wanted to say something, but I really couldn't. When she stood beside me on the porch, I tried to meet her eyes.

"Can I come in?"

I just walked inside. She could follow if she wanted, I supposed. I wasn't going to tackle her to the ground or anything.

When we reached the living room, she screeched—one of the dangling plastic centipedes we'd hung from the ceiling had slapped against her face.

"What the hell!"

I watched her eyes widen by candlelight as she scanned the room. My anatomical skeleton looked horrific in the light of lanterns covered in green and blue film, jutting from a cardboard coffin, organs pulled out and draping down to the floor. Cobwebs coated every bookshelf and table. I was heading for my room, but Liz stopped as we passed through the kitchen to the dining room. We'd decked out this part of the cabin in a Poe and Dickens crossover party. The dinner table was laden with lace and a half-dilapidated cake Mom had spent hours stacking up just so we could smack it with a mallet, giggling like sadistic ghouls. There was a swinging foam pendulum in the entranceway, and we'd lifted some of the floorboards to shove a papier-mâché heart underneath, although, of course, it had no telltale beating.

"Wow, Ollie. You went all out."

We'd spent so much time trying to make the table look as

though it hadn't been touched in decades, and now it would never be touched after all.

I walked up the stairs without a word. She followed me past black lace curtains into the chaos of my bedroom. I sat on the bed. I didn't bother moving the canvases and comics.

"I have a present for you." She held out a pink package; when I didn't take it, she set it on my cluttered desk. "So say something, please."

"So *everyone* had driver's training, right?"

I had never seen her so uncertain. She was wearing a lot of makeup, biting her lip.

"I didn't invite anyone. I didn't even tell anyone." She sat down beside me, laying her bag at her feet. It was glowing softly; she couldn't come over without her phone anymore. "But your decorations are really something. You know, there's going to be a Halloween dance in a couple weeks, at school. And it won't look half as amazing as this. Your costume's great, too."

"Yeah, zombies are easier to pull off when you're me," I said. "So you can just come here instead, hey. We can leave the decorations up for a few weeks. No biggie."

Liz sighed. "I'm going to the dance. With Martin Mulligan."

"Because I know who that is." My blood rang in my ears. This was it. She was finally done with the hopeless hermit.

"He's a senior. He's going to study computer engineering at State. You'd like him. He's really nice. Smart, like you."

"I don't think I would like him, although I might like kicking him between the legs."

First she was angry. Then she put her hand on mine. "If things were different . . ."

"If I were anyone else," I said, trying to grin. "I can never listen to electronica. I can never study engineering."

"It's not that. After all this time, you think—*Ollie!* It's not the fact that you're trapped in the woods—it's that you're trapped in yourself!"

I stood up. My face felt numb, but not because of electricity. Because of other charges in the air between us. Because I wanted to repel the truth of what she was saying. "What is that supposed to mean?"

"Tell me, Ollie. How many siblings have I got?"

"I—"

"What's my favorite subject?"

"You—"

"Or my favorite color, even? My favorite food?"

"You never talk about those things!"

Or what she does on rainy days. Something twisted in my stomach.

"You never ask about them, Ollie. You don't care about anything that goes on that you're not a part of. It's like you think the rest of the world doesn't matter!"

"That's not true. I care about other people. I care about Moritz."

She threw her hands up in the air. "You mean the pen pal you never have to meet. The one you'll never have to deal with in person. The one who's only ever going to exist inside your head!"

"Shut up."

"Tell me, Ollie. When's *my* birthday?"

I didn't know the answer, Moritz. I closed my mouth.

After a moment, Liz got up to go to the bathroom. Her tears were messing up all that mascara.

I had to do something. I was losing her. I was losing everything.

She'd left her backpack on the floor. It didn't take a lot of digging to find what I was looking for. It was one of the things that people seem to superglue to themselves, a little square of metal with earbuds dangling from it. I put the earbuds in my ears. My fingers hovered over the triangular button. When I heard the toilet flush, I pressed it.

A viridian, amorphous surge of electricity engulfed me.

When Liz came back, she knew something was wrong. She was probably tipped off by the bulging of my eyes or the way my head kept thrusting itself back and forth, back and forth against the headboard.

"Ollie!"

"N-New Wave." I tried to smile, but my face went slack. Liquid slipped from my bottom lip. More than saliva, because I'd bitten my tongue burning red.

Her eyes widened. She tried to pull the player from me, but my fingers tightened around it.

That wasn't the oncoming seizure doing that, I swear. I couldn't tell her that the sounds from the buds were so different from anything I'd ever felt that I would have died to hear more. There were . . . poundings? Bass? And something that must have been a synthesizer, punching my eardrums.

If it hadn't been *her* face, *her* eyes imploring me to stop, I never would have let go. When she yanked the earbuds from my ears, there was blood on them. She kept clawing at my hands.

I unclenched my fingers. Hot blood spewed from my nose as she threw the machine out my window, into the rain. But it still felt like I was holding it, like its vibrations were shaking my brain against my skull. I was trying my hardest not to let the tremors win. But when a seizure takes you, you're powerless.

Mom told me that she came in right then, right when I lost consciousness and started convulsing outright. It didn't take her long to understand what had happened. She told Liz to leave.

Liz went.

I wondered if all she had ever wanted was an excuse.

Later, I opened the package, and inside was that stupid old book light again. Passing the torch, I guess. Or another good-bye.

Hey, Moritz. Have I ever asked you when your birthday is? If being raised in a laboratory made you a monster, what did being raised in the middle of nowhere make me?

I wish it would stop raining already, but that's selfish, too.

~ Ollie

chapter twenty-five
THE ROSE-COLORED SPECTACLES

Do not think that my silence has been because I blame you for the harrowing events relayed in your camping confessional letter. That letter left me gasping in sympathy.

Hear me now. Hear me in ALL CAPS:

IT WAS NEVER YOUR FAULT.

The guilt you feel is no more unusual than it is justified. I know how difficult it is not to feel responsible for terrible things that happen when you are helpless to change them.

My birthday falls on July 3. Can you believe I'm a summer child?

Ollie, you have given me all the kindness I never deserved. If that is selfishness, then I do not know the meaning of the word.

I did not mean to abandon you like this, sad and alone in the wake of both my neglect and Liz's. But I am so lost. I have been feeling very low for what felt like an eternity. Doubtless Father told you.

I wanted to hurt him. When I realized he had forwarded my letter to you without my consent. But his face. It was on the verge of dissolution. I can't hurt him. He saved me once, twice. I haven't told you. But the man I call Father saved me.

I do not know what has become of Lenz Monk. I have not left the apartment. I dare not tell Father what happened. I cannot face his disappointment.

It has taken me so long to tell even you. Your confessions shed light on my own experiences, and now I tremble at my desk. Your honesty about your suffering—your confounded honesty!—has at last given me cause to share my own trials with you.

Long before the disaster with Lenz, other memories made me monstrous.

I began writing down my beginnings some time ago.

Here is a concept you might not have read about: *Vergangenheitsbewältigung*. The word roughly translates to "working through the past." This is difficult to describe to you. You are not German. But the people of Germany, as you have hinted before, do have a dark history behind them. We are haunted.

On a personal level, I am also haunted. All of us may have darkness in our past, Oliver. Some of us are haunted by those who came before us.

I said I would not speak of this. I try to see the laboratory as you imagine it: a factory that produces dolphin-wavy superheroes in bright colors? Perhaps a workshop full of vials and potions? Where men are given adamantium skeletons? Where the dead return to life? But this is not science fiction, Ollie.

In the hopes that it will strengthen the friendship that has grown between us, in fear that it is just as likely to rend us asunder, I want to tell you of my mother and the initiative she founded. I want to tell you about the children she worked with.

The children like us.

I won't apologize for withholding. Despite your disdain, I want to spare your ears whenever possible. I did not consider myself bound by linearity. Whenever you spoke of your mother, I recalled my own mother in vivid bursts that all but left me gasping. Your mother's electric fences and locks, smothering as they seem to you, are better than what raised me.

There is no pacemaker for this manner of heartache.

Like my mother before me, I am a weakhearted fool.

The name of my cardiovascular disease is cardiomyopathy. My brand of this disease is hypertrophic. My heart is weak, Anatomy Expert. This is due to an inexplicable thickening of the arteries within the cardiac muscle. This thickening restrains my blood flow. Chokes my heart out from the left ventricle.

This disease is often passed down in families. The heaviest inheritance. My mother knew to look for it even when I was a fetus. Not because she was a renowned doctor, which she was, but because a swollen heart claimed her sister. It stole her cousin, and a distant uncle.

It is this disease that leaves me frequently breathless. That swells my legs into tree trunks and makes my heartbeat rhythm-less. It is this disease that has often claimed young people at unawares. During sports matches or at nightclubs or in the moments when they are most excited. When their hearts fail to keep up with their hopes. Did you wonder why I am such a pessimist?

It is this illness that my mother passed down to me. This illness that she once spent every spare moment of her life working to cure. When she founded the laboratory that made me how I am, Oliver, she did so with good intentions: to study and amend cardiomyopathy and other genetic conditions in utero. To spare infants lives of inherited pain. Pains as small as color-blindness, as large as sickle-cell anemia.

Vergangenheitsbewältigung: correcting a broken past for the sake of the future.

When most people reminisce about dear ones lost, they see those dear ones through rose-colored spectacles. I'm not sentimental. I see my mother as she was.

There was something deflated about her appearance. She could put on the nicest patent leather shoes and a skirt and a silk blouse beneath her lab coat and just seem to sag inside them. Her eyes were ringed by circles a corpse would envy. She smiled rarely, and even then a misalignment of her jaw that made her top and bottom gums level ensured that her smiles were inevitably sharkish, displaying all her teeth at once. Perhaps this was fitting. Her smiles were calculated.

Of course I loved her. Does a child consider anything else? I did not consider how she never looked at me. She fed me and clothed me and raised me. That was love.

My mother never spoke of my father. She acted as though he had never existed. Implied that he was no more tangible than an anonymous donor. He mattered no more than a strand of DNA in a vial.

Perhaps she was more human before he left her. Perhaps not. I have no way of knowing. I wouldn't have known he was a man of flesh and blood at all, except that in my youth I overheard my nanny saying over the phone that a "good-for-nothing" had left my mother alone with "a retard in her belly."

Some things you forget as a child. Some things you do not.

My mother studied medicine in Berlin before she ever worked at the laboratory.

Yes, Ollie. A laboratory. *The* laboratory. However fantastical your hypothesis, you are a good detective. Soon you might wish, more than ever, that you were wrong.

Doubtless this was the same laboratory that your father spent time in. I imagine your father was a kind man, just as many of my doctors were.

Most of the doctors who began working at the initiative had noble intentions, Oliver. They wanted to fix us before we even existed. They manipulated fetal DNA. They spotted diseases in amniotic fluid and endeavored to undo them. They plucked and pulled at genes to defy kidney disease, to purge Tay-Sachs from the womb, to deter fragile X chromosomes. To take hardships from the very beginnings of people. Sometimes epilepsy is genetic, isn't it, Oliver?

In the beginning, they meant well. I don't know when this changed, but it did. By the time I was toddling, the scientists were no longer seeking cures to diseases. They were seeking evolution. They were seeking dangerous frontiers. Science for the sake of science is a terrifying thing, Ollie.

I know this in my weak heart. In my gut. I know this because this laboratory was my second home. The people working there were my family. The laboratory is here in Saxony, likely within one hundred kilometers of Kreiszig.

In the workday hours, my mother worked at a clinic in Kreiszig. Treating colds and fevers. Fungal growths and eczema. I remained at home with that cold-natured nanny. My mother did not want me coddled.

On the weekends, we traveled to the laboratory, where she served as the medical and experimental director. To my memory, she was the highest authority in the facility. The founder of what seemed to be an international initiative.

Every weekend, she strapped me into my car seat. Hushed me with a finger to halt my clicking. Then she pulled out into the streets and away from the city. I slept in the car when we traveled. Already, transportation made me uncomfortable. I remember the roads were winding, but I could not see them. It could not have been very far from where we lived. We always arrived within an hour or so. We parked in an underground garage that led directly into the facility.

You would not believe the ordinariness of the "secret" laboratory you are so curious about, Ollie. It seemed no different from any wing of any given hospital. It smelled like antiseptic, sweetened by a latex-y odor that dried out the nostrils. There was always a receptionist sitting at a counter by the entrance. Magazines littered the tables. Clipboards in slots on the walls. Wheelchairs beside the automatic doors. Several waiting rooms were spread across two floors and a basement level, although there were no windows. The laboratory was fully staffed with scientists. Doctors and nurses and maintenance men and women from every continent. More than all this, though, there were patients. The patients were children. Perhaps they had originally been diseased. Now they were experiments.

You would not believe how far the laboratory had strayed. The scientists' nightmarish curiosity had resulted in nightmarish results. *Unbelievable* results, even. I question my memories. Could the children have been as bizarre as I recall? Or have my *Alpträume*—my bad dreams—merged with reality?

Regardless, the other children in the laboratory were not superheroes any more than I am.

I remember a girl with curly hair. Either I am delusional, or she had a second mouth on the back of her head that she had to feed on a constant basis. Very often, she sat holding a slurpie cup in her hand with a long, twisting straw winding over her shoulder to satiate that maw. At nighttime, she strapped a pacifier to the back of her head.

Could I have dreamed her up?

And even she was not the strangest. There was a pale, hairless boy whose arms and legs were jointed the wrong way. He could turn his head around almost 190 degrees, and always did so whenever I passed by. What possible "noble intention" could have resulted in that?

I have memories, real or no, of dozen-fingered toddlers and a lipless boy who disgorged his esophagus—a parasitic-looking tube lined with two rows of tiny teeth—whenever he wanted to eat. Once I witnessed him devour beef stew in the laboratory cafeteria. The sight of him sucking up chunks of beef was unappetizing. It looked as if a worm had burst from his throat to sip sewage.

Maybe their ailments were more typical than I recall. Time has warped my recollections. I never spoke to these other children. My mother carried me everywhere when I was small. Perhaps just so I would not speak to them. She would spare a few minutes to tote me around the halls and observation rooms of the complex. I was a trophy. The scientists and doctors she worked with would fawn over me. Prod me. Perform casual, clandestine experiments on the eyeless child.

There was a man by the name of Dr. Rostschnurrbart who took interest not only in my oddities, but in my well-being also. He would stop us in the hallway every time I arrived.

"Peekaboo!" he'd say, but cover one of my ears rather than his eyes. He'd use his other hand to hold up a number of fingers. Wait for me to match his number with my own.

Sometimes my mother would accompany him to rooms full of scanners. My weekly physical. She was always distracted. Always looking away whenever anyone addressed her. I could hear how her stuttering heartbeat matched my own. I could hear it. Even as a toddler it upset me. Rost-schnurrbart and the other scientists became disgruntled: her proximity disrupted their results. So she would leave me there alone and attend to work elsewhere.

She never told me what she was doing. She put her hand on my chest some evenings after work and then her other hand on her own. Looked at me as properly as she ever would, eyes on my chest if not on my face. I believed then that her work was for my sake.

For the sake of our weak hearts.

We did not often speak in my family, Ollie. We were never like you.

I harbor scattered memories of my experiences in the laboratory.

Every few months, men in suits toured the facility. The doctors were always aflutter in these weeks. Dressing us nicely. Washing our faces. Presenting the best sides of us. Demanding that we smile and wave at visitors from all around the globe.

I smiled the brightest. Imagine that, Ollie. I felt privileged to be there even as a kindergartner. The scientists were always kind when they sat me down with nodes attached to my scalp and asked me to listen to recordings. When they muffled or plugged my ears and asked me to describe objects on the other side of the room. They claimed other children would envy the microchip behind my left ear: "You're like an android! So *cool*!" (Several scientists were native English speakers. That was where I attained English fluency at an early age.)

Every test was presented as a game.

I remember playing sports that mostly involved smiling men and women in lab coats throwing various projectiles at me to measure the extent of my reflexes. They cheered when I caught every object they threw at me. Cheered and scribbled on notepads and typed my success into computers. High fives and applause!

I was so proud. So beloved. And a few of the other children, some of whom never left the facility, took notice.

When I was eight, Rostschnurrbart sent me to a vending machine with a fistful of coins after my "exceptional work" during a "game" that involved dunking me into a water tank to see how my vision fluctuated underwater. I stood in the hallway, dripping onto the linoleum. Shivering in my bathing suit. Quietly pleased. Torn between potato crisps and a chocolate bar.

My MBV was alerted to motion behind me. I angled my left ear toward the disturbance.

"May I help you?" Politely, as I'd been taught.

The girl with two mouths stood behind me, arms pressed against the sides of her dress.

"Hello, Prince Moritz." She popped gum between the teeth in the back of her skull. "Why don't you ever look at anyone?"

"Beg pardon. I am always looking." Rostschnurrbart was teaching me proper manners and social mannerisms. I reminded myself to face her when I spoke to her. I turned around.

"Why don't you ever talk to any of us, Prince Moritz? Even in the cafeteria."

"Why are you calling me Prince?"

She didn't answer but smiled wide. That chewing sound was wearing. I kept seeing the curls of her hair and the creases in the malformed lips in sharp relief. Whether or not I wished to.

"Well, I should be going back. They're waiting for me."

"They're always waiting for *you*." She giggled.

Typically I would have left her there. Left her while she smiled beatifically. But my heart thumped with something like hope, Ollie.

"Would . . . would you like to come with me? Perhaps you can go swimming, too."

"Really?" She closed her eyes and grinned all the wider. Those second teeth still chomped away at that gum. "Ooh, please! We don't get to do the things you do, Prince Moritz."

She took my hand and I forgot to choose my snack.

I showed her to the observation room that housed the water tank. A shaggy-haired janitor was mopping some of the splashed water from the floor. He looked up as we entered but as usual said nothing.

"What is she doing here, Moritz?" said Dr. Merrill, peeking out from behind his laptop on the opposite side of the room.

Merrill was relatively new to the staff. I did not know him well, but he was almost always grinning and bobbing his head in agreement. High-fiving me. He wore large glasses that gave him something of a clownish appearance that was enhanced by the way he flip-flopped along the tiles on overlarge feet. He tended to cling to my mother, rattling off his ideas for chromosomal manipulation as a means for progressing humanity as a species. One of the zealots, Ollie. Of course Mother hardly noticed him. She was always elsewhere in her head. Studying something kilometers away.

This was the first time I had ever seen Merrill frown. "Moritz?"

"Well . . ." My face grew hot. "I don't know her name."

The girl laughed. "It's Molly."

"I know who she is, Moritz; she belongs in the children's ward. She shouldn't be in here."

"I was hoping she could play in the pool with me," I mumbled.

"This isn't a playroom." He gave us another sad-clown frown. "What would your mom say?"

Dr. Rostschnurrbart came in from the hand-washing room. He blinked at us. His face crinkled into a smile. "Oh, let them have their fun."

Merrill returned to his computer. Rostschnurrbart ducked away again while Molly and I approached the water tank. It wasn't large. Perhaps two meters deep and two meters across.

"Ladies first. Do you have a bathing suit?"

"Oh, no," she said. "But that's all right. I'll just watch you go in."

Somewhere at the back of her head, the mouth gulped and swallowed its gum.

"All right!" I was always monitored during activities. Her request did not strike me as peculiar.

All her teeth were bared in a grin as I climbed the slippery ladder and stepped into the lukewarm pool. She perched halfway up the ladder. Looked down at me while I treaded water.

"Can you see underwater?" she asked as I paddled around.

"Yes! But the sound waves get slower, so everything becomes blurred."

"Really?" she cooed. "Ooh, but I don't even know how to swim. Please show me!"

I plugged my nose. Allowed myself a small smile. In the millisecond before I submerged myself in the water, I heard both sets of her teeth grit. Both sets of her lips twisted downward, but it was too late to alter my course. And my hearing was muffled and she was pressing her hand against the top of my head, holding me underwater. I clawed at her arms, but she would not let go, and my heart was skipping, seizing up, panicking—

Dr. Merrill sat at his computer, eagerly jotting notes about my panicked heart rate as the janitor yanked Molly off me and pulled me out. I was gasping. Ears popping, heart pounding. Tried to steady myself. My heartbeat was all but limping. I could not find air.

Molly had been thrown to the floor. Her arms were soaking wet. So was her dress. Rostschnurrbart took my hand while the janitor restrained her.

"It's *your* fault," Molly cried.

I could not fathom what she meant. Pangs in my chest were restricting my lungs. I wished I could not see how her second mouth at the nape of her neck was hissing and spitting like an angry cat.

I wished I could not see that my mother was standing in the doorway with cold eyes that certainly meant I would never see Molly at the laboratory again. Maybe she didn't ever have two mouths; maybe I imagined them. A manifestation of her cruelty. A way to assuage my guilt.

The thing about having no eyes is you can never close them.

Sure enough, Molly was not at the laboratory the following weekend. I dared not ask my mother what became of her. I sat with Rostschnurrbart in the cafeteria. The other children sat as far away from me as possible. Not as though I missed their conversation, because when had we ever spoken?

But their gazes felt malevolent now. My hand trembled. I dropped my spoon.

"Don't fret over it," said Rostschnurrbart, wiping soup from the table. "She tried to hurt you. I should never have left you alone with her."

"I wasn't alone. Dr. Merrill was there. And the janitor."

"Herr Farber."

"Pardon?"

"The janitor who saved you. His name's Herr Farber. Be sure to thank him."

"Oh." I nodded. "Of course."

"Chin up, Moritz."

"What did I ever do to her? What was my fault?"

Rostschnurrbart sighed and pinched the bridge of his nose. "Nothing. You did nothing wrong."

Owen Abend could never know what handing me a pair of goggles meant to me, because he could never know about Molly.

There are more stories to tell. More unpleasantries to share. Unpleasantries that might explain why I am not trusting. That explain why I am huddled in this room and could not face my reflection even if I could see it.

I will share them with you, so that you are not alone in unsavory memories. Or, if you would prefer, I will speak only of happy things. Of apple tea and warm day trips to the mining town of Freiberg and, yes, of bacon.

I am sorry about your party, Ollie. Perhaps it took you sinking into your own despair to give me courage to face mine.

If you no longer wish to speak to me, for the worm I am and the secrets I keep, I will understand. I am not so different from the scientists. My intentions were noble, but maybe keeping quiet has harmed us.

chapter twenty-six
THE COAT

Sure, I'm just going to stop talking to the only person who ever got to know me and didn't run away. Yeah, that's likely.

Moritz! Gah! That was what kids might call a mindfluff. It doesn't seem to matter anymore that I guessed right about top secret laboratories. It doesn't sound like science fiction. Like fun. I'm so stupid.

I should never have joked about needles.

Thanks for writing me back at last. Thanks for every time you put up with my antics and wrote me. I never thought of you as a void. I guess maybe Liz was right about how I just get stuck in my own head.

I won't pretend that your letter didn't horrify me a bit. I can't even make funnies about it. (There has to be a plethora of jokes I could make about girls with maybe-extra-mouths trying to drown you, but . . . I'm not seeing any.)

Even though I asked you from the start if you knew anything

about what sort of, eh, tomfoolery our parents got up to years ago, I never thought you would actually drop that anvil. I'm so used to needling failures!

How can I criticize you without calling myself Emperor of Hypocrites? All this time I was writing you not just because I have a hard time focusing, but mostly because of what happened to Joe and with Liz. Because I couldn't really deal all that well.

Now I'm sighing a bit because of *Vergangenheitsbewhatchamacallit*, and not only because that word looks totally ridiculous.

So you spent part of your letter telling me about how German folks have to buck up and work through their issues with their lederhosen strapped tight and their *Bier* tankards firmly in hand (I haven't made enough stupid German jokes yet, okay, and it's been eating me up inside), but then you say that you're down with it if I can't deal the same way?

Look, I'm not German. I'm not even American. I'm Hermit Supreme. And I resent that you think the fine people of Hermitopia can't move past things, either. You think I'm somehow justified in disliking you from here on in because you didn't rush to the bedside of the kid who treated you like shit? After people treated you like shit? Give me more credit!

Just because Owen and Fieke turned out to be crappy friends doesn't mean I am.

Who am I to judge?

Hermit Supreme is a master of making a mess of things.

After the seizure, Auburn-Stache put me on bed rest. Like I wanted to get up and do anything anyhow. He placed his hand on my forehead and sighed.

"Oliver, I'm the most broken of records. But your mother does not need this."

"Why should you care? You don't love her." I don't know what made me say it. But right then, Auburn-Stache closed his eyes and he didn't argue.

All those times I called him a kook, Moritz. I wasn't really right about it. The more I think about him, the less I remember him laughing. Maybe that's my fault, too.

I could see the garage through the window, even from my bed. The glass was streaked with water. I swear it's been raining nonstop ever since I last wrote you.

"What is it, Ollie?"

I said it fast: "So is she going to die, or what?"

"We're all going to die, Ollie." He didn't smile. "For now you've more pressing worries."

"Like what?"

"You're young and in love, right?" He put his hand on my shoulder.

"Or something."

"Yes, well. That's usually what it feels like. Don't waste it."

"What does that mean?"

"I already said." He let me go. "We're all going to die. Don't waste it."

He got up, but I grabbed his sleeve.

"Ollie?"

"Auburn-Stache. Am I selfish?"

"I've never met a soul that wasn't. I've met a lot of people who don't bother wondering."

Auburn-Stache gave me a sedative and went downstairs to talk to Mom. They must have thought I'd fallen asleep, but I'd spat the pills into my hand and shoved them under my fitted sheet beside the others and a sci-fi novel with busty cat people on the cover.

"Do you think he'll be all right?"

"Being a teenager 'blows a fat one,' if you recall. Being in love is no better."

"Say it ain't so, Doc." She sighed. "Nowadays he's just like his father was."

"In what way?"

"I can never decide whether he's a big, goofy kid or a small, sad adult."

"And is Ollie also incapable of tying his shoes properly?"

"*Tch!* God, Greg! I'd almost forgotten that. Seb always made two bunny ears, didn't he? He was always tripping over his laces. The first day I met him on campus, he was wearing scrubs and a lab coat and glasses. He looked so professional, apart from those damn untied shoes." Did Mom laugh? "I thought I was the only one who noticed that about him."

"Now, now. Breathe in."

I don't have your hearing, but I could hear her wheezing even through the wooden floor.

"I never thought it would be like this, Greg."

"Do you ever wish you'd made different decisions?"

I should have covered my ears. But sometimes you have to hear things. They were talking about the owner of that lab coat, Moritz.

"Not really," said Mom. "If I hadn't gone abroad, I'd never have met him, which makes me think I never would have realized how to be silly. I mean, really, really happy silly. Seb. God, he used to buy Chiclets and jam them over his teeth whenever we rode buses, just so he could waggle his eyebrows and grin at people like a buck-toothed ape. Nearly gave an old man a hernia once."

"I'm sorry I never saw that, but it does not surprise me."

"He was silly about everything, apart from his work. I wish he'd been silly about that."

"Lean forward." The chair creaked; I guess he was pressing a stethoscope against her back.

"If I hadn't met him, I'd never have had Ollie. It'd be silly to regret the things that made you. I mean, *tch*—do you regret the past?"

"Sometimes more than anything," said Auburn-Stache, "but not always for the same reasons."

"You know," said Mom, "he could never knot his ties properly, either."

I covered my ears with my comforter. One of them had started crying, very softly.

I couldn't stay in that house. It was just coughing and wheezing and weeping and silences that no number of books and bottled ships could drown out, and lying around like a slug wasn't changing any part of that.

So I climbed out of bed for the first time in a week, pulled the sticky gauze off my tongue, put on my boots, and went downstairs. Mom was just sitting at the kitchen table, staring at the lace-patterned tablecloth, running her fingers over the bumps and details. She'd crocheted the tablecloth herself, a few years back when she got really into making doilies and washcloths and stuff. Now she doesn't make anything. All her hobbies have fallen away from her.

"I'm going for a bike ride. Please don't lock yourself in the garage."

She didn't even wince.

"Wear a coat," she said. "It isn't summer anymore."

"Right. Can I ask you something?"

"Are you going to needle me about the lab?"

"No." I stared at her. "Did Dad have epilepsy, too?"

She didn't blink. "He did."

"How come you've never told me that?" I sat down; the seat creaked. "Did you think I wouldn't care? You think I'd rather have a mystery?"

"The mystery of your father has always been better than knowing the truth about him."

"What do you mean?"

She cradled her head in skeletal hands. "He made mistakes. He tried to make you better, but made you worse. He tried to give you the world, but took it from you instead. I wonder what he'd think if he could see us now, stuck out here in a cabin."

"We don't have to be." I raised my voice. "Maybe you should let me go."

Her eyes were buried in her arms, now. Her shoulders trembled just like my fists did. I flipped open the book light. The buzz was nothing to the aching in my head. I slid it across the table. She raised seeping eyes to look at it.

"Mom," I said, "if I could go, you could go, too. You could go anywhere. You don't have to be stuck because of me." I pinched the bridge of my nose, ran a sleeve over my eyes. "I hate that you're stuck because of me."

"I was stuck before that, Oliver. Out here, I don't have to make excuses." She stared at me. "Out here, no one expects me to move on."

I wonder if she still sleeps under the coat sometimes, Moritz.

"Why is there an electric fence surrounding our property?"

She stood up from the table and dragged her feet to the window. "I was a college student when I got pregnant. I never graduated. I've been worried that's not enough to keep you."

"The fence, Mom," I said. "Why did you have to put up the fence?"

She turned to look at me. "I'm telling you. To keep you."

"Right." I pulled up my hood, wiped my nose, and headed for the door. "So you could preserve me like one of Joe's stuffed deer? Okay."

She tried to stop me, but her arms are like flimsy straws now, and so instead she said, "Wait!"

I remembered the sobbing. I waited.

"I didn't keep you here for my sake. It was to keep you from being out there."

"What?"

"The digital watch," she murmured. "It stopped working."

"Tell me what you mean!" I didn't mean to shout, Moritz.

Her eyes were bright, foggy somehow. "When you were maybe two years old, Greg tried to—look. He had one of your father's old watches. Tiny battery. He remembered the paddles when he resuscitated you, and he wanted to see how you'd react."

The day they'd argued, the day of the house fire.

"He could have *killed* you. I walked into the living room and he was holding it out to you, and you were huddled in the far corner of your playpen, just shaking. I shouted at him; you heard me and got upset. You screamed. When you screamed, the watch *sparked*."

I tried to pull away from her. "What are you saying?"

"I'm saying that it goes both ways. Electricity hurts you, but you hurt it, too. The screen cracked. The watch still won't work."

"Electromagnetism . . ."

"Greg thought that maybe we could build your tolerance. They do that with peanut allergies, you know. Gradually increase the dosage so a body can become immune. Maybe that's why he gave you the watch. He wasn't *trying* to hurt you." Suddenly she seemed more aware. "But you weren't *his* son."

"I know where I learned to be so selfish."

"It's not selfish to love people." Her eyes narrowed, lit on every part of my face. Rain battered the windows. Her hand was clenched around my sleeve, so tight it was starting to hurt.

"If there was even just a chance I could go to *school* and you could go to work. If I could go to Germany and you could study astrophysics . . ." I took a deep breath. "*How* could you not tell me?"

"All people do out there is hurt each other," she said, and her eyes were strangely unfocused. "You'll go out and hurt someone, Ollie. You can't even help it."

I thought of the phone, the stupid phone that shorted and how I couldn't stop it from hurting Liz.

"People hurt each other here, too, Mom."

I pulled her fingers from my arm and burst out of the house and onto the porch, into the rain. She doesn't bother with locks anymore. I haven't tried to leave in ages.

"Ollie!" she cried. "Your coat!"

I got on my battered old bike and rode toward the power line, spitting rainwater from my mouth. I didn't look back to see if she lingered on the porch, silhouetted in the dim yellow light seeping from the cabin. I just didn't even look.

The sky overhead was gray and brooding, and some of the clouds had a purple tinge that meant they might spit lightning in a little while. The driveway was more overgrown than before. I didn't slow down until I could see bolts of orange up ahead, flashing above the trees.

I squeezed the brakes and came to a stop when the cable was still a little shadow on the horizon, a draping line of black surrounded by an orange haze. It was still raining, but drizzling more than pouring. The air was sharp and cold in my nostrils.

"We're ending this," I said, showing my teeth. I should have worn my fedora. "I'm going to a dance. And then I'm going to Kreiszig, motherfluffer. To drag a friend from newfound hermitdom."

Because Liz is right, Moritz. It *has* been all about me. I don't want it to stay that way. I don't want to be selfish and alone in a cabin for the rest of my life. I want to go out there and get hurt. I want what everyone else has: not just power sockets, but conversation. Memories! I want to see things and meet people and become something more than myself.

So even if it hurts Mom, I have to leave. Both of us can start living.

The cable didn't sway. It was like the little orange tentacles hadn't sniffed me out yet. They were hanging limply, ignoring my threat. Or maybe they just were indifferent to my challenge.

Not for long.

I stepped back onto my pedals and started pumping my legs with all my might. I gained speed faster than I've ever bothered to before, huffing and puffing within seconds and splashing mud and rainwater all up my jeans.

About half the distance from the power line, the electricity took notice. The tendrils reared back and up, and then seemed to intensify as I pedaled closer. I wanted to scream, but instead buckled down against the handlebars as icy rain hit my face.

My tires shook in the mud, the seat post knocked me up and down, and the great orange cascade of light formed itself into a tsunami and reared back, ready to crash to earth and make smithereens of me.

I was going to pass under. This time I was going to.

The nausea hit me before the wave began descending. I could feel a nerve in my temple going, but all I did was pedal, pedal, pedal and close my eyes, and the wave of harsh light came down on top of me.

I roared against it.

My front tire twisted sideways in the mud.

I crashed into the wooden support post.

There was an almighty snapping sound as the cable split in two overhead, throwing a shower of sparks down onto the driveway. Not a digital watch. Not a phone. My nemesis, split in two because I wasn't going to spend my whole life on one end of a driveway, Mo. The things that trapped me here, that held me here, couldn't hold me forever. They wouldn't.

My head was pounding, my heart was racing, and I was still on the wrong side of the cable, lying in the underbrush yet again.

But I wasn't seizing. I was conscious.

And maybe I could walk past that sparking, broken cable.

Maybe I was still selfish. I still wanted the whole world.

I got on my feet and hobbled closer.

Shut my eyes.

Took slow, deliberate steps forward . . .

And walked past it.

The air, again, was the same air on the other side, soaked in rain, and I remembered very suddenly what I'd told Liz on the day I'd met her, while we sat on the Ghettomobile in the junkyard, about how I didn't want to cross the power line if it meant I couldn't go back.

Mom is never going to leave the woods again, is she, Moritz?

I was panting, suddenly feeling queasy once more. As if my allergies had caught up with me. I stepped backward across the line.

The tendrils were trying to grab me once more. They gathered their rage into a ball of something like fire where the cable was broken.

They groped at me the whole time I pedaled away. I could feel them on my back, boring into my spine.

At home, the door was still open. Mom wasn't in the house. From my bedroom window, I could see the garage lights glowing. I could see the cloud of crimson emanating from the small generator.

She hasn't come out since. I haven't been able to apologize.

Maybe we're on the wrong side of some metaphorical bridge where the grass is crusty and not grass at all, but sharp little spines of glass. I dunno, Moritz.

But the one little speck of green that I get is your letters, so please never stop writing me.

You got that?

Never stop.

Because you'll never meet me, and it's the closest we can get even if I beat all the power lines between here and Kreiszig.

chapter twenty-seven

THE CHAMBER

I would give you the world. But you might not want it. After this letter, you may wish to break me just like you broke your power line.

I have to tell you something now that I should have told you before. Before I even permitted myself to speak to you.

I have to tell you about Dr. Merrill's anechoic chamber.

Dr. Merrill finally finished building an anechoic chamber inside the research facility. An anechoic chamber is a sound-proof room, padded with jutting squares and triangles of foam insulation that absorb even the smallest whisper of sound. Even the floor is no more than a grate suspended above insulation underfoot. An ideal anechoic chamber creates a vacuum of sound. A body could scream in such a space and someone four centimeters away would hear no more than the tiniest whisper.

I was eleven. I saw him coming before he arrived. Recognized him from the telltale way he smacked his feet against the tiles in the hallway.

"There you are, Moritz!" Merrill said, popping his head through the doorway. He found me where my mother had deposited me. In one of the waiting rooms. There were a few young women waiting there as well, biting their lips. I rearranged my hair atop my goggles. One woman set aside her magazine. Gave me a hesitant smile. I walked out the door. Nudged it shut behind me.

"Wait till you get a load of this." Merrill grabbed me by the arm. Steered me down the hall. "It'll blow your mind."

"You don't need to drag me." He led me to the elevator. "I can walk on my own."

"I finally finished the chamber. It's amazing! It negates sound to the extent of negative twenty-eight point two decibels. It's the best one in the world. We beat out Sweden. Ha!"

"Ah." I had known about the proposed anechoic chamber. Merrill had longed for one ever since he joined the staff. "I take it you want me to test it for you?"

He chuckled. "No, no. I want *it* to test *you*, Moritz! How would you adapt to an *absence* of sound, hey? Let's find out!"

He pressed the button for the basement. The doors slid closed. I tensed, wishing that he would release my arm. Resenting that if he did, the buzzing in the walls would dizzy me.

"But if it's a soundproof room, I won't be able to see." I swallowed. "It'll be worse than the water tank was."

I did not say: "I am frightened."

The elevator door opened. Merrill led me out into the narrow basement hallway. Our footsteps echoed in my head. There were cobwebs down here, even; they tickled my hearing in a way that made me shiver. It was like walking through a meat cooler.

"Don't underestimate yourself," Merrill said. "Did you know that over the past decade, you have been the most extensively researched subject here? Other subjects have come and gone, but you're their muse, you know. The original. They just can't get enough of the echolocation kid."

"I'm aware."

"Yeah, I guess you would be. I mean, you were the one dodging projectiles for your entire life. Heh. Good thing you've only ever gotten better at dodging things, according to the data. Your echolocation just gets stronger as you get older, and may spike again when you hit puberty. Maybe by then you'll be dodging bullets!"

"My reflexes have very little to do with my mother's research into treating cardiomy—"

"Oh, come on, Moritz," he said. "You're a clever kid. You know your mother's not bothered much about your heart. Not anymore. I mean, you started it all! You're the reason I came here in the first place."

If I could have scowled. "You don't know what you're talking about."

But Merrill was steering me into an unobtrusive observation room, devoid of chairs and cupboards. At one end of it was a substantial metal vault that spanned the distance from the floor to the ceiling. I clicked at it. Iron. Durable and cold.

"Isn't she a beauty? I wanna paint her cherry red, like a Corvette."

I crossed my arms.

"Oh yeah. I suppose that doesn't matter much to you, eh, Momo?"

"Do not call me that."

"Lighten up, kid. This is fun! Here."

He pushed nose plugs into my hand.

"What are these for?"

"Well, some of the insulation smells a bit funny still because it hasn't set entirely. It isn't toxic or anything, but it reeks."

"I'd rather not."

"Don't be a party pooper! Please. I'm so stoked about this."

I jabbed the plugs into my nostrils. Bowed my head in defeat. I'd seen that mad gleam plenty of times before. Scientists in that state of mind cannot be reasoned with. "Fine. If we must."

Merrill opened the door to the vault and stopped my breath.

Beyond the door was nothingness. An absence of anything. Blank space. Impulsively I clicked my tongue at the open door. Rapid-fire clicks, sharp and clear. And I experienced the impossible, Ollie: an absolute lack of feedback in reply.

I shivered. "What does it . . . look like to you?"

"Like a bunch of foam books stacked up in horizontal and vertical lines, sticking out of the walls and ceiling and most of the floor. A whacked-out bouncy castle. So you really can't see it, huh?"

I bit my tongue to stop the clicking. "It's like staring into nothing."

He smiled. "Well, come on in, then! Let's see what you make of it."

Dr. Merrill stepped backward into the gaping quiet. The moment he entered, he all but vanished from my sight. I could only hear him and see him at all because the door was open.

"Come in," he said.

"I don't think I should." I could not help but notice the lack of monitors in the room. What did he mean to measure? And how? Surely some of the other staff should have been in attendance. Where was the ever-present group of women and men with clipboards? Where were the folks in face masks?

I was climbing the ladder to another water tank. Why didn't I run, Ollie?

Merrill popped his head out of the vault. I could see only the sketchy outline of his torso, so he appeared to me like a disembodied head floating in midair. The momentary shock was enough that I let him grab my elbow.

"Come in!" He yanked me forward into the chamber.

Before I could say a word, he slammed the door behind us.

And then I knew what black was.

I could not see. Could not hear. Could not sense *anything*. I was blind as I have never been.

There was nothingness around me. Creeping inside me.

I couldn't feel a solitary sensation but Merrill's hand wrapped around my forearm. I couldn't smell the chemicals he had warned me about. It was a black hole, an abyss. It was hell.

Can you blame my heart for tripping over its own beats? Can you blame my lungs for limping?

It became worse when he released his hold on me. Then I felt I was caught in the blackest reaches of outer space, falling into pitch darkness. I cried out and could only just hear my own voice, only just feel the faint echo of the vibrations in my throat.

Merrill could see well enough. There were lights in the chamber, lights that have never meant a thing to me. He didn't rely on his ears. It must have *fascinated* him, watching me flounder in that minuscule chamber. I fell to my knees. Tried to reach out to the foam walls to orient myself. To do something about the way my chest was heaving, my heart was skipping beats. To make noise enough to see by. To little avail. The walls were far enough that I could not reach them. I gasped. Clung to the platform we stood on, as insubstantial as the cold metal of it felt when I could not see it.

Merrill did not help me up. Of course he would not. He pressed fingers to my throat to take my pulse, probably taking notes on his clipboard. Then he cupped a hand against my right ear while I gasped on the floor.

"Come on, Moritz! What's with that heart rate? Get a grip on yourself! This doesn't look good for us, you know?" He was shouting, but it was coming out in whispers. It was everything in a vault of sensory deprivation. I clicked and clicked, and there was nothing. Nothing but his distorted voice. I could only listen. "You're supposed to be our *golden boy*. Most fetuses we tweak aren't lucky enough to land supersonic hearing. Some kids end up tiny and with no legs and no arms and half a brain. They're going to cut funding if we can't prove you kids useful. And even you've still got cardiomyopathy, don't you? The initiative's a failure if you're not superhuman, Momo! Prove yourself! So click louder! Quit panicking!"

He jammed a finger against the monitor implant behind my ear; it beeped, illuminating my skull. Doubtless the device told him how my heart was failing, how my temperature was rising and my ears were straining. Could it tell him what I was trying to?

Could it tell him to stop?

Was he writing this down? What were the numbers telling him when all I was telling myself was that this wasn't worth living through?

"This is so disappointing, Momo!"

I was gasping. Light-headed. Weeping just to feel the warmth of water on my cheeks. The spikes of pain in my chest were worsening, constant. But every word that went straight into my head was more painful. He was so indifferent, Oliver.

I was a fruit fly in a vial. He would squish me between his thumb and a hard surface, to see what color my blood was.

"Please," I wanted to say, but I could not hear my voice. I clutched at his pants.

Somehow he made himself heard. Put his mouth so close to my ear that the warmth of his breath seemed to prick the inside of my skull. "Those women in the waiting room. They're still hoping to avoid cystic fibrosis, you know? They don't realize that we're aiming for the *future*. But if even our muse can be defeated by *foam blocks*, what am I *doing* here? How are *you* inspiring?"

The pain was unbearable now. My lungs were lifeless sacks. Breathing seemed futile. I must have been in the throes of cardiac arrest.

"Look, it's all because of you, Moritz. All those failures in the children's ward, in the name of improving you. Because even you're still diseased! So prove we haven't wasted our time!"

"*Please.*" It was only a gasp in my constricting throat. Was I being crumpled by a mighty fist, ribs through lungs and bone shards through muscle? And underneath it all, what pained my heart more? My disease?

Or the knowledge that my existence diseased everyone else?

This was when I died, Oliver. If you were wondering.

I was unconscious during my liberation from the anechoic chamber.

Rostschnurrbart ran into Dr. Merrill in the elevator. Asked if Merrill had spoken to me that morning. Merrill shrugged. But on the ground floor, when Rostschnurrbart asked after me in the waiting room, the woman who smiled told him that an odd man had shown me away.

Rostschnurrbart did not hesitate. He told me while I was lying in recovery that he had long since found something unsettling about that grin. He had been careful not to leave us two alone together. Rostschnurrbart recalled the incident with the water tank. Recalled that Merrill made no effort to save me from drowning, but instead recorded data while I flailed behind the glass.

When Rostschnurrbart pulled me from the chamber, my lungs had collapsed. I had no pulse when he lifted me out.

Rostschnurrbart had to press the defibrillators into my chest to restart my heart. I did not repel them.

My mother installed my pacemaker that same day. I did not wake for almost a week. Merrill was long gone. My mother did not listen to his claims. He grabbed her lapels. Declared that his actions were for the sake of progress, couldn't she see? The place was stagnating! *Look!*

Rostschnurrbart struck him in the face. He was not grinning then.

My mother never truly looked at me. She was logical; she knew that no matter which way she was facing, in a room of sufficient sound waves I could see her. She should not *have* to look at me.

It never bothered me until I was lying in rehabilitation after the anechoic incident.

When she was switching out one of my IVs, I found the courage to speak to her. I had considered, carefully, my course of action. Which questions to ask her.

"Mother," I said while she pushed a needle into my arm. Her fingers were icy inside her gloves. We weakhearted fools have poor circulation. "Mother, did you make me this way?"

"I did." She pulled the needle out again. "Somehow I did."

"Not on purpose?"

"Not on purpose. I only meant to repair your heart, not take your eyes. Genetic manipulation is a mysterious field. We are still learning."

"Were you trying to . . . repair the others, too?"

She pulled medical tape from her pocket. "No. Not only repair them. I was trying to improve them. As I unintentionally improved you."

"But why *not* only repair them? If they could have been normal?"

The threads of the medical tape she laid on the needle already pulled at my skin.

"Normal people have done little for the dying world, *mein Kind*. The world needs abnormal vision. As it stands, there are flaws in humanity that no genetic manipulation can change." Her impassive face flickered. "Normal people are monstrous."

"My father was normal."

"Without a doubt." She sighed, for once like a person. "And he left us. Too late to change him."

I asked a final question.

"Would . . . would you still love me if I were . . . *normal*?"

"Do you have to ask?" She left the room.

I did have to ask. In a soulless house, you must ask such things.

I have wondered what would have happened if my mother had not accidentally taken my eyes from me. If her meddling in my genes had simply fixed my cardiomyopathy and left me unremarkably normal. Utterly human. If the research in the lab had not been twisted to bizarre purposes.

Your ailment could be my fault, Oliver Paulot. I do not know how far my mother's needles reached. How many children across the world are pale, twisted shadows of super-humans. How many parents with genetic conditions applied to her testing program hoping she'd spare their children disease, not realizing she'd only do so if she could give them "abnormal vision."

I do not deserve normalcy, Oliver. Not if my existence deprived others of it. I am the prototype of your suffering. It may be because of me that you cannot visit the garage that houses your family's grief. That you cannot go to a cinema. Or be irritated by cartoons.

If I had been born with eyes, would you be dancing to New Wave on Halloween?

Do you wonder why I could not tell you of this sooner?

You wanted me to cure your boredom. You did not want me to haunt you.

And I . . . I did not want to be the monster who sent you to the woods.

Moritz

P.S. You think I am leaping to conclusions. You think that your illness could be unrelated to the lab in Saxony. If only, Ollie.

I didn't want to tell you. In the laboratory that injected young women with chemicals, the man who played peekaboo with me and raised me from the dead with defibrillators:

His name was not Rostschnurrbart. I misled you.

You should know that *Rostschnurrbart* translated into English is "Rust Mustache," or perhaps "Auburn-Stache." He wore paisley shirts and leather shoes. He moved in a stuttering, stop-motion fashion.

chapter twenty-eight
THE NEEDLES

I'm sorry you were locked in a dark chamber. I know the feeling.

Screw hypocrisy: you should have told me all this sooner.

The thing about Auburn-Stache—how the hell am I supposed to trust him now? How could you let me, knowing what you know about him? How do I know he doesn't spend all the time he isn't here working in Germany, jabbing needles into people?

Right from the start we became friends because we needed someone to trust in, to confide in, right?

But you still can't see me as a confidant. Even now. Even after what I told you about Joe, about Liz, you were holding back things that massively shape both our lives. I want to think it doesn't matter.

Why did you lie to me? How could you?

How could you do what everyone else does?

chapter twenty-nine
THE WOMBLE

Ollie,

Perhaps I should have told you all this sooner. But much of
our friendship is founded on encouragement. You have been
such a light. You had confidence in your autobiography. Why
would I take that from you?

Why would I want to reveal the horrors of me to the only
person who ever saw me as heroic?

I think, perhaps, you are asking the wrong question. It
should not be "Why did you lie to me?" but rather "Why did
you decide to tell me the truth?"

Knowing the stakes, why should I ever risk it?

I haven't told you about the night before we confronted Lenz.
The night we returned to *Partygänger*. Mel didn't even sigh
when he let us in. Another night of music and noise and

illumination and the kind of company that was beginning to comfort me. Company that no longer made me look over my shoulder in trepidation.

We danced. We laughed. Owen mouthed along to words and I acted like a fool to the beat. The world wept to see my terrible dancing. I danced anyhow.

And at one point while a song crescendoed and broke like waves on the shore, Owen leaned forward and kissed me out there on the dance floor. Hyper-real in the vibrations of the bass and bodies and breath and motion. He pulled my head toward his and held me close so that you might have thought I could not breathe. For once my weak heart did nothing. Felt nothing.

For a moment I understood silence. I pulled away from him. I left him standing alone in a field of movement. Even as I turned around, of course I could still see him. Could see how his face crumpled as I retreated.

I pushed through nameless torsos to the bar. Fieke pounded me on the back. If only I could blink my thoughts from my head.

"Well? You've gotta be fluffin' pleased."

I shook my head. "Beg pardon?"

"What?" She scowled. "All that chasing after my brother and you *ditched* him? Are you shitting me?"

I allowed her to shove me that time. I could see Owen headed for the exit, pushing past people. Harried. Losing his innate rhythm.

"What the fluff were you thinking? Are you even human?" As angry as Fieke ever was with me, this was the angriest.

"I don't love him," I said.

"As if you know what the hell it is to love anybody, you android."

She did not stomp away. She glared at me until I had to leave. Until the noise was showing me too much of Owen's painful absence.

But I do know what it is to love anybody. I realized it the moment Owen pressed himself against me and the rest was only silence.

I can confess because I am already doomed.

Doomed, not only that I love a boy far away, but that I love a ghost. I love a boy who will forever be a stranger to me and my crippling heart. It is also that you have been, since the moment I first knew you existed, completely in love with someone else. And I loved you anyway. Despite or because of Liz's impenetrability.

I love the way you fail to stay on topic. Your admittedly lame sense of humor. Those self-effacing comments you make that demonstrate the extraordinariness of your heart. I love the way you feign optimism for the sake of those around you.

It causes me no end of grief, loving you. Ollie, you cause me no end of grief with the way you counteract yourself. With the way you bring misery onto yourself and act like an idiot for the sake of a girl who does not appreciate you. Who cannot appreciate the loneliness and the silence.

Forgive my bluntness.

Now you cannot say I do not trust you. I have shown you my beating heart. Pacemaker and all, confidant.

Now that I have trusted you with the darkest depths of me, I have sent you this package. Inside you will find a womble, a rubber hazmat suit that my mother once wore in the laboratory. Perhaps your father wore one, too. I beg you to go out and stand up for yourself. Stand up for the girl you're in lovesickness over.

Win the girl and take her away into the night after your masquerade ball.

I am going to the hospital. Nothing can hurt me now that I've faced the power line that is you.

Worry about your weakhearted fool of a pen pal no longer.

Yours,

Mo

chapter thirty
THE BLACKBERRIES

I hope that one more thing you can forgive me for—or love me for or whatever—is my bad habit of being a complete ass.

I'm sorry. And now I'm terrified. What are you doing? What will happen to you if you turn yourself in? What will you do when you get to the hospital?

No, screw it. There's more I need to say to you.

Mo, I can't hate you for loving me. Although I can wonder whether you're on drugs—not because I'm a boy, which, whatever, Oscar Wilde. But because I've been such an idiot all the time.

Maybe if I'd met you first, out by the power line with pockets full of berries—not Liz, but you—I mean, who knows? I don't know anything about love except that it stings a bit and makes people act like cat-pissing doofuses.

Never mind.

What I'm saying is this:

I didn't mean to blame you for one second about what your

mother did. I was so scared, so angry, and I took it all out on you. Because Mom can't walk anymore, and Auburn-Stache said nothing the last time I asked again if she was going to die.

If *Vorgaggingdon'tmakemewriteitagaindamnit* is all about moving past the actions of a previous generation, how can you just sit there all shaken with guilt about your mother's bad choices? I mean it.

Let me put it more artistically, with greater sophistication:

They left us in the toilet. In the deepest pile of shit. And we're coated in the crappy residue of their decisions. But that does not mean we are the one who pooped, Moritz. And neither are we the poop.

Never think that. We are not the poop.

I think that analogy puts it straight. And don't argue with it. Don't even try.

Moritz, you are not the poop.

(I can't wait for you to cringe through this. I hope you can still laugh at my lame humor.)

But, god, I'm not laughing. I'm terrified. I'm scared that you've ended up like your mother somehow, buried under the weight of her bullshit. And then there's me, powerless to do anything about it. Powerless yet again.

Moritz, don't go anywhere.

chapter thirty-one
THE HANDS

Father will not look at me. I told him what happened. Told him the awfulness of what I did to Lenz under the bridge. He contacted Lenz's father. A phone conversation that I left the room for. That I plugged my ears to make myself blind for.

Father told me to get in his car. He didn't turn on the radio. He sighs in his throat, and I can hear the echoes of how he can't bear what I've done. What I may have become. Am I so different from the girl who tried to drown me?

I gave him the address of the Abend residence. When we passed under the bridge, I could not see it.

The basement apartment seemed shabbier than I remembered. I walked right down the steps and took a deep breath. Knocked on the door.

After a moment, Owen eased the door open. His gaze shifted to his feet. I could hardly see him despite the way his pulse trilled. He soon withdrew. Of course he did, after my inhumanity on the dance floor. My violence under the *Südbrücke*.

Fieke appeared in the foreground, pulling out the chain latch.

"Look what crawled out of its cave." All her piercings had been removed. Her face was actually soft-featured without those rings and studs. I saw the little girl in her again. She looked in dire need of sleep.

I coughed. Straightened myself up. Tried to project confident dolphin-waves. For whatever good it could do. "I am going to see Lenz. I am going to tell his father what happened."

"What, did you grow a pair? He's been lying there for ages. It's a bit late."

"I came to ask you to accompany me."

"Fluff off," said Fieke. "Why would I ever want to see him again?"

"Because you're sorry for what happened. Because you can't sleep, either."

"You don't know shit."

"He never touched you," I said. "He wasn't the one who hurt you."

Again I let her hit me. The smack of her palm on my cheek confirmed my words. It wasn't Lenz. But it was someone, anyone else. It was the parents neither of them speak of. The reason they live alone in an apartment in disrepair without proper heating. Why Fieke is nineteen years old but still in *Hauptschule*. This is their inheritance.

The slap echoed in my head. I retreated up the steps. A

bus passing on the street bombarded me with sound that I wished I could vanish into. No matter what, I will always hear my rushing blood and creaking bones. I slipped into the passenger seat beside Father.

He finally looked at me. Switched the car into first. My stomach roiled.

"I thought they were my friends," I said.

"They are."

I like to imagine that Owen ran out to the street as we pulled away, his hand outstretched.

But of course I could not see him.

Father has been apologizing to Lenz's family. It is a family as small as mine. A family that is only a father, a man who wrings large hands and frowns. Father does not ask whether they want to press charges. Neither man says anything of the kind. Of course they would not do so in front of me.

God, does this waiting room haunt me. It looks like all waiting rooms.

I cannot talk. I scribble in this notebook. I hope that no one will speak to me. Half an hour ago, I met Lenz's father. Afterward, I had to run to the restroom to vomit up the shameful bile in my stomach. I clung to the toilet bowl and gagged. The sound echoed and illuminated nothing so much as my own face, creased in self-disgust.

Because I have seen Lenz's father before. I recognize those hands, of all things. I recognize them for their crevices. They are a baker's hands. I knew then who Lenz was. How I made him scream as a child in the bakery. How I made him scream and scream at the nothingness of me. And suddenly Lenz's hatred makes some sort of sense to me.

I left the room to sit in the hallway. Tried not to overhear my father or the baker.

I rested my elbow on my knees. My chin in my palm. Listened to the feet of the hospital staff as they passed by. The familiar swishing of scrubs and squeaking of plastic shoes. I listened and my throat burned, and I knew I was on the sidelines again, Ollie.

The lightest of footsteps drew near. A set of unfamiliar tennis shoes appeared.

"Budge over." Fieke slumped into the chair beside me. Diminished without her boots.

I swallowed. "Thank you for coming."

"*Pffft*. I didn't want to. Owen wouldn't stop tugging my arm and staring at me with his freak eyes, and finally I agreed to let him follow after his eyeless loser of a girlfriend. No offense, *Brille*."

I felt her lean over to look at me. Why is the act of looking so vital to other people?

Why is it so vital to me? Because I can never look away?

I spent so long being unseen. Until you wrote me, no one would follow me to dark places.

Fieke wore a knitted sweater pocked with holes, and her eyes were always narrowed, but she was here. Someone normal might have hugged her.

"Owen's in the bathroom, if you're wondering. Took one look at your depressing face and slunk backward into a toilet stall to escape the overwhelming stench of self-pity." She coughed, that old wheeze and something deeper. "Sorry it took us so long."

I shook my head. "Please, no. Don't apologize. I'm the one who can never apologize enough."

"For what happened with Lenz? Or what you said to me before? Because yeah, you don't know shit about what raised me, Moritz. It's not only freaks who have wretched upbringings."

"For that. For everything. For things I can't even verbalize."

I could hear the beeping of monitors all down the hallway, calling the surfaces of walls and floor and ceiling to life. Which were the sounds of Lenz?

I pressed the heel of my hand against my chin. Allowed my shaking fingers to cover my mouth.

"*Brille*, are you crying?"

"I'm eyeless," I said. "I can't cry."

Fieke pulled my head onto her shoulder. "Of course you can."

I had not spoken to my mother in weeks. She had not allowed me to leave the laboratory since the anechoic incident. Sometimes I heard her weak heartbeat as she passed through the hallway outside my room (my cell). She never told me whether her love for me existed or was infinite. More than ever she was unknowable. She would not look at me. Her feelings were never clear to me or anyone else.

You may think you do not know your mother because of

her secrets, Ollie. But I knew my mother's secrets and she was a stranger.

Doctors advised me to stay in a wheelchair during recovery. Advised me not to put further strain on my heart. Auburn-Stache treated me as he does you:

"Moritz, please eat."

I lacked your witty retorts. I only slumped. I only shivered.

I had days like you've had, Ollie. Days when I did little more than sit alone in the cafeteria.

We had not done well on the last inspection. Hardly any countries sent representatives to visit; two frowning men and a woman with arms folded, who only yawned at what I recall as triple-armed and reptile-scaled and heartless infants. I had become a resident, but the other children were leaving. One by one, walked or wheeled away.

My mother knew that her work had not "progressed" in years. Perhaps the initiative's funding was being cut. A lot of her staff had followed after Merrill.

Her broken children were not equipped to repair the world.

My mother was a distant woman, but I cannot believe that she was heartless. She did not kill the children she dismissed from the facility. She allowed Auburn-Stache to place them with their families. Or in facilities and foster homes across the world. In cabins in the woods across the sea, Oliver. She was not so monstrous as to murder her failures.

I think about her when I wake on weekend mornings. How far away she seemed even when she carried me, heart-to-heart, hundreds of Saturdays ago, to my car seat. Maybe

it wasn't the irregularity of her heartbeat that frightened me.
Maybe it was the irregularity of her heart.

My mother did not *feel* in the way others do. She pro-
cessed the *echoes* of feelings. Their resonance did not reach
her until long after the events that inspired them. She did
not realize the pain she caused until it had reverberated for
years. Maybe she felt that realization when I died.

Maybe this was the real, human reason she did not look
at me.

It was a November morning. I was sitting in the cafeteria with
Dr. Auburn-Stache. He was helping me study for a test that
would determine whether I could attend *Gymnasium*. I saw
little point in it. I doubted I would ever leave the laboratory, let
alone attend public school. I was by now aware of all the things
I was not worthy of. He was always trying to make me feel like
any other child. He encouraged me to get better at spelling, if I
could not read. To get better at speaking, if I could not read.

I was reciting the answers to division equations to him
and then, suddenly, I heard her absence. I said nothing of it.
But as the day wore long and the remaining staff went about
their business, dismantling machines and packing away equipment, no matter where I was in the hospital, I heard not a
single pulse from her jarring heartbeat. At some point in the
afternoon, Dr. Auburn-Stache asked:

"Moritz, have you seen her today?"

I shook my head. He told me to wait where I was. He
ground his teeth as he left.

I began listening, as I was accidentally born to.

I wheeled down the hallways. Wheeled toward the elevator. Something gave me courage to ride that elevator down to the basement. There was only one place in the hospital that she could be. One place where I could not hear her.

I knew she was in the anechoic chamber.

The dreaded vault was open. I stood up from my wheelchair. Felt a sharp dagger in my chest, pulls at my stitches. Stepped toward the echoless void. The last thing I ever wanted was to reenter it.

And I couldn't, Ollie. I couldn't cross my power line.

But I knew she was lying inside it. I knew.

Dr. Auburn-Stache appeared beside me, as he tends to.

"What does she look like?" I said numbly. "I can't see her body."

"It isn't there, Moritz," he said. "She isn't in there, kiddo."

"How can I believe you?"

"I'm telling you. She's not here, Moritz."

"Then where is she?"

He shook his head. "I don't know. She's gone."

Dr. Auburn-Stache tried to lead me from the room. I dislodged his grasp. He left me to find help.

I wanted to look in the chamber. I did not want to. I dared not.

Auburn-Stache returned. Trailed by the janitor who'd saved me from drowning.

"I appreciate this, Herr Farber. I'll arrange somewhere more appropriate for him to stay as soon as possible."

The janitor nodded. As we left the room, I could feel the

vibrations of Dr. Auburn-Stache. He shook from head to foot.

How long did it take for the echoes of us to reach *him*, Ollie?

We left the laboratory through the parking garage. I would not return.

The man who would later adopt me did not speak. He treated me to silence. Why bother with quiet? The quiet illuminates nothing. It is nothingness; it does not carry. It should not mean a thing. Still, I heard it over the noise of the car and rested my face against the cold glass of the window.

When I began clutching at my lurching heart halfway through the journey, when Herr Farber saw me gasping in his passenger seat, clicking to see the walls, to find something close that still *existed*, he reached forward and switched on the stereo.

Bass and rhythmic speaking and horns. The first time I ever heard N.W.A, Ollie. Voices bidding me to express myself carried us from the darkness.

I have not missed the laboratory. I have no idea whether it still functions. I do not ask Dr. Auburn-Stache.

He visits me every few weeks, just as he visits you. Just as he visits other children like us. It is he who monitors the effectiveness of my pacemaker.

He still tells me my mother is not dead, Oliver. She did not have an excuse so rich as her demise to explain why I am without her. She simply left me behind and vanished into the world. Not unlike the way she often vanished into her thoughts.

The hospital room hadn't begun to take on aspects of a second home. There were no photos on the nightstand. Few *Get Well* cards. Lenz was not well liked. Although he had been in this room for weeks, he had only been unconscious for a few hours after admission. He would be in the hospital for a while longer, to be sure that his lungs did not fill with fluid or become infected for a second time; he had fractured a rib after all. Perhaps his chest twinges as mine does.

He did not look half so thuggish as before, thin and propped on pillows. A tracheotomy tube dangling from his throat. Bandages around his skull. He no longer smelled of pumpernickel bread.

He did not want to see me. I did not want to see him. When I stepped around the curtain to face him, I wished that he would vanish as my mother did. But I can't let him rot, Ollie.

He can't even speak properly right now. He has been made temporarily as mute as Owen. I was nearly petrified by all he could not say.

Lenz tore his gaze from the window. I looked at him. I did not know how to begin.

"Lenz," I said. "I don't know how to begin."

He shook his head. Closed his eyes.

"I am wary of words. I thought I might say 'sorry,' but . . . did you ever say it? When you smashed my face into the floor? When you did the same to Owen? The others?"

He opened his eyes. Looked right at me.

I took a deep breath. "Even so . . . I *am* sorry. I am sorry for all of us. All the time. Laboratory or bakery or basement apartment . . . or anywhere. I am sorry the world is frightening."

I trailed off. Do not ask me if what I said made any impact on him. Perhaps he was plotting how best to beat me when he got back on his feet. Perhaps that is what I deserve.

But if he aims a fist at me this time, Oliver, I will peel off my goggles. I will duck, but I will not hit back. Not if I can ever help it.

"Ollie is better at speeches."

He narrowed his eyes.

"That's his gayboy crush from across the sea, if you were wondering," said Fieke from the doorway. Owen was standing beside her. Fingers fluttering.

All we misfits blinked at one another in silence. But I could hear every heartbeat, every bothered breath. The awkward shuffling of our feet. Lenz's hands clenching on his bedspread.

"What?" Fieke scowled at me.

"I didn't say anything."

"You were looking at me."

Owen sighed.

"I am always looking at everyone. But since you've brought attention to it. Have we begun to, ah, clear the air? Should we all shake hands?"

"Fluff off," Fieke said. Even Owen cringed. Lenz mustered the strength to give me the finger.

I was rushing things. Yet looking at us all, standing in one hospital room, bruised and battered with our aches of various origins, we were a comical bunch.

Perhaps you *have* seen a shit-com, Oliver. Perhaps I've shown you one.

Father waited in the hallway. I could hear that some of his anxiety had shifted. Had settled into the calmer depths of him. Was he relieved? His eyes widened when we met him. He blinked at Owen. At Fieke. Did he almost speak?

From nowhere, Frau Pruwitt rushed forth. A bat out of Hades! I nearly would have rather ducked back inside and dealt with Lenz's glare again than face the sight of her toting books in her arms. It was as if she meant to beat me with them. Not steel, not titanium. Adamantium.

"*You*. You think any *Gymnasium* will have you if you've dropped out of *Hauptschule*?"

"I—" She deposited the stack of books into my arms. My shoulders sagged.

She flicked me on the nose. "The transfer assessment. It's tomorrow morning at the *Zentrumschule*. Seven AM. You'll be sitting the exam in a closed space, with audio to assist you. You. Will. Be. There. Any questions?"

Would she drag me to the test center by the ears?

"No questions. Thank you."

"Good." She showed her arched eyebrow to Fieke, who had the grace to cow a bit in her presence. She eyed Owen. He grabbed my hand. His palm was warm and welcome.

"And then, on Monday, you and your merry band of fools

will be at school, and you'll be completing community service in the library."

Owen nodded.

Fieke chilled me with a smile: "Yes, ma'am. We'd be fluffin' delighted."

"Will I wake up soon?" I said, to no one in particular.

Will I, Ollie? Must I?

Moritz

chapter thirty-two

THE CONFETTI

Dear Moritz,

So much has happened to this lovesick hermit in the woods since I last wrote you. I hope you're all right and I hope you passed your exam (I *know* you did, you clever doofus.) It was nice to see so much hope in your last letter.

Did you mean to put it there?

It was the day of the Halloween dance. Mom was out in the garage somewhere, probably. I hadn't seen her since the power line fell. I hadn't seen her since I hurt her, Moritz.

I was curled up under my blankets with my back to the door; I'd been lying like that for most of the past few days. I heard someone coming up the stairs.

I knew those twitching footsteps. I thought about jumping out of bed and slamming the door.

"What do you want," I said, without turning.

"Ollie," said Auburn-Stache, "I've been in the garage."

"What?" I looked at him out of the corner of my eye. "Why? You want my permission to jab needles into Mom? Perform more tests? Throw her in a water tank? Make some more superhuman babies? Stick a microchip in her head?"

He sat down at the foot of the bed. He didn't look surprised. He didn't look anything. "It took so long for Moritz to tell you."

"Yeah. Well. Maybe he didn't want me realizing I trusted a monster."

He frowned. "Call me a monster. But don't say you can't trust me. I pulled you from a burning building. I've bandaged you more times than either of us can count."

"Are you trying to guilt me? *You?*"

He put his head in his hands. "No, Oliver. It's just . . . I thought I had done right by you."

"Again, I don't know what you actually mean."

"Your father was my intern, you know." He pulled his hands away. "I put out an ad for a child therapist, and he applied while he was still a graduate student. It had hardly occurred to many of the staff that what these children needed was someone to care about their feelings."

"Dad . . . was a therapist?" I forgot to sound angry. Therapists aren't so different from social workers, Moritz. Therapists don't cut people up. (Maybe I was relieved.)

"He hoped to be, Ollie." Auburn-Stache cleared his throat. "By the time he arrived, I was thoroughly disheartened by our whole enterprise. I had seen the amazing prototype that was Moritz, but I had also seen our failures. I had seen disembodied lungs that cried for air. I saw . . . oh, kiddo. I saw things that should never have been."

"Then . . . why did you keep working there?" I raised my head. "I thought you were a good person."

"The initiative began as a gathering of scientific minds interested in *stopping* disease. We had such ambition in the beginning!" He put his finger up. "We were going to save lives! Cure all but death!" His finger curled inward. "The optimists dropped out early, when the first children emerged sickly. It wasn't only the subjects who mutated, but the scientists. Suddenly I was surrounded by cold-eyed strangers who saw experiments rather than children. If I left . . . who would look after them? How many kids would drown? I have made mistakes, but I could not leave them."

He couldn't let you rot, Mo.

"Then your father joined us, smirking on a winter's morning. Imagine it! Simply strolled right into my office with his hands in his pockets and asked me when he could meet everyone. I told him there would be a staff meeting later that afternoon.

" 'No,' he said. 'When can I meet the kids?'

"I took him to the children's ward, somewhat dumbfounded. He crossed his arms behind his head and chattered about how excited he was to be working there, about the heavy snowfall, about his beautiful fiancée he had met on campus, a girl who played guitar and was expecting. When I unlocked the second door and we entered the ward in our protective suits, I expected him to recoil. Some of the specimens in those days were scarce recognizable as human beings. Some of them were radioactive. Others were not much more than wriggling feelers.

"But your father paused at every bed, every cell and container, to greet each and every one of them. He asked them for their names; when they lacked the ability or the organs to reply, he asked me to speak for them.

" 'Hey,' he told them, 'I'm Seb. What's it like to be you?'

"Some of the children spoke to him. Some of the children reached for him, and he never flinched. Some of them betrayed their humanity for the first time. The ward became a nursery.

"We both missed the staff meeting entirely. When we finally left the room, I followed in his wake. I could not think of what to say. In the face of his optimism, I felt like an infant—I felt ancient.

"When we returned to my office, he gestured for me to sit down at my own desk.

" 'Don't think I've forgotten about you,' he said. 'What's it like to be you, Dr. Auburn-Stache?' "

Auburn-Stache paused to clear his throat. I stared at my hands on the bedspread. Wriggling feelers.

"So . . . he got sick because he spent so much time with sick kids?"

"We can't be sure, Ollie." Auburn-Stache sighed. "Cancer comes from so many places. Your father may have been sick even before I met him."

"I mean. I always assumed that he died because . . . I dunno? He and Mom volunteered for daring genetic experiments or something. In my head it was a lot more . . . adventurous."

You told me it wasn't science fiction, Mo, but I wanted to believe in storytelling.

"Your mother *did* undergo experimental treatment, Ollie. But only because she nearly miscarried in the early months of her pregnancy. Only because . . . there were signs you'd be unwell."

"What?" My heart beat in my ears.

I didn't think I would be able to keep you.

"Seb—your father—told me that he had undisclosed motives for joining the lab.

" 'The doctors say something might be wrong with the baby,' he told me. We were in my office. 'Maybe the same something I've got, probably something worse. Hard to tell.'

"I remember that I sighed. I had thought your father was entirely selfless and here solely for the sake of the kids. But it was also for the sake of his own. I was disappointed, until I saw the tears in his eyes. 'We need help, Greg.'

" 'And you come to me,' I told him. 'I can't promise that we've helped anyone here. You've met the children. You've seen how many of them suffer. We have no idea what the long-term effects are, on the subjects or their mothers. Think of your fiancée.'

" 'Thinking isn't my area. But Meredith and I have talked, which is something I am good at! People suffer everywhere. At least in this place, you guys are working on it, right?'

" 'That . . . that's right.' "

"Your father had a lot of faith—a lot of hope in the initiative. He saw it as what it was founded as: a place that helped people. He wouldn't have thought twice about using it to help his wife and son. He had not seen the gradual shift in purpose. Beyond that—he did not see failures as failures, only as people."

This story wasn't the heroic one I'd wanted, Moritz. My dad really did sound just like . . . just like some big kid.

"So Dad just gave Mom experimental treatment as if he didn't care that she might get sick." I clenched my fists. "He *was* an idiot."

"Don't ever say that," said Auburn-Stache. "It worked. He saved you."

"Saved me! Wow. Bully for the world."

"Don't you dare sit there and shrug as though that means nothing! That is *everything*, Ollie! *Every* goddamn thing to your mother and me."

I had never seen Auburn-Stache like this. I had never seen him look so terrible and sad and scared and tired of it all, and I shut my mouth because I probably looked the same way. After a moment, I nodded.

"Okay. Okay."

Auburn-Stache stood and walked to the window. His fingers flicked against the glass. "Your father spent so much time with the unknown, at his own expense. But when he got sicker, he was still smiling. He sat in my office and he asked me . . . when he knew that was it for him, when he aged before my eyes and strolled no longer, when the optimism left him empty . . . he asked me to look after you. Even though I was standing there with syringes and all those screaming children behind me, with countless experiments already done and nameless more on the horizon, your father trusted me with his unborn son. And after he . . . was gone, after you were born and I took you out to the woods, I knew what you were to me. Even while I was still working at the lab, I could visit you. I could visit your happiness. Your mom's."

I wanted to scream, but he looked so old with his head in his hands. Like someone's grandfather or something.

"I've spent so long trying to be a better person. I like to think that for you, I was. You redeemed me." His voice was hoarse. "After he was gone, that was all I had."

"What about all the others? The other kids."

"Ah." He swallowed. "Yes. I visit some of them, but it's not enough, is it? Perhaps I haven't actually done a decent job here, either."

"I'm fine." Anger took too much energy. And no one had ever really talked to me about Dad before. That was something, I guess. Words are the next-closest thing to meeting someone.

He winced and pulled the package you'd sent out from under his seat. "What's this?"

"It's a womble. Supposed to be electricity-proof, I guess."

"Yes," he said, peering inside. "We used to wear ones just like it."

"And you never thought to give me one," I mumbled.

Auburn-Stache's eyes flashed with that old manic gleam. "Oh, I did think of it. You should see the solutions I designed for you, Ollie. Nonconducting bodysuits and rock wool caps to obscure the sensitive pressure points at your temples. Rubber headbands with skin-tight seals. I drew up plans for a translucent lotion that hardened into a second, insulated skin, and would ideally be invisible to those who weren't looking for it. God, did I plot for you to live like everyone else. I plotted for you to leave here."

I sat up straight. "Then why haven't I?"

"Oliver," said Auburn-Stache, "the risk went beyond your safety. I fear that you are just as likely to make the world tremble as it is to make you seize. So long as you're growing, you lack control of your emotions. So long as you lack control of your emotions, you lack control of your electromagnetic tendencies. What do you think would happen if you got upset on a freeway and stalled every vehicle alongside you? What if you removed your womble at an airport and sneezed a plane from the sky?" Auburn-Stache smirked, but it was a dark smirk. "Other lads worry about their voices cracking. But, Ollie, you've never been other lads."

I tried not to think about the phone that hit Liz's face. The power line, blown apart. Mom telling me I'd only hurt people.

"You think I'd murder phones," I said quietly.

"I don't think you'd ever intentionally hurt a soul on the planet. But fate is cruel."

"No *Schicksal*, Sherlock," I said.

Auburn-Stache lifted the arm of the womble, ran his fingers along its surface. "Why did he send it, Oliver?"

"Because he loves me, I guess."

"Really?" He choked on a laugh. "Well, what do you know."

"And . . ." I slumped into my pillows again. "For a Halloween dance I'm not going to. Because dances are juvenile."

I could hear Auburn-Stache's shuddery fingers squeezing the plastic, and his laughter was gone again.

"Oliver, I need you to put this on."

"Go away."

Auburn-Stache held up the womble with shaking hands.

"You need to put it on."

I didn't want to hear it. I bit my lip and closed my eyes but heard it anyway:

"Oliver. She may never leave the garage again."

Minutes after he left, I climbed out of bed, pieced it together, pulled it on, and stood in front of the mirror.

"Not a freak. Wicked."

Auburn-Stache waited for me at the foot of the stairs.

"Will it work?" I said through the filtered mouth of the gas mask. Sweating, I lifted one heavy arm of the thick rubber–coated canvas suit.

"It should." Moistness in his eyes, fogging his glasses.

It took a while to get the hang of walking in the suit, but Auburn-Stache helped me traverse the lawn, walking ahead and pointing me around dips in the grass as we approached the overwhelming red-gold luminescence of the garage. It was dusk and the building was glowing like some alien mothership. My breath caught in my throat as I stepped right into the light—

I didn't seize. The red electricity gently tickled the lines of my suit and let me be.

Auburn-Stache held the door open for me.

I entered the garage.

There were things in there I'd known about: a freezer, her truck, a phone tacked to the wall. Rainbow bursts of color.

But there was also a lot more.

What was in the garage was a hospital bed, IVs and monitors and cabinets full of medication. A sink and a toilet and a hazardous-waste bag. And a leather chair that I recognized as being the sort of place people sat during chemotherapy.

"Mom," I whispered.

She was lying in the middle of the setup, entirely bald and thin and looking like a child, tubes in her arms and in her nose, and I wondered whether her brain was still in her head or if it had finally been eaten away. The light of the machinery she was attached to shrouded her in half the color spectrum.

She blinked at me a bit blearily as I approached. I wanted to hug her, but I worried I would dislodge a tube or hurt her or crush her—why didn't I hug her the day she told me summer was over? Why was I awful to her? Why didn't I wear the coat? It was raining and she was just worried about me, but I was so—

Focus, Ollie.

"You'll knock her dead with that costume," she gasped. "I made a corsage for you to give her. With a fiery chrysanthemum. In the freezer."

"Mom . . . I shouldn't have said—I mean, I know you're trying to help me."

"*Tch.* It's old hat. And the dance starts soon, right?" She clenched my hand in hers, a skeleton grip on my rubber gloves.

There was no way I was going to the dance. But Auburn-Stache stepped forward with the corsage in hand. The orange mum was framed in maroon aster petals. She'd spent a few months last year arranging flowers. Another lost hobby.

"Mom. Dances . . . they're something. I mean, dances are juvenile."

But her tears slipped down the canvas on my arms and she shook her head.

"I promised I'd let you go."

Right then, I didn't want her to.

"What did you used to do on rainy days, Mom?"

She smiled. "Puddle-hopping, Oliver."

We took her truck, whatever color it was.

We approached the broken power line and I held my breath. But with the womble, I almost hated how easy it was to drive under it. I breathed a sigh into the mask when we passed unhindered below the limp tendrils. They were as threatening as spaghetti noodles. They didn't mean a damn thing, Moritz.

I could see enough through the goggles and the windshield to know that the engine was propelling us forward at speeds my bike could never achieve. I didn't seize, despite the dizzying bouts of color that assailed me as he drove. I had never looked out car windows before, but I didn't enjoy it much. I kept thinking of how Mom tried to smile as we pulled out of the garage. She tried, and it hurt to breathe when I thought about it.

But at least I wasn't seizing. Either the womble was working or I had fooled myself.

We pulled onto the main roads of town. Piercing cobalts and ceruleans swarmed around billboards, jabs of amber lashed out from streetlamps. Congealing browns overtook us as we passed other drivers. I didn't appreciate it like I should have.

Auburn-Stache kept glancing at me, as if looking away might puncture the suit.

When we pulled up in front of the school, I struggled to breathe. There were *people* out there, heading from the darkness to the colors of the flat-roofed building.

I almost whimpered. "This is crazy. What are we doing?"

"Sometimes you have to take a plunge. For better or for worse."

He helped me out of the truck and tucked a wad of cash into my hand. "For tickets."

"Oh. Yeah. Money. That's a thing."

"It is."

"Come pick me up at ten, okay?" I tried to sound confident. I thought I was hallucinating.

"There are all kinds of adventures in the world, Ollie."

* * *

I stumbled into the school alongside other monstrous shapes, flinching away from lightbulbs overhead, twitching at the sight of phones in hands and the feel of the beat emanating through the floor. Both my fists were closed; I handed a mummy at the ticket table ten dollars. He gestured to the double doors that said "GYM."

That room was sensory murder. The usual pain wasn't there, but I could feel the weight of electricity suffused around me. The colors were unbearable. I could hardly see the dancers and the DJ through the clouds in the air around them. Individual shades, individual auras were impossible to pluck out. They were tangled and smeared together in a seething mass that circumvented dozens of laughing kids.

It could have been worse. I think it was easier for me to see witches, superheroes, and vampires through womble eyes than it would have been to see normal teenagers through my own.

Of course I recognized her, even in costume. Liz's dress was black with glow-in-the-dark bones on it; her torso looked like the model skeleton in my room. Her face had been paled with makeup. She'd put shadows under her eyes, beneath her cheekbones.

She looked like me, only beautiful.

But she wasn't standing alone. She was attached to a blond boy dressed as a knight in foil armor. If I kicked him between the legs, I'd probably be kicking homemade chain mail.

I trudged to her, pushing against dancers who swore at me. The suit was working, but it wouldn't for long. The hot perspiration, the flashing from all sides, and the din of voices that I was unaccustomed to, the onslaught of light . . . I was being smothered.

Colors swallowed me as I reached for her.

*   *   *

My glove wrapped around her arm. She pulled away. "The heck?"

"Hey." Martin Mulligan squinted at me, half smiling. "Who's this? Brian? Great costume, man!"

I unclenched my other fist and pushed Liz's corsage and music player into her hand. I'd cleaned the blood and water off. She frowned at it. Then her eyes looked straight into my goggles.

"*Ollie?*"

"Liz!" I spoke as loudly as I could. The heat was excruciating. I pointed at the DJ. "Electronica?"

"Ollie, what—how—?" Through the haze I think I saw her eyes widen.

"No . . . biggie." My legs gave out.

Martin Mulligan caught me with cardboard arms. "Man, you're hyperventilating. Take that thing off!"

"I . . . can't."

Martin misunderstood. He thought he was helping me. That was the worst thing—knowing that he really *was* a decent guy. Maybe I would have liked him after all, the bastard.

"No!" cried Liz.

"Here," said Martin Mulligan, and he yanked my gas mask off.

My head exploded. A barrage of malevolent electricities stabbed me in the eye sockets. It was beyond pain—it was concentrated anguish at the base of my neck, expanding and searing as I waited for my brains to splatter onto my shoes.

I screamed as blood vessels in my eyes burst, as my hands started flapping. I screamed twice as loud as I ever had until the sound reverberated up to the gymnasium rafters. And when I fell to the floor, I screamed even louder, and my skull threw itself against the wood.

I screamed.

The world ended.

And I *wanted* it to end.

Because it was finally too much. And I mean all of it was too much, all of it was swirling through my skeleton and nerves until it was imploding inside me in this twisted spiral of pain or something so much worse, and I swear that lights switched over in my eyes and then I saw more than Liz beside me, horrified in the gym.

I saw my dad tripping over his untied laces, but all the wriggling feelers stretching out of incubators were ready to catch him. I saw daylilies sprouting from dilapidated birthday cake no one ever ate. I saw the fishbowl in shards painted redder than blackberry juice. Liz's hand getting sucked back into the cardboard television. Joe flying right back up into his tree. The automobile bones in the junkyard creaking and standing up on huge metal stilts with feet at the ends. I saw Dorian Gray lit with electricity and I saw us wearing layers of mud puddles as thick as winter coats and I saw planes go down because I sneezed and I saw, I saw, I saw all sorts of things I could never see and the weight of it all was pulling me under and I could have happily fallen back into the feelers of the things in incubators, too, right? That seemed easiest.

But then I saw you. You were in the deer blind again, Moritz. I saw you, smiling with holes in your face, reaching down into the collapsing chamber of things that held me, saying only "It was never your fault!" and pulling me up and out and closer to you.

It was almost like I met you, Mo.

And the thought of that was enough to send all of the imploding mass of horror spinning out of me ALL AT ONCE in a roaring scream that no one heard, that no words, no ALL CAPS, could capture.

*   *   *

So the world only ended for the DJ. All his speakers blew out in the exact instant that his laptop died. The lights above sputtered, went out. Phones sparked and people dropped them. All that was electric died with my scream.

I made the world convulse instead.

I was on my back. The sound of stampeding, costumed teenagers shouting in the dark shook me to the bones.

"Is he okay?" Martin Mulligan, my knight? Screw that. "I'll get— get help." His footsteps joined those of the exiting, hollering masses.

I opened my eyes. Liz was leaning over me. I could see her face in the glow of her skeleton dress, although it hurt to stare through the red haze of broken blood vessels.

"I brought the . . . house down," I said, all stumbling tongue.

"You're crazy." Her relief was almost tangible, like another color.

I didn't look away. "You wanna dance?"

"You didn't bring your glockenspiel." She laughed, or maybe choked.

I could see her eyes, just barely. She didn't look bored. I thought her freckles were piercing through the makeup. And when she hugged me in the emptying gym, a current passed between us.

She held out her hand.

"Do you wanna stand, Ollie?" A hint of that old grin. "Or do you wanna lie there and bleed some more?"

I stood.

Liz and I kicked balloons and untangled orange and black streamers from our shoes. We stepped out of the school through a fire exit.

I was riding some kind of high, face open to the air, dragging my gas mask behind me. I was still grinning like an idiot as she pulled me away from the school, despite the blood cooling on my face. The streetlamps overhead burst as I passed under them. When the first bulb shattered, Liz yelped and I ended up dragging her too, but the air was cool and fresh and new, and there was blacktop under my feet for the first time ever, and I wanted to think only of this moment.

But she stopped halfway across the large parking lot to catch her breath and we were alone, and I didn't even know what to say. I looked at her and peeled my womble farther down from my face. We walked slowly across the remainder of the lot. It just felt like we should keep moving or I would have to stop and think, and I did not want to.

"So you beat the power line," she said. There was pumpkin-shaped confetti in her hair.

"I had help."

"But hey, maybe you can start coming to school here now."

Overhead, another streetlight went out. I felt the slightest release of pressure in my temple as the colors faded, but nothing more.

"I'm not sure that's the best idea."

"Who needs computers if you've got origami?" She was beaming. "It'll work."

We'd stopped walking, standing behind the lone vehicle in the back lot, an old minivan that made me nostalgic. When I stood near it, my stomach clenched and its black smog vanished. Maybe we were going to kiss again.

But . . .

"I've got a better idea!"

"I know that look," she said, but I didn't want to think about why she was frowning or why maybe I should be frowning, too, so I grabbed her hand and pulled her forward, toward the road that ran behind the school.

"We could go anywhere! Where do you think we should go, Liz? Where's a good place to eat? Maybe a sushi joint, because I'd probably take out ovens if I got too close. And after that, how do you feel about Kreiszig? I don't know whether I could get on a plane." I chortled, yanking her forward, walking down the yellow lines in the road. I forgot that roads *had* such a thing. Genius!

"Ollie!" Liz cowered as another bulb burst overhead. "Can't you shut it off?"

"I mean, maybe if I got in a plane it would crash, but maybe not. Maybe I could rein it in a bit. Or we could get a skiff. Either way I'll see the ocean. The *ocean*, Liz! I bet confessions are even bigger at ocean sunsets! Stands to reason."

Liz pulled her hand away. I couldn't see her expression beneath the makeup, but her teeth were showing. "You're manic again!"

"No, no, I'm not." I showed my teeth, too. "Just excited!"

"What's happened?"

Man, she knows me well, Moritz. My smile slipped. And as it did, I felt queasy. The electric aura from the next streetlight suddenly seemed stronger than I was and I took a step back.

"Nothing's happened," I said. "I just don't want to go home."

"Ollie?" she said. "Calm down. Breathe." She put her hands on my shoulders. Since when was I crouching? "Is it your mom?"

I didn't answer. She helped me up and started walking me back toward the school, back across the parking lot. That womble was so heavy. My feet were so heavy.

"Come on. Pull on your mask. Let's go."

"Auburn-Stache . . . he isn't coming back until ten PM."

"I'll drive. I wasn't lying about driver's training."

It didn't end there, Moritz. But the moments I have left with Mom are running out, and right now I'd rather be at her bedside than writing you.

Thanks for the womble. Send me more hope?

chapter thirty-three

THE MICROPHONE

Ollie, I would pull you from every darkness, if I ever met you.

Bernholdt-Regen did not welcome our merry band back with willing arms. But it seemed Lenz's father truly had influence. I had feared he would want to pursue further punishment for me. Facing him in the hospital had been even harder than facing Lenz. The way he'd stared at me with bags beneath his eyes. Cracking his dry knuckles. But he'd said, "My son has been known to ask for trouble. I told the authorities he fell from the bridge. I told them not to trace the emergency call. I told them he is clumsy, like me."

"He . . . fell."

"I know some of what he's done to you. To the other boy who frightened him."

Frightened him?

"Goodness knows he's hospitalized a classmate before.

Goodness knows I did, in my day. Like father, like son." He tried to chuckle. It didn't reach his eyes. "Clumsy, like me." He sighed a deep sigh that seemed to reach the bottom of him. "I did not mean to raise him like me."

"I'm as . . . *clumsy* as he is."

I felt his eyes crinkle up. "You were also raised by someone. We follow examples. I . . . I have been a bad example since his mother passed. I shooed you from my bakery, years ago. What was I teaching him?"

"But it has to be more than following examples," I told him. "I have to be more than that."

"Maybe you are. Some of us never get there." I heard his bones creak. His knuckles tightened on his knees. "It is very hard, to be human."

I clutched my shoulders. "It really is."

He held out one cracked hand. With a burning throat, I shook it. His palm was as warm as mine.

Fieke and Owen awaited my arrival in the courtyard at school. My heart leapt, Ollie, but this was not a sign of breathlessness or fear. I didn't pay much attention to what the other students were doing. It was enough that the Abends were chattering away, sending their own waves back to me. Not in color but in vivid detail. Owen laughed and wiggled his fingers. He's trying to teach me sign language. It is as difficult as reading!

Pruwitt demands I keep up with reading. She handed me a stack of manga the other day, which must please you, Ollie.

As we walked, Fieke said she might actually attend class for once. Her teacher will wonder when Siouxsie Sioux registered for his course! Ha!

We shared lunch together. I spoke. Owen spoke in his way, holding my hand beneath the table. I doubt you will mind, Oliver. Despite your kind words about meetings under power lines.

This is not science fiction. But I almost feel I am in a fantasy world.

Except when I think of you. This is not fantasy. In a fantasy world, your mother would not be in such pain. And neither would you. If I could tell you this in person, you could hear the truth in my voice.

But perhaps one day I shall meet you, now that you have the womble. After all, you overcame the power line. Perhaps one day you'll be able to find the happy medium between your polarities—between rejecting electricity and it rejecting you.

I am not afraid that you will hurt me. If you do, the scars won't last for eternity. People hurt each other all the time. Especially when they care for each other.

Lately I have been dwelling. I asked Father where the laboratory that made us is. I had no idea whether it was still operational. Whether it still smelled of antiseptic and windowlessness. My father wrote the latitude and longitude down.

"I never thought you'd ask for this," he said as he wrote.

"Neither did I," I said. "But . . ."

He nodded. *"Vergangenheitsbewältigung."*

* * *

At the Sickly Poet, I laid the folded coordinates before Fieke and Owen.

"What's this? You couldn't even throw it at me?" she said while Owen unfolded the paper airplane. I am only capable of the simplest origami, Ollie.

Owen's eyes widened. He signed a symbol similar to "hospital" to my untrained ears.

Fieke frowned in a clinking sound. "You mean the place where you were raised?"

Owen frowned at me as well. Or perhaps frowned at the obnoxious racket that the current performer was making on the evening stage. Wailing ineptly along to K-pop songs. Help, Ollie.

"Why the fluff would you wanna go back there? Are you looking for your sociopathic mother?"

"She wasn't sociopathic. And no."

Fieke opened her mouth. Owen put his hand up to her face and nodded.

"I was hoping one of you could google how I can get there. If it isn't too much trouble."

Owen held the unfolded plane close to his face. Set it down again. Moved his hands at Fieke.

"Owen can find anything online. So when are we going?"

I shook my head. "I don't expect you to accompany me."

"God, you're a prat," said Fieke.

Owen kicked her under the table. He looked frightened, but he pointed to himself.

Once this might have upset me. Their recklessness. Their

curiosity about the source of my childhood torment. As if this were a field trip. Once I might have been angry.

"I'll come," grumbled Fieke, "if your next performance isn't shit, *Brille*."

I looked at the two of them. Two people, Oliver, who are content to follow me into the dark. Fieke's cheeks twitching, despite her fixed scowl. Owen's eyes, wide but determined.

I made my way to the stage. Pushed past the quiet crowd of regulars. Climbed into the spotlight. Adjusted the microphone. Finally, I peeled off my goggles.

Perhaps someone gasped. Perhaps the bartender dropped a glass. But I was not listening for it. Such a hullabaloo was coming from the table in the corner. Such a large amount of whooping and foot-stamping and table-pounding. It ricocheted off all the walls of the *Kneipe* and shook my very soul.

Lenz met us at the train station. Standing on the platform, looming over Fieke's shoulder. He cracked his knuckles as Owen and I approached. Fieke showed her teeth and squeezed his forearm.

"I passed him by the good old bridge this morning. He offered to help me."

I could see evidence that he had changed, at least physically: a dent at the back of his head. A dent I put there.

"Hallo," he murmured.

Fieke grinned like a proud mother.

He nodded and set down her satchel and left us. As he turned I remembered once more the day I'd first seen him: the day the sight of me had set him to screaming.

Perhaps he'll head off and hurt someone again.

Perhaps he thinks the same thing when he looks at me.

For all I knew, there was a dead mouse in his pocket.

But I hope not.

Freiberg was once a small village, but with the excavation of its ore mines over the centuries, it grew to prominence. Now Freiberg is home to a technical university. It attracts additional tourists because of the ruins of Freudenstein Castle. There are old, crumbling walls scattered here and there among the town houses and shops. Scraps of an old world displaced in time. You live in America, where things are still new. In Germany, the old and the new exist side by side.

The area surrounding Freiberg is said to be "green" and scenic, due to its proximity to Tharandt Forest, an ancient sprawl of trees and sandstone caves. The forest is listed among the most beautiful places in Saxony.

We did not enter the national park there, but rather we climbed a fence along the lines of the forest. Owen led us through those aging woods. The air was cool beneath the canopy. Thick moss drooped from the trees, sweet-smelling. Peculiar in its familiarity. Had I smelled this from the car seat where I drowsed? While my mother drove me in dizzying silence to the laboratory?

We hit a dirt road somewhere amid the trees. I imagined we might have stumbled onto your driveway. Wish as I might, heart swelling as my companions stopped so that I might catch my breath, at the end of the driveway was no triangular cabin.

Hidden in the sandstone cliffs was the entrance to an underground car park. It was dark within. I asked the others to hold on to me. We formed a human chain, and I led them through the damp garage. They held their phones aloft for additional light. Grass had invaded even here, and the entire lot was empty. Devoid of machinery. Of any sign that once the place was the source of so much strangeness and pain.

We approached closed automatic doors. I hesitated. Fieke stepped forward and kicked in the glass with her boots. As if she did such things on a frequent basis. Of course she does, Ollie.

I stopped in the familiar reception area. No lights buzzed inside. The wallpaper was curling with water damage. Everything smelled cold. We could all sense it. The entire facility was vacant.

"Ghost town," said Fieke.

We wandered the halls that used to house me, calling to what I used to be and hearing no reply. All the medical equipment was gone. Posters had been torn down. There was nothing. Not even paper litter. Just dampness and silence and empty counters. Even the clipboards were absent from the walls. Even the magazines were absent from their tables.

I half expected to see anxious women sitting in the waiting rooms after all this time.

"Yeah, I can believe you used to live here," said Fieke, stopping outside the cafeteria across from the stairwell. "It explains why you're such a mopey bastard." The fire was gone from her voice. Everything sounded hollow in that hallway.

"I have been trying to smile more."

Fieke let out a nervous bark of a laugh. "As if that isn't the saddest part of all."

I cannot see darkness, but I could feel it gathering down those steps as I pushed open the door to the stairwell. The air was icier. Smelled fouler. I took a deep breath and a step forward.

Owen grabbed my arm. He shook his head and began to tap a message to me. I put my hand on his fingers to stop him.

"I'll return before you can even ponder missing me."

He released my arm, finger by finger. Despite his silence, I knew all that he was saying and was stronger for it.

I descended alone.

The door to the anechoic chamber remained open. It remained a gaping vault of blackness. I forced myself forward and fell to my hands and knees. I crawled into the soundless void.

I could feel my heartbeat. Could feel the grate beneath my fingers as I listened. I shouted once, just to be certain. The foam pallets had moldered enough that the room was not so silent as I recalled. It was not so good at swallowing everything up.

She was not there, Ollie.

I put a hand over my mouth and breathed through my nose, again and again.

If I made any sound after that, the walls halfway absorbed it.

Upstairs, Owen and Fieke waited on benches in the cafeteria. Owen met me when I pushed the doors open. For once, Fieke did not speak.

"It's all gone." The sound of my voice echoed in the halls. Halls that used to house me. "There's no one. Nothing's here."

Fieke sighed. "So what are we meant to do now?"

Though no one could see me do it, I smiled.

"Anything we fluffing want," I said.

Frau Pruwitt showed up on my doorstep to deliver the results of my transfer assessment. She came into the kitchen and nearly smiled when Father gave her a coffee. I could hear the creases in her face protesting the unfamiliarity.

My father smiled, too. Oliver, romance might not be impossible for *all* of us.

"You passed," she said. "Not a big fuss. Here is a list of potential schools you may consider transferring to."

"Not a big fuss. But worth hiking up five flights of stairs to inform me."

She sniffed.

Father grabbed my hand. "I'm proud, Moritz."

He didn't have to say it aloud. I felt it in his posture. But he's trying to speak more. We both are.

"You should also start considering universities. You're behind, Mr. Farber."

"I'll leave that until I get back."

"What do you mean, until you get back?"

"After *Gymnasium* I'm going to take advantage of the grace year. Postpone pursuing higher academia. Travel."

It is traditional for German students to spend one year abroad before beginning university. A year to see the world or work and discover what it is they would like to do with their lives.

Frau Pruwitt clearly wanted to throw a book at me.

"Let me tell you something, Moritz. Going out looking for the woman who left you won't make any of us happier. You've found a good father here in Herr Farber."

"And he has a son in me," I said, "and he understands me well enough to know I'm serious." I smiled. "I'm not looking for her. But if I meet my mother in my travels, well, I suppose I can finally accuse her of being the one who pooped."

Even father looked shocked.

How uncouth you've made me, Ollie.

One day, I will meet you. I will meet you and neither of us will die for it. By then you'll have seen more than enough humidifiers to sicken you.

In one year, I hope to be where you are, Oliver Paulot. I am saving pennies. In the meantime, the handful of friends you've helped me gather will be enough to deal with.

Perhaps I'll surprise you even sooner.

Perhaps I am in your driveway. Not far from where you sit folding origami dragons. Tapping your fingers against the bones of your glock. Painting electricity.

Perhaps I am already at your door, arms and weak heart open.

Here is a children's rhyme you already know:

Ready or not, here I come.

All my love,

Moritz Farber

chapter thirty-four
THE DOORWAY

The funny thing about character arcs, Moritz, is how you can decide to see them in almost anyone if you look.

You could argue that Rochester starts off as an asshat in *Jane Eyre* and ends up as the same asshat but with worse eyesight, and that would be true. Or you could say that he grew as a person by falling in love and acknowledging his twisted past (namely, "Oops, maybe it was weird of me to lock my crazy wife in the attic for years").

You could argue that Tess in *Tess of the d'Urbervilles* starts and ends her life in misery, and all the things that happen to her are awful and don't stop her from being an innocent fool for eternity. Or you could say she fought her crappy fate in quiet, ultimately futile ways that nevertheless proved her resilience.

You could argue that Harry Potter started off a brave little kid and ended up a brave young man and we never doubted for a second that he'd get there, or you could say you bit your nails the whole way and watched him grow with your heart in your throat.

You could argue that people change or don't change, and you could probably make a pretty damn convincing case for both sides.

You could argue that Mom didn't get a fair shot, stranded out in the woods with me for years.

Or you could argue that she made a lot of her time here. So much of the house is shaped by her presence: cross-stitched tapestries on the walls, knit blankets on the couches, furniture she whittled herself, and bowls and plates and spoons she made from porcelain, and flowers she planted that are perennials, which means they'll bloom for years and years and years even now that she's gone.

And so much of me is shaped by her presence, too.

It sounds a bit morbid, but we buried Mom in the backyard where I buried Dorian Gray. She didn't die the night of the dance, or even the day after. She died about two weeks after that, and during those last weeks Liz basically lived at the cabin with us. She and Auburn-Stache were there the whole time, and when I kissed Mom good-bye through the gas mask, they were standing behind me, ready to catch me. But I didn't fall. I didn't.

I have to live without a kickstand now.

We even had a funeral.

I wore a suit, and so did Auburn-Stache and the rest. A few people showed up, actually—from Liz's family to the local state park guy, who cried so hard that I wonder whether he and Mom did more than play poker, to the mailman and Lucy from the pharmacy. I didn't want to talk to anyone, and we didn't make people check their phones at the door. It gave me an excuse not to approach people.

That excuse might not always work.

Because Auburn-Stache talked to me about it, one day while we were at her bedside and she couldn't open her eyes and her breathing was sharp and short. Auburn-Stache thinks what you do: that maybe there's a middle ground and I'll have to focus, focus harder than any sci-fi laser beam, but maybe with his help and in the hopes of meeting you, I can learn to put up with electricity. And all those electricities will learn to put up with me as well.

"So . . . I wouldn't have a seizure *or* blow things up?"

"Hopefully. And in the meantime we could find something less awkward for you to wear in public."

"Forget that. You're saying I could watch a movie?"

"Yes."

"And explore the Interwebz?"

"Y—"

"And use a humidifier?"

"All the humidifiers, Ollie."

Snot ran down my face.

"Here I come, world," I said.

As it is, I kind of just dart around the waves of color when I see them and make sure that if I start to sense a stronger aura—if I smell cinnamon or feel really dizzy or sneezy—I get the hell away.

We were in the open backyard, in the long grass, so there were plenty of places to run to if I needed to. But I didn't.

Junkyard Joe showed up in his wheelchair, but he couldn't go onto the grass. He waved at me from the porch. He could have been simulating ornithology again. I was scared to get close to him, what with his respirator, so perhaps that was for the best. He was a lot thinner than before. I didn't know what to say about it all, and maybe he felt the same way.

*　*　*

"Uncle Joe demanded to come, you know," Liz told me. We were walking down the driveway to where she'd parked her car. I was relieved to leave the murmuring guests behind. "Said your mom's 'No Trespassing' signs gave him enough deer pelts over the years to reupholster every vehicle in his lot, and he owed her."

"He still talks about hunting?"

She rolled her eyes. "Half the reason he tries so hard in physical therapy is so that he can climb right back up into a deer blind again. I told you, Ollie. He's a crackpot."

The trees on either side of us seemed shorter than I remembered. I could see more of the sky than I'd ever appreciated, above the driveway.

"So, look at you," she said. "I've got a phone in my pocket and you aren't squealing like a girl."

I had noticed the green glow of it through her jacket, over her heart. "I never squealed like a girl. I squealed like a girly boy, thank you."

She shoved me gently. "Anyhow, girly—how long until you're ready to come to school? Everyone's still talking about the dance. It took them two days to sort out the generators. If I told them that four-day weekend was your doing, all the kids would start singing your praises."

I lifted my chin. "I did my duty for school and country. But I don't think I'll be going back."

"Hey! Never let your illness define you." She elbowed me. "Give it time, Ollie."

I swallowed. "Yeah. That's what people say. But I'm going to do more than that, I think."

She was kicking absentmindedly at stones as she walked. "Oh, how so?"

"I'm going on a road trip with Auburn-Stache."

She stopped short, so that for once she was behind me.

"Whoa, what's with that face?"

She was frowning: strands of hair in her eyes, lines around her mouth. "I just never considered that one day you might not be here."

I choked on a laugh that wasn't really a laugh. "Funny. I considered that every day."

And then she ran forward, threw her arms around my neck, and pressed herself against my heart, and I could feel that phone in her jacket pocket buzzing against my chest and I swear it made me gasp.

Is that what you feel like all the time, Moritz?

"I'm coming with you," she said, breathless.

"Nope," I said, and shrugged her off. I turned around before she could see me cringe. I wanted to play it cool as a cucumber. I wanted to laugh it off, but my feet were heavy. We were almost at the power line.

She followed behind me, trying to catch my eye, asking me to wait. I kept walking until she grabbed my jacket.

"Wait, damn it! Ollie . . . didn't you come to that dance to get me?"

"Yeah, kind of. But that wasn't all of it."

"You went for your mom."

I looked up at the trees. "A big part of it was just . . . standing up. Like I asked Moritz to do. Like I'm going to do, taking this little vacation from here." I looked at the dead ends of the cable dangling overhead. "As much as I love you to pieces, I think that's sometimes a problem. No offense. But you were right. I think I have to go figure myself out first, or something, before I can become the sort of person who asks what other people do on rainy days." I cleared my throat. "Then I can come back all wise and handsome and dashing for you."

I thought she would laugh, but she was obviously trying to wrap her mouth around something.

"So what—um . . ." I could feel that old habit of hers. That ingrained need to be socially aware. "Do you think you might be, um, romantically interested in him?"

"Are you asking me whether I'm gay for Moritz?"

"I would never say it like that."

"No, you wouldn't." I grinned. "And no, I don't think so. If you don't know who I'm in love with by now, then I must be an unusually subtle person."

She smiled a bit. "You definitely aren't."

"But . . . hmm . . . have you read about Shakespearean love?"

"What, you mean bromance?"

I blinked. "Whoa. That word. It's wondrous. Is that a thing?"

"An Internet thing."

I laughed. "One day I want to surf it! There. I admitted it."

"And so? Why can't I come with you?"

"Martin seems like a nice guy, the total bastard."

She looked me dead in the eyes. "Spit it all the way out, Ollie."

"You're awesome, Liz. Not because I say so, but because you *are*. What the hell are you running for? You're bigger than high school. The next time someone calls you trashy, you pull a Fieke and punch them in the face. And then you can guilt yourself about it and learn some life lessons and get a bit tougher for it."

"What's a Fie—oh, never mind."

She wrapped her arms around me once more, gently this time,

and I swear she smelled like autumn and all the things I don't want to forget about when I leave Hermitopia.

"I'm going to miss you, doofus."

"Likewise, you know."

She kissed me on the mouth, and it didn't suck this time. And she walked away. Not into the woods, not with blackberries in her pockets. But still and always Liz.

Auburn-Stache helped me pack up my things the next day, although I got really annoyed when he told me I couldn't bring my anatomical model or all my graphic novels or the stag tapestry. Hey, I'm not used to not having those things around. I'll feel downright naked out in the real world, Moritz. I put my foot down when he tried to unpack my fishbowl and glock.

He's got a phone he keeps wrapped in a rubber poncho; he says he'll text your dad whatever address we end up at next. We're riding south to visit a kid in Ohio. From what I've read about Ohio, it's a state that grows lots of astronauts. Either that means Ohio is really damn cool, or it's exactly the kind of state you can't wait to get as far away from as possible.

Either way, I'm pretty excited.

"How many of us are there, Auburn-Stache?" I asked while we loaded up his Impala. I'm so used to this womble now that I forget I'm wearing it.

"'Us'? You mean . . ."

"FREAK LABORATORY SPAWN."

"Hey now. This isn't a comic book, Specimen 17."

"Ha. Ha."

"As far as I know, there were thirty-seven, ah, partial successes in the human enhancement program before the dissolution of the facility and the funding. Several are in Germany, others all around the world, in New Zealand and Taiwan and England. I visit the stateside ones on a regular rotation."

"Can we help them all?"

"Help them do what?"

"I dunno." I scratched the canvas at the back of my head. "Deal with emotional teenage nonsense. See if any of them are worthy of comics. Nothing major."

Auburn-Stache's face crinkled up again and he stilled his fidgeting for once.

"If you can find a way to deal with emotional nonsense, I need to come along for my own sake."

"And here I was hoping that emotional nonsense was something I could grow out of."

"Sorry, kiddo. Nope."

I looked back at the triangular cabin in the woods as we reversed out of the garage. I looked back at the doorway where she wasn't standing and I took a deep breath. I was glad that underneath the womble, I'd remembered to wear my coat.

I'm writing this in the car. We've only been on the road for an hour, but I've seen fast-food restaurants and semitrucks and so many splatters of color that my head might metaphorically explode, and I think Mom would be happy about that, so long as I don't have to actually implode to see it all. It's several hours' drive from the Upper Peninsula all the way down to Ohio, but I'm not even a little bored. I could write so much to you.

Should I write about the kid we're going to see first, the girl who stashes her heart in a lunch box far away from her body so she doesn't have to feel things?

Or about the one I want to visit afterward—a boy who can't heal any of his injuries, so he's as careful about moving around as he might be if he were made of glass and paper?

But the kid I'm dying to meet is you. I want to tell you stories in person. And you know, maybe we're getting closer to that. Keep your chin up. Goggles off.

One day I'll see you in Kreiszig.

With all my heart,

Ollie Ollie UpandFree

ACKNOWLEDGMENTS

I can't believe I get to write acknowledgments. I can't help but think that's a job for fancier people. Not that I don't have people to thank! They are legion.

First and foremost, the fanciest people of all: my editor, Mary Kate Castellani, and all the others at Bloomsbury. Tons of people worked behind the scenes to put this book together. Work I can hardly fathom! I am astounded and grateful.

My agent is a super-agent and I'll never forget that she found me first. Lana, m'dear, there aren't words enough to give you. I give you hugs instead.

My first readers kept it real. Kali Wallace, my BNF forever (and I'm hers, too, so back off!). Erin Thomas, the miraculous person this book is dedicated to. Karin Tidbeck, who helps me weather brainstorms. And Tamsyn Muir, who rooted for my boys before I did. I love you all to tiny bits.

There are all sorts of people who raised me to be a writer, from fantastic teachers to fantastic coworkers. I also need to thank my family, extended family, friends, and fellow cosplayers for indulging my weirdness. My peers and instructors at Clarion 2010, for helping that weirdness blossom into something greater. ("Your title sucks!") Here, too, goes a special nod to Ann and Jeff VanderMeer, who have been supportive and awesome to the point of excess.

Because I'm a dork and I can't write without headphones glued to my ears, I want to acknowledge the musicians who unwittingly helped me fight this fight. Primarily: Perfume Genius, Youth Lagoon, Los Campesinos!, and Owen Pallett. I also can't write without sustenance. I wrote more than half of draft zero at Picnic Café (野餐咖啡) in Taipei. Your tea and scones worked magic. The city as a whole worked its fair share.

And finally to my readers, whoever you may be. You're the very reason I write. I don't have to meet you to know that you're wonderful.

Ollie and Moritz's unique friendship continues . . .

NOWHERE

NEAR

YOU

Author of *Because You'll Never Meet Me*

leah thomas

BLOOMSBURY

Read on for a sneak peek!

THE BILLBOARDS

Moritz, you know me.

You know that usually I'd be the first person to say I'm awesome.

Behold! The Teenage Lord of Glockenspieling! I've got the astronomical charts for the next six months memorized, at least for the small patch of sky that hangs over northern Michigan. Did *you* know a comet's going to be soaring over my cabin in seventeen weeks? The Teenage Lord of Glockenspieling knows.

Keep on beholding, though! Because thanks to all the letters we've written this year, when it comes to getting epistolary, I am basically motherfluffin' Alexander Hamilton.

But here's my slice of humble pie: I've never been all that awesome at *patience*.

How did I handle the suspense of knowing I was actually on my way to meet other experimental kids like us, Moritz? With hazmat pants full of proverbial ants.

And how did I handle riding in a car out of the woods into real-life society for the first time?

Basically, I smeared my gas-masked face against the window for hours while Auburn-Stache chauffeured me down the freeway. He wouldn't let me turn on the radio (as if I could figure out the buttons!) and slapped my hand away whenever I reached across him to point at things.

"Whoa! Those windmills! They're moving! I can see them *moving*!"

"Glad I packed tranquilizers," murmured Auburn-Stache, but his goatee twitched.

"I thought windmills were little wooden houses with wings! Nobody told me they'd be white and *electric* and look like, like *gargantuan futuristic spaceship flowers*, 'Stache!"

"*Ollie*, I'm going deaf in my right ear. Spare me."

Although my allergies are still my ultimate kryptonite and electricity loves clouding my eyes with puffy swatches of color, I've gotten better at seeing past the swatches to what's underneath. I do this sort of squinting thing and scrunch my nose up in a way that might make Liz want to dump me for real. Then I can actually see almost like normal people do. The modified hazmat suit, the womble, absorbs the worst of the electricity, so these days I'm mostly only sneezing in the face of glowing screens. Sneezing beats seizing, so I'll take it.

And, Moritz, I have to tell you how outclassed my old power line nemesis was. For years I thought of the cable halfway down my driveway as actual Voldemort, burning orange in my aura, but that thing was only the lowest level of Death Eater (think Wormtail). Now I've seen power grids! They light up every horizon. I can't get over the towers that support those fiery lines in almost every direction. During that drive, to me they looked like stick people holding out cable jump ropes made of lava, and those lava ropes could have caught the world on fire if those other tower-people didn't help out and lift those ropes away from the fields—

Squinting too hard made me hiccup.

Auburn-Stache put a firm hand on my shoulder and shoved me back down into my seat.

"Ollie, I'm not daft enough to ask you to sit still. But sitting *down* would be a start."

"I'm just appreciating the beautiful things in life, you kook. Hey, do you think the kids we're going to meet will mind if I'm unfocused? Because I can't help being unfocused, but I don't want them to realize I'm less than cool. I have my hermit pride."

"Cross that bridge when we come to it."

"I want to seem *suave*. I should try to be aloof like Moritz." I sat up straight. "If I'm documenting their lives, they have to take me seriously. Right?"

Moritz, I'm on a storytelling mission. I figure being raised a woodland weirdo without even electric-coffeemaker experience to my name means I'll never be a good applicant for, you know, *office jobs*. But you told me I'm a good storyteller, and plenty of writers are antisocial! Some of them go off to live in cabins on *purpose* and do crap like stare at ponds for weeks. If you really think about it, my whole life's been a writing retreat. The TLoG is very qualified in this area.

So I'm going to conduct interviews. I'm going to write authoritative accounts of the lives of our fellow weirdos, the kids created in the laboratory and then scattered around the world. I'm going to meet them and tell their stories, and tell them right.

I like them all already. And I know it shouldn't matter, but I've always been a halfway-friendless electro-sensitive hermit, so I also want them to like me back.

"Do you think they'll tell me what it's like being them, Auburn-Stache?"

"Ollie. Wait and see."

"But—"

"Ollie. Please. You're doing my head in."

He really won't say much about the kids we're going to meet, Moritz, which is typical in an obnoxious sort of way, since that's the whole reason I'm *on* this trip. Aren't we all done with secrets already?

I guess old habits are vampires, immortal and hungry to exist. Because yeah, Auburn-Stache *is* like the dad I never had, but he's the kind of dad who spent a decade and a half of my life lying to me about basically everything important. I don't know. Maybe all dads do that, Moritz? Maybe if you cut anyone open, secrets wriggle out? (At least you and me are way past that!)

Right now it doesn't matter. Right now there's a whole world falling open in front of me instead, making me queasy in all the brightest ways. If I were serious and aloof like you, I'd sit still and let it wash over me.

My shoulder blades hit the passenger seat for maybe the first time.

But two milliseconds later, I rested my head on the dashboard, trying to angle the womble gas mask so I could get a good squint at the overpasses we kept driving under. The smog of cars flowed over the sides of bridges in gunpowder waterfalls, but for moments after we drove through them, the clear air underneath made me feel like we were floating in hidden caves.

"Spelunking!"

"Ollie! Seat belt!"

"How can anyone see anything with a seat belt on?" I twisted to look out the rear window.

"Not everyone is so thrilled by the panoramic views of a freeway commute."

"Holy crap! Is that a motorcycle?"

"What else would it be, Ollie?!"

Heck, it could have been anything. I didn't have time to focus on whatever lay beyond the electric clouds. All I saw was what looked like a severed head, speeding by on top of a black smog-horse.

"Can I get one? I shall name it Brom Bones, and it will strike fear in the hearts of mopeds!"

"Pissing Nora, no! Sit. Down. Before you overheat."

"I'm not an engine." I made a huffing noise through the filter of my gas mask.

He smirked. "The little engine that could."

I tried to ignore the doomed, unrequited desire to wipe sweat from my forehead. I considered napping, but that seemed risky.

What if I missed something miraculous?

Moritz, basically everything in the world is miraculous.

The countless colors invading my aura started mimicking autumn: those power lines draping orange curtains, planes miles (or kilometers, Mo) above trailing wisps of bronze through the clouds, blackened RVs and HOLY CRAP SEMITRUCKS roaring next to us with their twenty-something wheels and magma-colored diesel engines. Puffs of umber bled through the cracks in the pavement—dissipating as cars tore through them—especially as the scenery shifted from woodsy to industrial.

Northern Michigan has pine trees and lakes, but downstate is no great beauteous shakes. The farther south we got in Auburn-Stache's Impala, the flatter the roads, the grayer the scenery, the more overpowering the vomity bouts of electric color stabbing my pupils became. Glowing signs on massive posts told me that restaurants are a pretty big deal, but the signs became distorted when they merged with electricities: fast-food restaurants in yellow turned to sulfur in my corneas; green gas-station signs browned like dying leaves. Again, kind of vomity.

Actually, after a while just about everything felt vomity.

I put my hand on my stomach, and when I squinted at the next billboard, an advertisement for the Detroit Zoo, my hiccup tasted like . . . you get the idea.

"I have a pickle for you, Auburn-Stache," I said, voice muffled by the gas mask. "You know how you told me to stop writing Moritz while you were driving, and how I wasn't allowed to read or paint or glock in the car because I might get carsick?"

"Ollie, you're noisy enough without glockenspiel accompaniment." He was tapping his fingers on the wheel with one hand, biting his nails with the other. (And he gets mad at *me* for fidgeting!)

"Well"—I shut my eyes—"turns out the carsickness doesn't think those qualifications matter. Maybe you should stop the car."

"I can't simply stop the car, Ollie." Why was he sweating? He wasn't the one encased in layers of rubber.

"Sorry. What's the phrase for nonhermit car people? Oh. Pull over, *pretty please*." We overtook a minivan. It reminded me of Liz and the Ghettomobile and leaving home; the reminder made me queasier. "I'm gonna be sick."

"I can't," he said. "There are too many cars around."

"Look, I'll whip the mask off and do my sticky business and whip it back on in a flash. It won't even take long enough for me to seize." I tried to laugh but burped again, and I really didn't have time to talk about this. "I'll be just dandy!"

"I'm sorry, Ollie." He glanced at the wing mirrors, at the line of cars behind us. "We're half a mile from a rest area. Hang in there for one minute. Just one minute. To avoid any accidents."

I wanted to shout at him that I was about to have an accident right here in his car, but when I opened my mouth, something sicker than words came out and splattered onto my own face, and I realized the accident had already happened and this suit was never going to smell the same, and it hadn't smelled like lilies to begin with.

"Ollie!" cried Auburn-Stache. "Ollie, breathe. Chin up." He signaled left.

"Fluff you," I mumbled through burbling spit, nostrils burning. I tried clawing the mask away from my face. He grabbed my hand and held it tight.

"You *can't*, Ollie. You're wound up enough that you might short us out. Not just my car but the batteries in the cars on either side of us. The cars behind us. Do you know how disastrous that could be? If even just one car stopped without warning?"

I swallowed a teaspoon of vomit and coughed, and I couldn't reply because, aside from my disgust and my anger and my scorching throat, what tasted worse was knowing he was right.

Moritz, if I'm not careful nowadays, I could send out a pulse just like I did during the Halloween dance. Like how I blew out all the gymnasium lights and people's phones and ruined the evening for the DJ. This is what happens when you're an electromagnetic loser and you don't have any say in the way you impact the world.

This is why Mom wanted me to never leave the woods.

I gasped again, a hot sob that came from nowhere or from the dark inside me.

"Ollie, we're almost there." His hand on my chest wasn't restrictive anymore, but more like he was trying to hold me in one piece.

But then I was thinking of her, and I don't think I would have been breathing right even if I weren't dealing with a mask full of puke. This felt like a brand-new kind of seizure.

Did she die, Moritz? It seems as unbelievable as giant stick people draped in cables. As impossible as four lanes of steel machines surrounding me in parallel lines, machines moving fast enough to bend metal and pulverize bones during collision.

Moritz, if things as deadly as cars can be part of the world, why can't I?

"You'll be all right," Auburn-Stache said as he turned onto an exit ramp and toward a brown flat-roofed rest area. He parked the car while I breathed hot acid through my nose.

No one was around to see him drag me out into the parking lot and across a narrow strip of grass, into the line of trees beyond a few picnic tables. No one but a scarred old man, leaning on his truck and chewing jerky, who blinked at us like he'd seen much stranger things in his life than a goateed doctor tearing a dripping gas mask off a sobbing teenage loser.

"Ollie, Ollie. Now, stop that, kiddo."

"Why did you . . . let me leave?" I gasped, stomach rolling, eyes streaming. "If you're so afraid I'm going to wreck the world, why did you agree to take me on this . . . trip?"

Auburn-Stache didn't reply until he'd caught his breath. I guess dragging me out of the car was a bit hard on him. He's older than ever and I'm taller than ever, and my legs felt like lumps of dead weight, even to me.

"Neither your mother nor father would have wanted you to spend your youth with only ghosts for company."

"Me and my dead parents." I wiped my mouth on my sleeve and stared up at the darkening sky. "Someone should write a book about an orphan named Oliver."

"Enough, Ollie," he said gently.

"The bright side, 'Stache: a lot of superheroes are orphans." I laughed weakly. "Maybe I'm just fulfilling an epic destiny."

"There's that fabled optimism." He patted my back.

"Hey. Do you think the kids we're going to meet will mind me smelling like damp compost?" And then, all hoarse: "Do you think they'll mind *me*?"

Liar-Dad's detailed, heartfelt answer? "Wait here. I'll go clean your mask."

I winced. "Do I have to wear it again?"

"I'm afraid so. For now."

Auburn-Stache soon returned with the mask and more: my toothbrush, a tube of toothpaste, a warm bottled water, and a washcloth. I rinsed out my mouth, brushed bits from my teeth, and washed my face. Auburn-Stache helped me wrap the damp cloth around my nose and mouth inside the mask, but that thing still reeked enough to knock approximately seventeen skunks unconscious when I shoved it back on. In the parking lot, we found the old man sitting in his truck, trying to start his engine. Is that called revving?

Revving and revving, but it wouldn't start. That was almost definitely my fault.

So was his dead phone, probably, and his semifried hearing aid. Where before I'd seen the usual smattering of electric shades, now there was nothing. And his bumper sticker said he was a veteran and everything.

Go, me.

While we waited for someone to come along and jump our batteries (because of course I'd shorted out the Impala, too), I sat in my stinking womble at the picnic table on the edge of the narrow line of fake woods, holding my knees and staring at the litter underfoot.

Moritz, I know *you* get it: there have to be dark parts in origin stories.

I just hope the other kids like us will get it, too.

Once or twice while Auburn-Stache laughed with the old man about how bizarre a coincidence it was that both of their car batteries died in the same parking lot, the old man craned his neck to peer at me and my suspicious radiation suit. You hardly ever see superheroes wearing suspicious radiation suits.

When we finally left the rest area, the sunny first day of our road trip had given way to an amethyst November evening; I wish electricity got darker with everything else. Instead, all the colors only seemed brighter, and nausea caught me again.

Auburn-Stache took his hand from the wheel and placed it above the womble goggles, the approximate area of my forehead.

"Bet you regret this already," I murmured. "This insane road trip."

"I won't if you don't."

"Fair deal, Auburn-Stache."

I'm still impatient, Moritz. Even if I'm finally getting a little taste of how terrifying strangers can be and a bigger appreciation of what it is to be you, alone in a crowd of people. This must be what it's like to go out without your goggles on.

I told Liz I wanted to take this trip to figure myself out, but it's not easy. My electromagnetism might always freak me out. Maybe I can't control my life if I can't control my own body. Maybe I really will short you and your pacemaker out, and I don't think it's as easy to jump a person's batteries as it is to restart a car.

Even knowing that, I still wish more than anything you were here to talk to. You said you're not worried about me hurting you, but honestly, Moritz? Maybe you should be. Because I might be willing to hurt you a little if it meant I'd get to meet you!

I want to meet *all* the kids like us. I want to write their origin stories, too, dark parts included. I want to give them a shorter nickname than "kids I'm going to meet." Oh, and help them with their emotional teenage nonsense. I want this to be my new life purpose!

But what I want most is one of those amphibious vehicles. Then Auburn-Stache and I could just drive right off the coast and aim straight for Germany. I'm sure there'd be gas stations along the way, floating on buoys out in the middle of the Atlantic. We could stop off at oil rigs, right?

That'd be the cherry, Moritz Farber. You're the ultimate cherry. And we're serious about cherries in Michigan.

Now! Shut up and tell the Teenage Lord of Glockenspieling what the sounds of your life look like, Ultimate Cherry Dolphin Mo-Man!

I know you're sighing in exasperation. Just like Mom used to.

Focus, Ollie.

~ O

P.S. Hey, since we're on the move, you can e-mail (!) your next reply to the account Auburn-Stache set up for me, and he'll go print it out. (Did you *know* about the existence of print shops? I stood outside the door when Auburn-Stache went in, and when he returned, I swear I smelled watermelons. Does ink come from all those black seeds we spit out?)

Anyhow: oxenfree@stache.org. I'm not even joking. *Stache.org*

P.P.S. There may be a handful of us weirdos stranded here in the colonies, Moritz, but after the eighty-seventh time I asked him, Auburn-Stache confessed there are more in Europe. Unlike me, you have access to the magical realm known as the *Internet*, with all its maps and search machines. You can use electricity to meet the X-Men (real nickname pending)! What d'you say?

© Jessica Hilt

leah thomas frequently loses battles of wits against her students and her stories. When she's not huddled in cafés, she's usually at home pricking her fingers in service of cosplay. Leah lives in San Diego, California, and is the author of *Nowhere Near You* and the William C. Morris YA Debut Award Finalist *Because You'll Never Meet Me*.